Until You Say My Name

Tatum Schroeder

spectrum
books

Contents

Chapter One

The trouble with childhood dreams becoming real is they never really hit like the version that lives only in your head. In fact, they run the risk of turning out to be the total opposite, and that's a quick and easy way to grow a few gray hairs.

For Mia Reyes, that childhood dream was getting into a state university. Sure, it wasn't the biggest or fanciest dream out there. But it was hers, and she had taken good care of it since fifth grade.

Some kids dream of becoming an astronaut or the President or publishing a New York Times bestseller or directing the Oscar winner for Best Picture, things like that. And yes, Mia liked to dream big, and any of those things sounded fucking amazing (if nothing else, because most of them would probably mean she never had to eat another instant meal packet). But she also knew that dreaming up something impossible was a good way to set yourself up for heartbreak, something she sure didn't need any more of. Even so, she would never forget the day her letter of admission arrived in the mail. It was one of those moments where you felt like you really could float away, defying gravity, and all your troubles forgot themselves for a second, and you know what, fuck it, you were right, Louis Armstrong; it really is a wonderful world.

That was months ago. Now, the dream she had tossed, turned over, and filled with every little detail in her mind had finally arrived. She had imagined how it would look, sound, even smell. Maybe some instrumental music by Randy Newman would fill the background. She'd be wearing clothes that, in this version, she could afford. And most of all, her voice, face, and body would all resemble her favorite female celebrities. Since age fifteen, Mia had known exactly whose nose she wanted, whose jaw she wanted, whose legs she wanted, and on and on it went, until she was a Frankenstein's monster made up of women she'd never meet.

But the moment was here. And not only was far from what she had hoped it would be, but all she wanted to do was run away from it. To hop back into her old sedan and speed right back down the road she came from.

Mia shifted her weight from one foot to another as she stared up at the residence hall. It loomed in front of her, a red brick giant with stone pillars and colonial windows. Large lion statues stood guard at the entrance, and rows of flower bushes lined up along the front wall. The sight of it made her blood run cold. Of course, the campus was breathtaking and her lineup for classes this semester was exciting. But she did not look like the girl she had hoped would be starting college today, not even close. She still wore ratty, faded hand-me-downs that weren't even fashionable in a vintage way, but just plain dull. She still hated everything about the way her face was shaped and the way her clothes covered her and the way she sounded when she talked.

Classic Mia, with the double standards, she mused. It's too much to dream up nabbing an Academy Award, but not too much to imagine that one day, by the grace of the tooth fairy or whoever the hell, she'd one day wake up looking like a Hollywood starlet. Go figure.

The truth of the matter was, she must have been hoping that by the time she got here, she would be someone different. The person who lived in her head would be just as visible to the rest of the world as she was to herself. But that never happened. Not that it ever could have; again, reiterating the dreaming-of-something-impossible thing. Still, it sure would have been nice to start college being that person, or at least looking somewhat like that person. Instead, she was still someone else. Still someone trapped in the underworld of what could be and what wasn't.

Maybe this would not turn out as she had hoped. It may have been just one big mistake. Probably a safe assumption, all things considered. Behind her, Mia dragged a long receipt of disappointments, setbacks, and hindrances, so the idea that this would be any different felt like a tablespoon of water in a huge vat of the messy, sticky, ugly oil that was all the events in her life leading up to this moment.

Then again, maybe she was doing that thing where her brain invented problems that weren't there. After all, she did drive across the entire country to get here. If she had had bad luck in her hometown, maybe she had left all of it behind, along with everything and everyone else who told her this would never happen. There was a small chance this time would be different.

Mia clutched the straps of her backpack, then picked up her duffel bag from the sidewalk. She glanced at the other students making their way around the brick pathways, and quickly realized how much she stood out. Many of them were dressed in brand name clothing, with trimmed or styled hair, wielding leather laptop bags and the latest phone models. Mia had seen this coming based on what she knew about the school, to say nothing of the meat grinder she endured just to get the scholarship. But seeing it up close rattled her. It forced her to reconcile the strange new world that she had thrown herself into.

She scratched at the dark stubble on her chin and took a deep breath. No. She couldn't even humor the idea. Driving all the way back home was out of the question. She had promised herself she wouldn't even look back, and the last thing she wanted was to prove everyone back home was right about her. Of course, the catch with that little promise was this: she could only look ahead now, and all she saw was clouded with shadow.

The future had never looked so uncertain. And that scared the hell out of her.

The volunteer blinked at her.

"This is it? This is all you have?" he asked, looking her up and down.

"You got it." Mia adjusted the backpack again. Aside from necessities like charging cords and documents, she had only brought several outfit changes, her old laptop, a few books, and a carton of menthol cigarettes. Although, in her defense, it hadn't been her choice to travel light. When she left last week, she took everything that belonged to her, and she had never had much to speak of, anyway. On the bright side, Mia liked to think that, at least in the physical sense, she had left nothing behind in her hometown. No trace that she had once lived there. Sort of like cutting off a metaphorical umbilical cord, or an extreme version of spring cleaning, but less for your bedroom and more for your entire life. Something about that notion made her feel cozy all over.

The volunteer just shrugged.

"Okay, then. Your room number is 14–B." He handed over her set of keys. "You're lucky. Single dorms get taken pretty fast."

She couldn't help but grin as she clipped the keys to her lanyard. This was really happening. She was a college student now. She was about to become somebody in this world who could stake out their place. Maybe even make a difference one day too, but time would tell for that one. As she walked up the stairs to her room, she jingled the keys in her hand.

The dorm was small, which she had expected. Nothing more than a bedroom, a small space for cooking, a bathroom, and a closet. But to Mia, it was plenty. In fact, it was the most she had ever had to speak of. Before she got to work settling in, she laid down on the bare bed and stared up at the ceiling for a few moments, just to take it all in. Her heart pounded as she clasped her student badge to her chest.

In the back of her mind, old voices trickled in. A long assembly line, as far back as kindergarten, who told her she would never make it this far. That she had wasted her time applying for scholarships and studying for tests. Many of her teachers even told her she wouldn't graduate high school, and if she was honest with herself, she couldn't blame them too much for that one. Mia had been what some folks like to call a 'problem child.' The kind of kid who got caught smoking in the bathroom as far back as sixth grade. But of course, no one had asked her about why she never had clean clothes, why she liked to shoplift junk food, or why she always sported bruises and cuts. Anger only at the symptoms of the problem, not the problem itself. Even the school counselor hadn't had much good to say to her.

"You keep this up and you'll never amount to anything. Do you want to go to juvie? Because that's where you'll end up if you keep heading in this direction," he had said almost exactly two years ago.

Look at her now. And yes, she liked to think it was her hard work, not sheer luck, that got her foot in the door. Every night staying up late to study and every day writing and rewriting her application letters had been worth it. She liked to think that she had succeeded in proving them wrong.

She planted a kiss on her student badge, then ran her fingers through her short black hair.

Commotion started outside her door. Mia hurried outside to see what was up. It turned out to be some freshmen having a pillow fight in the hall, much to the frustration of those who were just trying to unpack and settle in. Mia debated joining them when she remembered how much she stood out around here already, which she already tried not to think about.

Yet she still felt the pull to at least try to fit in. To assert if not to them, then at least to herself that she belonged, and this wasn't some prank she was playing on herself.

Mia glanced up and down the hall, then did it again to take in what she was seeing. Some of these guys must have brought enough stuff to fill a school bus. Piles and piles of suitcases, sports gear, electronics, furniture, clothes, and everything else. Then again, she had grown up having to fit all her belongings into a garbage bag, maybe two if the adults were feeling generous. She never got in the habit of accumulating things for that reason.

A pillow flew at her. Her reflexes helped her catch it just in time and throw it back to him. It struck the guy right in the face, and his buddies laughed. They engaged in the fight for a little while longer until a volunteer rushed in and told them to settle down. Mia glanced at the others and smiled with them as they watched the volunteer leave.

"Someone has a stick up his ass," she said to the freshman nearest to her, a tall, strong boy with dirty blonde hair. Not exactly her type, but she did find him cute.

He looked back at her with a teasing grin.

"His dad works here, so be careful who hears you say that."

"Oh, right. Because nerds are terrifying." She rolled her eyes.

"What's your name again?" he asked, holding the pillow he had thrown at her moments ago.

She bit her lip.

"I'm Carlos. Carlos Reyes. Yours?"

"Rhett Nilsson. We're all getting together for pizza in the common room later. You should come." He slugged her on the arm.

She forced a smile and slugged him back. This was an easy role to play. She fit in with the guys so well, acting like she was one of them. If only they knew what she was really like. The person she hid from them with all the expertise of someone far too used to this sort of game.

"Yeah, maybe." She shrugged.

"Oh, and don't tell anyone, but we're all going to bring some liquor, too. You can bring some too if you're not a pussy." He laughed.

Her well-practiced self-control helped her not to wince. But it still stung, as always. She really, *really* hated hearing that word used like a punchline. It was like hand sanitizer on a paper cut.

"We'll see. I'll catch you later." She ducked back into her dorm. Of course, she had a pretty good idea of what would happen if anyone here found out about her. You only had to spend two minutes online reading more than enough horror stories to scare you right back into the masquerade. Even in a city and college like this, which self-advertised as accepting of all demographics, Mia knew better than to buy it. To her, those words held just as much substance as when her school stated it had zero tolerance for bullying. Words thrown around so they could feel better about themselves and dismiss any accusations of behavior that proved otherwise.

You're going to be fine, she reminded herself. *You made it to college, for fuck's sake. You're going to be fine.*

Mia woke up the next morning to several text messages on her phone. It was a cheap touchscreen model and could only hold a few apps and maybe one or two games. For a few seconds, she forgot where she was, but before a wave of panic crashed over her, yesterday's memories kicked in.

All the texts were from Alan, the first friend she had made who wasn't from her hometown. She smiled a little.

Alan: How's college life so far??

She rolled over on her stomach, feeling a headache coming on. She fumbled to message him back.

Carlos: Hungover (oops). Ready for first day of classes.

Against her better judgment, she had stayed up eating pizza and drinking with the guys down the hall, including Rhett. She even forced herself to make a few jokes that made her feel sick afterwards, the kind that reduced women to just little pieces boys could gaze at, mock, and hold them to as much as they wanted. It was a language she learned all too well starting around middle school, and she hated herself for her fluency. Actually, the list of things she liked about herself was much shorter than the list of things she hated, but this definitely ranked around the top ten, maybe fifteen things.

But what choice did she have, other than being known as that one guy who wasn't any fun to be around? Because if you were 'that guy' who said you shouldn't talk like that, suddenly that invited them to come to all kinds of conclusions about you. Conclusions that, to them, were the worst thing that could happen to a guy. Yeah. She'd been down that path. Wasn't making that mistake again. At least not right away.

She could have said something, commented on the way they described people they had no idea were listening. *Should* have said something. And she promised herself she would next time. But fuck it, it was only her first night here; she deserved a small break.

Alan: Sounds like the best possible way to start college lol

She met Alan the first week at her new part-time job at an auto repair shop, which she took on at the start of the month. The scholarship only helped so much, of course. And in those few weeks before she moved into her dorm, Mia had had no choice but to rotate between staying at cheap motels or sleeping in her car. It was fun the first three or four nights, made her feel like a real adventurer, but it got old fast. One day, while Alan had been paying for his oil change, they struck up a conversation because they happened to be wearing the same band shirt. Just her luck. It turned out Alan borrowed the shirt from his husband, Julian, so they didn't listen to the same music after all. On the bright side, once Alan discovered she was new in town, he invited her out for drinks. Mia, realizing she needed to start somewhere in this town, had no ounce of strength left to politely decline his offer. Alan eventually introduced her to Julian, a dashing gent who reminded Mia of herself. Or that is, the man people expected her to be, and who she could see herself being if she was one.

She liked the couple. A lot. Alan was a TTRPG-loving Chicago native who worked in cybersecurity. Meanwhile, Julian was from SoCal and had a rising career as a professional chef, but he also hoped to foster rescue animals on the side one day.

But more than all their interests and accomplishments, Mia loved seeing them express their affection so openly. She loved watching them kiss and hold hands and not be afraid of what anyone else might think. It almost comforted her to know that such a thing was not impossible—well, at least for some people. In her hometown, if you were different in any way, no one was going to know. You buried it deep down and prayed no one picked up on any signs.

She knew all too well how to hide. How to play the game they instilled in her from an early age.

Alan: Try to stay out of trouble but don't forget to have fun. Enjoy your first day!

After a quick text back, Mia hopped into the shower. By half-past eight, she was scurrying into her first class, textbook and notebooks tucked under her arm. She found her seat and gazed around the classroom, trying not to lock eyes on anyone already seated. Eye contact was one of those things Mia had struggled with as long as she could remember. It was not unlike trying to cross an ice rink without skates but also without slipping and while also balancing a tray full of glasses filled to the rim; that, but for your eyes. But the last thing she needed on her first day of college was people thinking she was some weird creep with no manners. Enough of that from high school. So, doing what she had learned to do years ago, she kept her head lowered, with mumbles of 'excuse me' and 'sorry', until she found a vacant seat. Finally. At last, sitting down, no more worrying about what to do with her weight and the way she stood or walked. She could focus.

Mia had barely settled in when the professor started in with introductions, followed by an outline of the semester and all the work they had to look forward to. The longer he went on and on, the more Mia felt her bones turn to jelly. The reality hit her of what the coming months would be like.

It was going to be a long year. But she had to stay positive. After all, she had gotten this far.

Chapter Two

A long day of classes left Mia with a pounding headache, along with a big appetizer of dizziness from hunger. One professor after another today had done more than enough to help her realize just how unprepared she really was for college. And to think she thought high school had been tough. It was like she had skipped the part of learning to ride a bike with the training wheels. Couldn't wait to fall flat on her face and skin her knees on repeat for the next four years.

Back in high school, she had a hard time getting assignments turned in on time, not to mention the bullying she had to put up with. By sophomore year, Mia figured out that if she wanted to get out of that hellhole of a town and have a shot at a better future, she would need to work hard. So, she spent every waking hour practicing her equations and problems or hiding in the library for hours on end to study. Her grades soared that year. And it got even better in junior and senior year. All those long nights were worth the looks on the faces of the people who said she wouldn't make it. She practically waved her diploma in the school counselor's face after the graduation ceremony.

College, however, was going to be a whole other ball game.

The confidence she brought with her, built and broken and rebuilt over all these years, had already begun to wear thin by the end of her first day. Here, no one cared that she was the foster kid who went from being in detention every other week to the top ten of her graduating class. No one cared that she pulled herself together without a mentor or group of friends by her side. Here, none of that mattered. She had come so far, and now she had to start all over again.

As she walked out of her last class for the day, a lump started to form in her throat, which Mia swallowed down like a whole lemon. Nope. No way she could let herself have a breakdown on the first day. That was not allowed.

Maybe she needed to give herself a small treat to reward herself for surviving the first day. That had to be it. She even had some spare change to afford one, too.

Before Mia could talk herself out of it, she pulled out her phone and texted Julian.

Carlos: Hey do you know of any good places close by to get a treat? Like a cafe or coffee shop or something?

Mia waited for him to reply, hoping there was somewhere decent within walking distance so she could save on gas. Iced coffee was one of her favorite treats. The more sugar and whipped cream, the better. Julian texted her back in seconds.

Julian: Corner of 15th and Main. It's right down the road from campus. Locally owned too. Real cozy! I used to go there all the time a couple years ago when I was working in a restaurant in the same neighborhood.

She texted back a thumbs-up emoji. Her phone told her the coffee shop was just a ten-minute walk away; perfect. That perfect time slot that gave your head enough time to clear, but not so much that you wore yourself out from the commute.

The coffee shop in question was small, with industrial décor, brick walls, and a high ceiling. The mismatched furniture looked cozy and inviting. And it really was mismatched; a second scan confirmed to Mia that there was no way two chairs or tables were bought from the same place. A soft alternative song from the early 2000s played on the speakers. It looked like just the sort of place that starving artists would camp out at to edit videos or write highbrow poetry…or, more likely, where lots of college students flocked to when they wanted to make a big statement about either avoiding the chain coffee shops or whatever nasty stuff they served in the campus cafeteria. Only two other folks were here and keeping to themselves in the back corner. Behind the counter was a large blackboard with a handwritten menu. Handwriting was as adorable as Mia wanted hers to be, but her fingers moved way too damn fast to so much as put little hearts over her lowercase 'I's. She looked up at it as she approached the counter, noting the options for flavored iced mochas and lattes. She could see why Julian used to come here a lot.

"Can I get a…" The sentence never finished coming out. In the past, she had been picked on for her coffee order. Guys liked to find the slightest thing that could be labeled as effeminate and attack it. Hell, girls did it too. Maybe she should just suck it up and try to choke down that disgusting, bitter, dark brew.

The barista was looking at her, waiting for her to finish, but nothing about him seemed impatient. He had dark blonde hair, and tiny glimpses of a tattoo could be seen peeking just above the collar of his black shirt.

"Small black of the dark roast. Please," she finally said, then kicked herself. *You idiot, you* hate *black coffee. What is wrong with you?! That's two, three bucks, gone, and for what? Scalding juice that tastes like ass, and not in the good way!*

"Sure. Dollar sixty-eight," he said with a voice that came out bolder than she had been expecting, like he was talking in a room filled with loud music.

"Ah, so close." As soon as she said it, she wanted to curl up into a ball. She truly had no idea why she said the dumbest jokes sometimes, like one part of her brain never matured past age twelve. Nevertheless, and to her relief a bit, she saw the barista fight back a smile as he prepared her order. As she watched him, she could not help but notice the university's logo on a metal plate hanging on the wall. "I take it lots of college students come here?"

"Yup. A lot of us work here, too."

"Oh. You go there too? I just started."

"It's a great school. You'll love it. I'm graduating this year." He set her cup on the counter; she noted the chipped black nail polish. He also wore a few black rings and two silver and black necklaces. And with that, Mia suddenly realized just how cute he was. Handsome *and* cute, a double whammy. Although she did always have a weakness for guys who were taller than her.

"Major?" She sipped her coffee and, no surprise, it tasted just as bad as she remembered. She dumped about four spoonsful of sugar into it, but that did about as much good as frosting on fresh cow manure. But she was not one to waste money, so she choked it down. Really, the whole thing made her feel bad for the cisgender straight guys out there who really wanted the pretty pink cocktails but were doomed to a life of choking down brewskis just to avoid social castration…well, just a little bad, that is. She only had so much sympathy to spare for the oppressor.

"Political Science. You?"

"Mechanical Engineering." A new customer walked in, cutting off their brief interaction. The cute and handsome *and* tall barista quickly finished wiping down the counter.

"Well, good luck," he said to her with the slightest hint of a playful smile.

Oh, Jesus Christ, he's really, really *cute,* she thought with an impending sense of horror.

"Thanks, man." She glanced at him, realized this local place didn't do name badges. Probably too intrusive to ask for it. Better to act chill. She shuffled away and settled on a spot on the far end of a flower pattern couch, still beating herself up inside for ordering black coffee. Once seated, she rolled her backpack off her shoulders and pulled out her first textbook. Thoughts of tall guys were shoved into the 'to do later' pile in her head. Now she had to organize and get to studying.

Two hours went by, which she did not even realize until she looked up from her book. Everyone else had left, and the cute barista was sweeping the floor.

"Shit, my bad. I didn't realize I stayed that long," she managed to say to him. She fumbled to shove all her books back in her backpack. Her brain hurt from so much studying.

"No worries. We don't close for another twenty minutes," he said, back turned to her.

She hurried out the door, embarrassed and flushing all the same as she hurried back to her dorm. Maybe there was another local coffee place she could go to, one where she wouldn't crack dumb jokes and didn't get flushed every time a cute guy so much as looked at her.

On Sunday night, Alan and Julian invited her out for a bite to eat at a local burger place. She ordered the cheapest appetizer, paying for her share of the bill in loose change. Once they had put in their order, they got comfortable at an outdoor table, from which they had a pleasant view of the downtown area. Being that Julian was a chef, he had good inside info on the best (and worst) places to eat in the city, so Mia trusted him.

"So, let's hear it. How's the college boy doing?" Alan asked with a teasing grin.

Mia rolled her eyes. She had already opened up to them a little about where she came from, but to date, she had spared the details. For all they had to know, she was a foster kid from the Bible Belt who came here for a fresh start. What more did one need to know? You had to keep them guessing at least a little.

"It's tough. Overwhelming. Worth it, though." She wrung her hands in front of her. *They'll understand if you tell them the truth. They won't push you away. I mean, look at them, they're a married gay couple and they haven't made one transphobic joke or remark since you met them, even when you gave them that huge chance to do it the other day. They're one of the good ones. If anyone's going to accept you it's going to be them.*

So why can't you just tell *them? What the fuck is holding you back?!*

"It won't feel like that forever. Trust me on that one," said Julian. "College was hell for me the first year, but I'm glad I stuck through it. And a pretty boy like you won't have to worry about staying single for long." He winked at her.

"Dude. Your husband is right there," Mia laughed.

"I know that."

"He has to flirt with all the cute guys." Alan rolled his eyes. "Clearly I'm not good enough for him."

"See what I'm doing? I'm making him jealous on purpose, so he has to prove how much he loves me."

"Or you could just, I don't know, ask?" Mia shrugged.

"Sure, but this is more fun." Julian tossed back his cocktail.

Mia sipped at her soda, watching them. They were the perfect couple. So perfect that it made her giddy and cranky at the same time, like a sugar high and sugar crash happening at once. Giddy that these two guys could be open about their identities and their love for each other with no fear, no shame, nothing holding them back. Cranky that no one had ever looked at her the way they looked at each other, and probably never would. Even their apartment, which she had stopped at once to get the full tour, had all the pride flag decorations, and right where the neighbors could see! They were so *vocal* about it, and so free.

What must that feel like? Being your true self, everyone knowing who you really are. And not just that, but loving who your true self was, rather than wishing it would just disappear or magically change so that you could be literally anyone in the world except for, well, *you.*

I should just tell them already…

She started to spit it out before she knew what she was saying.

"Oh, by the way, guys? There's something I should let you know."

They turned to her, both wearing carefree expressions. They had no idea of the heavy weight she was about to release. How long it had been sitting there, aching to be let out and be heard for once in her life.

But before they could so much as hit the runway that was her tongue, the words got stuck in her throat, like trying to climb out of quicksand. Silence fell over their little table.

"Yeah? What is it?" Alan asked.

"It's, uh…"

Half of her screamed to just say the words. To finally say that she was not Carlos. She was *Mia*. That she had been secretly living as Mia for years. That she had gone through hell and back every time kids at school or foster parents noticed there was something even a bit different about her, a little off from what she was supposed to be. That she had found answers to the misery but had no idea how to show herself to the world.

The words never came out. Like herself, they were hidden too deep.

"Just…thanks. For everything. For being my friend and helping me adjust here. It's been helping me a lot." She couldn't look either of them in the eye.

"Of course! Anytime," Julian said, and the genuine warmth and kindness in his voice made her want to burst into tears. She still couldn't figure out why they were so nice to her. It wasn't like she had done anything to deserve it.

"Stop being so cheesy. You'll win him over, and I'm not sharing!" Alan grabbed Julian by the arm and smiled.

"Then hold on to the guy a little tighter," Mia laughed with him. Inside, all she could do was push down the hurt.

Next time. Yeah. You can always tell them next time. There's always a next time.

Chapter Three

Mia went back to the same coffee shop after classes the next day, smoking a couple of menthols on the way there. Once again, her backpack was heavy with books and study notes, but this time she also brought her laptop along to pull up some files the professor sent the class.

Luckily, the cute barista was here to take her order. Today, he wore a black tank top, which meant she got a much better look at the tattoos on his chest and arms.

She forced herself not to ask his name or about his classes. She didn't want to come off as a stalker or anything. But she did order a nice blended iced mocha today, having worked up the courage on the way here. He smiled as he topped it with a swirl of caramel syrup, and she dreaded what might be on his mind. Here comes the joke about what kind of a man orders a girly drink, as if she hadn't heard every version of it already.

"Is something funny?" Mia asked with a frown. She couldn't help it.

"Nothing. Just glad to see you ordering something you like today," he said. Once again, his voice was still just a tad too loud and bold for the atmosphere. It was as if someone was taking a jackhammer to the floor ten feet away and he was the only one who could hear it. Their fingers brushed a bit as he handed her the beverage.

"What?" She blinked at him.

He looked down, as if ashamed he had said anything.

"Not that it's my business, but you hated that black coffee and didn't say anything. If you don't like it, you can just tell me and I can make you a new drink. It's really not a problem."

She wasn't sure if she should be flattered that he remembered her, or if he just remembered all the customers who walked in. Or maybe, on the flip side, she should be concerned that something about her appearance made her memorable. Just the idea of existing as an entity in a stranger's head made her whole body flush with panic, because there's not much you can do to change that image they've built about you, and his was definitely one of the weird, gangly brown kid with old, boring clothes and a girly beverage and a funny way of talking. The more she thought about how she appeared to other people the more she spiraled until she was just about ready to move to the most remote place on earth and only be perceived by wildlife.

"Well, I didn't want to be rude." She adjusted her backpack's weight to her other shoulder.

He gave a halfhearted shrug.

"That's a good one, by the way. I got addicted to those for a month when I first started here," he remarked, motioning to the drink in her hand.

She took a long sip, feeling instant relief in her body. It was almost as bad as her nicotine addiction.

"Oh, yeah, I can really see why. Thanks." She nodded to him.

As the barista went back to cleaning, her gaze lingered on him. He had a tattoo on his upper right shoulder that sprawled onto his upper back and biceps. It was a big tapestry of various mythical animals, all shaded in black and gray, aside from a few bits of red. Farther down his right arm he had two different year dates and an inverted cross. His left arm was decorated with a handful of small to medium size black and gray tattoos such as fly agaric mushrooms, an octopus impaled by spears, a scorpion, a shattered anatomically accurate heart, and few wilting roses.

So he's a goth. Possibly a former mall goth. A dash of punk, maybe? I've really got to read up on those again.

She had to admit, that whole crowd had never been her first choice. When it came to men, Mia tended to go for the sporty gym rats, beach bums, and so on. You know, the kind of guys whose selfies you could smell. Although, to be fair, she did recall having a huge crush on a boy in freshmen year who dyed his hair black and wore thick eyeliner all the time, so it wasn't like she had ruled out the entire community. As for girls, she was still trying to work out which parts were genuine attraction, which parts were gender envy, and which parts were both, so it was overall a downright mess.

Still puzzling on the differences between 'goth,' 'punk,' and 'emo,' Mia hurried to the floral pattern sofa in the back and got to work studying. Of course, just her luck. She had come in during the slow period, and there was just one other customer. The music in the background had shifted to a soft 1970s rock theme, and she mouthed the lyrics to herself as she got out her books.

The barista spoke up. It startled her out of her seat. Why did he have to talk so loudly?

"How's your first week going?"

"Uh…fine? I guess?" She wasn't sure why he had even asked. She started up her laptop. The poor thing was missing a few keys, so she had to pull up an on-screen keyboard. Someday she was going to get the darn thing fixed.

"It's a good school. There's a lot you can get involved in if you're interested."

"I'm not ready to think about that yet. I'm mostly thinking about keeping my head above water." She slurped at her coffee and decided it tasted so good it was worth the risk of being teased for it. "What kind of stuff do they have, anyway?"

"Oh, there's a lot." He was cleaning the espresso machine. "Depends on what you like, what you're interested in. I like to think there's something for everyone."

"Well, then give me some examples."

He hesitated, frowning. As if trying to decide what or what not to say next.

"I'm actually a group coordinator for one of them. Not to self-promote or anything."

"No shit. What is it?" she dared to ask. She expected him to say he led a book review club where they only read 'intellectual' novels, or maybe a tattoo club, if those were even a thing. Did goths have a club where they talked about being sad and weird together?

Now, come on, Mia, that's not nice. As if you wouldn't fit right in with a group all about being sad and weird.

"It's more of a support group for students in the LGBTQ+ community. We get together, talk about what's going on, offer help or resources or just somewhere to go. Sometimes we host fundraisers or events but haven't been able to pull that off this year yet, but I have a couple ideas."

Mia frowned and sat up a little taller. Now she found herself trying to figure out which of those letters he was. She would believe it if he said he was bisexual or pansexual. Or was he just an ally? She stared at him, and she knew how rude that was considering what he just told her, but she couldn't help herself. The barista finally looked up from his work once he realized she had not said anything since this small revelation.

"So, what, you're gay or something?" The words were barely out of her mouth, and she already wanted to melt into the floor.

Jesus H. Christ. You've always had such a fine way with words, haven't you? I just know insert-famous-poet here would be quaking in their boots.

He gave her a slight smile. The smile that indicated Mia had asked a question he had been waiting for her to answer.

"I'm trans. Oh, and my name's River."

Mia felt her mouth turn dry. Her eyes darted up and down his body. All the while beating herself up inside for being so crude as to search for some indication, some *sign* that might have given away that he wasn't cisgender. But no matter how much she scanned him, she was just coming up short. He seemed so...no, *normal* was not the word she was looking for. Not at all. Well, whatever the word was, he looked it.

It was the first time she had heard the word spoken aloud by somebody. Back in her hometown, words like that had been hidden well, and if they were used, it came in the form of ugly slurs you were encouraged to use against them. That was the only exposure she got until she landed upon some resources in the public library, then in a few movies and shows she'd pirate online. In those days, she had to find out on her own who you could be, who you could love, and that there was no shame in it, or at least there shouldn't be. Of course, even when she discovered the words for what she felt, she knew better than to tell anyone. Not even the few classmates she had loosely defined as 'friends' had known, even if they may have had suspicions that she was a little different from them. Mostly, they just told her she was 'weird' or 'girly.'

And now, here was this tall, tattooed barista just saying a word like 'trans' as easily as if she had asked his favorite ice cream flavor. It felt like a kick to the stomach, making her feel out of place, like she had walked into a movie set. Question A: what world did this guy live in where you could just *say* something like that to a complete stranger? Question B: how the hell did she get out of this world and enter that one?

Now she sensed the barista—River—was shifting his weight from one foot to the other. He had just come out to her, and she had replied with the most awkward period of silence known to the postmodern world.

"Wow. I never..." She swallowed. "I never would have guessed...and, uh...I mean that as a big compliment, of course. You look like...you know..."

River's eyes lit up. The words had come out even worse than they sounded in her head. But either he understood her intent, or he had gotten used to hearing that.

"Well, thank you. I try my best," he said, stretching his shoulders back. And just like that, he went back to scrubbing at the espresso machine. "Anyway, that's just one of many groups you can join around campus. Whatever piques your interest or whatever you want to do."

Mia dried her palms on her jeans and cleared her throat. Was this possibly her way in? Were these the people who could finally understand what she was going through?

"Sure. I mean...I could check it out. I have a couple gay friends so I'm kind of curious about all the gay stuff. I'm Carlos, by the way," she said as casually as possible, hoping he would not detect any desperation.

"Yeah, I got you. We meet in Williams Hall every Friday night at seven-thirty."

"Cool. Maybe I'll come sometime." She rushed back to her coffee and computer. This paper would not write itself, and she needed to focus. Even so, now and then she would steal glances at him, her heart aching to barrage him with all the questions she needed to know:

'How did you do it?' 'Did you lose any friends when you came out?' 'How did you get on hormones?' 'How do you keep doing it?' 'Was it worth coming out?' 'Does it get better?'

It went about as painlessly as ripping out one's own fingernails, but she managed to at least get out the first draft of her paper. For the rest of the day, she asked herself if she was ready for such a thing as going to a support group. Perhaps a better question was if she would ever be ready, and if it was not about being ready but if this was what she needed. She had gotten so used to going about the world living in this shadow, this fear, that at this point it came as second nature. Like a rock in her shoe that she had learned to shuffle around for minimal discomfort.

And yet, whenever she considered the possibility that maybe, just maybe, River and those other kids would be able to help her, she couldn't let it go. She kept circling back to it, like a never-ending cycle of her own self-inflicted torment.

That night, Mia had nightmares. Nightmares about her first foster father dragging her down the hall by her arm, his breath stinking of gin as he dislocated her shoulder. They only took her to the hospital when she wouldn't stop screaming. She dreamed of her foster mother's best friend laughing at her when she wet the bed, and even she had not understood why she kept doing that. And then she dreamed about the night red and blue flashing lights filled her dark little world, coloring all the stained walls, and a woman wrapped her in a blanket and carried her outside into the cold.

River Solinski watched the new student shuffle out of the coffee shop yet again. As always, the look of surprise when he said he was trans never ceased to amuse him. True, he passed very well, but no one appeared to see it coming. Not that that was a bad thing, of course. He just got a kick out of it every time.

However, he thought about the kid as his day went on and he tried to find stuff to do to help his shift go by faster. There was something about Carlos that seemed…different. River couldn't quite put his finger on it. He just sensed there was a whole other level to the kid that maybe Carlos himself wasn't aware of.

But River had noticed the little things in the guy that were not all that unfamiliar to him. Like the way Carlos talked too fast, or the way he constantly pulled at his clothes. The way he shuffled around and tried not to draw attention to himself. It was like watching someone pretend they weren't covered in bug bites, or someone having to wear a costume they despised.

Maybe River was wrong. He could be reading into it too deep. And it wasn't fair to make assumptions so large of a person he hardly knew. But still, he could not help but wonder.

Chapter Four

Mia had been in college for a month when she finally worked up the courage to go to River's support group.

She kept making up excuses for herself, which wasn't hard. She had lots of studying to do. She needed to pick up extra hours at her job to afford groceries ('groceries', of course, being defined as frozen dinners and iced coffees). Or she just wasn't up for being around people if she could help it.

But almost every time she went to get her usual delicacy at the coffee shop, she got to see River. River usually had something funny to say to her as he made her order, like his latest idea for the name of a new menu item or an observation he had about one of the college professors. Although, to be fair, she thought he was so cute that he could read off a math problem and she'd laugh. He never brought up the support group, but he didn't have to. She could tell the question was lingering somewhere. Still, at least she slowly got to know River's sense of humor, which was off-beat and unpredictable, like she was always three steps behind his train of thought or like she had missed the first half of the joke. But she liked it. He didn't seem to care how peculiar or nonsensical he came across. As if he was either completely tuned out of social cues, or he just didn't bother to keep up with them.

Finally, after lots of trying and failing to talk herself out of it, she caved in.

That Friday, at a quarter past seven, Mia stepped into Williams Hall, a small library and study area. The support group met in one of the back rooms, where a large bay window provided a view of the wooded area on campus. A long coffee table had cups of hot tea, a bowl of snacks, and a stack of papers and folders. River was there, wearing a black hoodie and comfy-looking black pants, and Mia felt herself breathe a little faster at seeing him. About a dozen other students were there too. What struck Mia was that none of them, at least in appearance, seemed to have anything in common. River had dark clothes and tattoos and sitting next to his left was a girl wearing a flowery dress and carrying a small pastel pink satchel. Another wore a basketball jersey, shorts, and gym shoes. Two others wore mismatched blouses and skirts. Another had a crop top, leggings, and combat boots. In fact, it seemed all they had in common was being in this group. It was also nice to not be the only person of color in the room for a change, which came as a relief.

And that was the whole point, wasn't it? They all belonged in this community, no matter what they looked like or what they did with their lives or what their other interests were. Maybe that meant she could fit in, too.

The girl in the flowery dress noticed her first and waved her over.

"Hey, Carlos, right? You're just in time," she said with a big smile.

Mia waved and took a seat to the right of River, then wondered if it had been a bad idea to pick a spot so close to the guy she was crushing on. But it was too late to move, or she would make it weirder, so she just stayed put and tried not to look at him. River, upon noticing her, grinned and offered her a fist bump.

"My favorite customer's here!" he said, this time even louder than his usual tone, which was already quite loud as it was.

She tried not to blush as she fist-bumped back.

"I bet you say that to all of them, loser."

"Yeah, well, you can't prove that." He glanced around the room and cleared his throat. "So I think almost everyone's here. Looks like we have three new faces so let's all introduce ourselves. Name, pronouns, and anything else you want to share. I'll go first. I'm River, and I use he/him pronouns." He glanced at the girl next to him who pulled back her long, black hair.

"I'll go next. I'm Grace, she/her pronouns and I'm bisexual," she said with the cutest smile Mia had ever seen in her life.

"Sean, they/them and he/him, and I'm also bi," the one in sports gear said next.

Mia, of course, was the last one to go. When it was her turn, she cleared her throat. She had had about forty seconds to think about how she was going to say this, and of course, it all decided to just up and leave her mind as she tried to say it.

"Hey, I'm Carlos. I use he/him, and, well...I guess you could say I'm...questioning. Curious. Open-minded?" She shrugged. She hoped that they wouldn't ask her any prodding questions or try to get her to open up more. But as the meeting went on, she realized it was less of an actual 'meeting' and more of an open discussion. It took them all of ten minutes to go from batting around ideas for the next fundraiser to energetic discourse on the movie that hit theaters last weekend, and she wasn't even sure how they ended up there. Now and then she chimed in a bit, offering a comment or a joke when appropriate. But just to be safe, Mia didn't say too much. She didn't want to be the focus of attention.

When they finished later that evening (cued by River glancing at his phone and saying, "Oh shitballs, we went over again. See you next week,"), Mia got up and considered slipping out before anyone could talk to her. And she was almost successful, too. She could have made her escape. Told herself that she went, she did it, and could go back to her life now like nothing happened.

But at the last moment, she found herself stopping, looking back at this group of people who were so openly themselves. River was chatting with two other guys, one of whom said a joke that made River laugh so loud it echoed off the walls.

You're going to regret this, a little voice told her. *They're all going to hate you.*

Of course, that was possible. She had been hated before, and she knew how to handle it. But a bigger question held her down, and that question made it impossible to just walk away.

What if they don't *hate you? What if this could be what you've been looking for?*

Mia drummed her fingers on her leg, and bit her lip. And then she finally walked up to Grace, then stood by waiting until Grace noticed her. She cleared her throat and said it before she could talk herself out of it.

"Hey, Grace? So, I was wondering if maybe I could…talk sometime. Maybe with you and River?" She tried not to cringe at her words. *Oof, yes, let's sound even more desperate next time.*

Grace lit up at that, as if she had been hoping for Mia to ask that.

"Of course! Do you want to exchange phone numbers?"

Mia nodded, and they swapped phones to text their numbers to themselves.

"Thanks. I'm busy this week, but maybe sometime we could chat. I kind of have some questions to ask you guys. If that's okay. Totally don't worry if it isn't."

"Sure thing. We'd be happy to chat with you! There's no wrong questions."

Mia just nodded. The immediate acceptance felt overwhelming. Like it was all too much at once. And she was afraid of latching on, spilling her life story to these people she barely knew only for them to figure out she was too much of a mess and backed off. She could see it now. She'd end up telling them all the details of her story and they would just ask, *"Well, if you really* are *transgender, why do you still live as Carlos? Isn't that hypocritical of you? Maybe you're just a big, fat faker."*

She took a deep breath and closed her eyes.

Calm down. Don't have a mental breakdown over something that hasn't even happened yet. Get out of your own head!

Later, as she sat down to get to studying, she felt a hurt in her chest. Not a physical ache, but a strain that dragged her down. She had no idea where it came from or why it was there and tried to ignore it, but all she could think about was the girl named Grace she met today.

It wasn't until Mia lay in her bed late that night that it came to her. Grace embodied so much of what she wished she could look like. The way she dressed, the way she carried herself, the way other people in public, be it a stranger or a friend, responded to her and approached her. The energy she brought to a room and how the room felt when she left.

All of it was what Mia could only wish to have. And Mia had no reason to hate Grace. She had been nothing but kind to her and could probably end up being one of the first people she ended up coming out to. She couldn't hate Grace for things that weren't Grace's fault.

But Mia wanted to. She wanted to be angry and jealous. Because did *any* of those girls have any idea how lucky they were? Did they have any idea how much they had been given?

Well, they'd better.

"Carlos. I need to talk to you for a minute," her professor of her Humanities class said before she could shuffle away.

Mia took a deep breath and turned around, expecting the worst. This professor had to be one of the most stubborn she had ever met. And to think she once imagined General Ed classes would be easy.

She grabbed a chair and sat down. It had been a couple of weeks since Mia attended the support group. She did want to talk to River and Grace, she really did. Ideally, she could get to know them first and, therefore, get a better idea of how or when to come out to them. But every time either of them said she had an afternoon open, something in Mia froze up and put its guard up and couldn't move, and she'd sputter out a hasty excuse about how she was busy. Plus, River had given her his number too so they could coordinate a time to meet up, and seeing his name in her notifications made her feel giddy; that didn't help. Maybe she was more into goth/emo/punk guys after all. Or maybe River was just that cute. Hell, she'd probably fall for him if he was a lumbersexual.

The professor pulled up his leather-seated stool.

"I know what you're going to say," Mia began. "My attendance has been…yeah."

"You've barely been showing up at all." He crossed his arms. "Now I don't make attendance mandatory. You know that. But if you want a shot at *not* failing, it wouldn't kill you to be here now and then."

Mia looked down at her hands. A ring of black was constantly around and underneath her fingernails from her job. She didn't hate this class. In fact, she kind of enjoyed it; who knew the history of western art was so gay? But between other classes and trying to work more hours just to afford her expenses, it happened to be one of the courses that slipped through the cracks.

When she didn't say anything for a solid thirty seconds, the professor sighed and adjusted his round wire-framed glasses.

"So what are you going to do? Are you going to drop out or are you going to start being here and turning in your assignments? Have you thought about joining a study group, maybe?"

"Sorry. Look, Professor Bowen. I'm going to have to be straight with you. I'm struggling a little." She winced, hating that it had come to this, but she didn't see any other way.

Professor Bowen's eyes narrowed. Nothing indicated surprise or sympathy.

"It's been hard. I'm trying. I really am. I don't want to fail this class."

"Have you talked to admission and counseling? They might be able to help you sort things out."

"But if you—"

"I'm not your friend, Mia. I'm your teacher. If you need help getting through the semester, those are the people you'll go to." He stood up and brushed off his pants. He grabbed a few books off his desk, sighing deeply. "I don't want you to fail, but you need to make a change."

Luckily for her, she had a job that provided a good escape from the rest of the world.

At the auto repair, the hours were long, but she enjoyed it. The old fridge in the front lobby hadn't worked in years and the whole place stunk of tires, oil, and cigarettes. Mia loved it. It felt like a home away from home, and not in a toxic capitalist 'we're not coworkers, we're family' way either. The paychecks kept her afloat, if only just above the surface, and the job could be a foot in the door for something better one day. She figured she could at least be grateful for how much worse it could be.

Working on cars had been her happy place since she was eleven. In those days, she would walk half a mile after school or during the summer and visit a mechanic who ran a small shop out of his garage. He was an older guy whose wife had passed away years ago and had no kids, but he was really nice and always had time for the weird little foster kid who stopped by. At first, she hung out in his shop just for the company, but then she started helping him out around the shop in exchange for a free soda or a snack. He started teaching her a thing or two, and within a couple of years she was tackling her own projects. Looking back, she realized that even with all the hours of kindness he gave her, he had been getting free labor that whole time, and he had known it. Which, if she overthought it, really fucked with her sense of trust in people and lack thereof.

But, in the end, she didn't regret it. She got good skill and experience out of the whole deal, so who was the real winner?

She was currently elbows-deep in her latest project, face covered in filth and engine oil. Her brain ached from studying, and this was all she needed to feel better. Hours later, Mia couldn't feel the tips of her fingers from working so long. She stood up and headed to the bathroom and scrubbed as much grease off herself as she could. The water hit like ice, and she heard her coworkers sharing a joke wafting from right outside the door.

"Carlos! Want to come have a drink with us?" one of her coworkers asked as he signed off on the sheet at the front desk.

Mia thought about what she had to do that night. Go back to her dorm, do some homework, shower, then jack off and pass out. Maybe it would all be a little better with some alcohol in her. She probably shouldn't drink, considering how her body reacted when she smelled liquor sometimes. But...she had had a long week.

Fuck it. It sounded like fun.

"Count me in." She threw her work cap at them.

She went with them to the bar, and she ordered a drink she hated because, typical Mia Reyes, she rarely ate or drank anything she liked because what if she ordered something that made everyone realize who she really was. And as she sat there, trying to figure out where to put her hands and how to sit in her chair, she listened to her coworkers talk about their girlfriends and other women in their lives in ways that Mia despised. Not just because of how awful it was, and it was awful, but because a little part of her actually *wanted* a man to talk about her that way. A part of her wanted to be the woman of interest in that conversation. To be thought of and desired in that way.

Fuck, what's the matter with you? You're just as bad as these guys.

"Want to do shots?" Someone nudged her in the side.

She did not have the self-control to say no.

Mia remembered little of the rest of the night. She just knew that when she got back to her dorm, she grabbed her razor and stared at it for a long time, before stripping and hopping in the tub. Without thinking about it, she got to work on the hairy mess covering her legs. Too drunk to think about the papers she needed to finish. Too drunk to think about how much her legs would itch the next day because she didn't use shaving cream. All she knew was she looked down at her legs and thought, 'This has got to go.'

When it was all said and done, she was staring down at the clumps of curly dark hair all over the small bathtub and her poor clogged up razor. And because she was still drunk enough, she reached up and shaved her armpits too.

Of course, she would regret it all in the morning and have a good talk with herself about what she had done and what people would say if they saw. But that wasn't for a few hours. Right now, she could enjoy herself and admire her smooth skin.

Chapter Five

Two weeks before the holiday break, Mia finally bit the bullet and agreed to meet up with River and Grace. They decided on a local deli that served typical soups, salads, and sandwiches, and had a lovely view of the downtown of their little college city. Mia showed up wearing one of her favorite shirts, a salmon pink tee that wasn't really all that 'feminine', but the color made it good enough for her, so it was sort of a comfort, like getting to carry around your own invisible security blanket. Plus, it hugged her sides in a way that made her feel nice if she squinted.

The two had arrived a few minutes before her and found a table in the back. As Mia was now realizing was typical of their fashion styles, River wore all black and Grace wore a cute dress. They could not have looked more different, especially with River being so tall while Grace was so petite, she would disappear in a crowd were it not for all the bright colors in her outfit. As soon as Grace spotted her, she waved Mia over.

"Carlos! It's good seeing you again. How have you been?" Grace asked.

"Busy. And you guys?"

"Busy too," said River. He was currently fixated on folding a straw wrapper into as tiny a square as possible. As she sat across from them, Mia noticed he had a faux-leather bag with him. A few notebooks and a laptop were poking out, along with a pair of expensive-looking headphones. Maybe he had rich parents paying for his college intuition, she mused. That would make him a spoiled brat, and then maybe she could stop feeling things for him.

"Yeah, well, college will do that to all of us," Mia said.

"And in a band on top of all that. Poor River hardly has time for anything! I've been having to pick up the slack at the group," Grace said, to which he rolled her eyes like this was an inside joke between them.

"A band? No kidding." *Of course he's in a fucking band. Wait, have I ever been into musicians before? I guess guys with electric guitars are kind of hot. And boy bands are kind of cute. Although I hated the band kids at school…oh god, focus, Mia.* "What's it called?"

"It's called, um…" River grabbed another straw, pulled off the wrapper, and started tying it into a ribbon. "…History of the Disillusioned."

"What do you sound like?"

He laughed, almost nervously.

"That's a good question. We're sort of indie gothic rock, with inspiration from Seattle grunge, early nineties nu metal, and Scandinavian avant-garde metal."

Mia just blinked at him. That was a lot of information with literally no reference points she knew of. Yes, she had 'basic' taste in music, and what of it? You like what you like.

"That is…huh. I'll have to go to a show to see whatever the hell that sounds like. Where do you play?"

"Just around the city, mostly at the bar on Eighteenth and Lincoln. But we're trying to get more gigs," said River. His eyes did not leave her, but he still kept playing with the straw wrapper.

"Remind me to get tickets sometime." She waited until their food arrived before she decided there was no more beating around the bush. "So…thanks for agreeing to talk with me. River, is it okay if I ask you a couple…personal questions?"

"Fuck yeah! A-M-L-A. Ask me literally anything," was the very River-typical answer River gave her.

This time, Mia felt she had come prepared. Or she liked to think she was prepared. Mostly because these were the very questions she had once told herself that, if she ever got to meet anyone like her, she would want to hear from them. Well, no turning back now.

"How long have you been out? How did you come out?"

He swiped a straw from the vacant table beside them and tore off the wrapper before he began to speak.

"Well, I came out to everyone when I was twelve. It was just before the school year started. My parents were going over the list of things we needed to get. And that included name tags on my stuff and new clothes. And in that moment, I just realized I couldn't take going back to school as a girl. I had been wondering about my gender for some time, and I knew a couple kids at my school who were also out and starting to transition, so I had an idea of what could be going on with me. But that moment sort of made everything crystal clear. It just hit me. So right there, I told them the truth. I told them I was a boy, I was always going to be a boy, and that I wasn't going to live as their daughter anymore."

"Holy shit. What did they say?" Somehow, that didn't surprise her about him. That River did not so much as come out of the closet but bust down the door, bulldoze his way into the rainbow, and demand to be heard.

River stopped folding the wrapper and looked down at his hands. Mia hesitated before digging into her food, self-conscious of her eating habits, which included scarfing meals down way too fast and not always using utensils when she should. River didn't even dig into his meal before continuing with the story.

"It was a mix. My parents have always been pretty open-minded, but it did give them a bit of a shock. Because it's one thing when your neighbors or friends are part of the community, another when your own kid is. They struggled and pushed back. They wanted me to be really, really sure I knew what I wanted. And that took a while. We fought, but then...it just kind of started to clear up. Once they got over that shock and sort of worked out what it meant for me and my future, they started to come around. They bought me boys' clothes. Got used to calling me by my chosen name. A few months after I came out, they took me to see a therapist who put me on hormone blockers. But...the rest of my family is a different story. Especially my siblings."

"How many?" she asked.

"Four brothers. And I'm the youngest."

"Ohhh...shit." She tried to imagine that. Of course, some of the foster homes she had lived in had had a few other kids, but she knew it wasn't the same. She had no concept of what having actual siblings was like, much less four big brothers.

"Yup. They'd go on about how I was taking away the only little sister they ever had, that I wasn't being fair, all that stuff. A couple of them were always pretty hard on me growing up and when I came out it got worse. They hated everything about it. A couple of them have warmed up to it and are mostly cool now, but I still have a couple brothers who don't want anything to do with it."

"Shit. I'm sorry." Mia's face fell. That was not the story she had been hoping to hear at all. She had hoped for a lot more sunshine and puppies and support and acceptance, not this messy, complicated stuff she supposed was, well, real life.

River shrugged and gave her a smile. She couldn't tell how much of it was forced.

"I mean, it is what it is. I can't make my brothers be okay with it, you know? And the rest of my family is kind of all over the place. My mom's parents are very progressive, so they were always on board. They live in the same neighborhood, so I would ride my bike over to their house all the time to get away from all the drama and they'd spoil me. My dad's parents are the complete opposite. Very uptight, rigid, hardcore conservative. But my dad cut himself off from them years ago, so it doesn't really matter what they think at all. They're just a bunch of paranoid MAGA-brainrotted assholes. Oh, and I have a couple aunts on my mom's side. They're all right. One of my uncles is *really* weird about it...I'm probably saying too much, aren't I?"

"No, no! This is good. It's...not what I expected, honestly," Mia said. "I don't know. I kind of imagined it would be all or nothing. Either your entire family accepts you or they reject you. I didn't think they would be all over the place."

"Yeah. Family reunions were full of enough drama before I came out, so you can imagine." He laughed. Another loud laugh. They had startled her the first few times, but she found herself starting to warm up to them, picking up the music within the cacophony. "I don't know how much of that story helps. Is there anything else you want to know?"

"I don't even know what to make of most of this stuff. I've known about it for a while, and I'm just…" She paused, and in the silence, she felt them waiting for her to explain more. "I'm in a questioning phase, you could say. I need to know more. Learn more."

River and Grace nodded together.

"I can help with that. Like I said, any questions, anything you want to know. I'm an open book," he said.

Their eyes locked, and there were a few moments in which they did nothing but regard each other. And for the briefest second Mia got the feeling that River was seeing right through her, and he knew who she really was, and that in a strange way they were both looking into a mirror. Then the moment ended when River took his fork and had a small bite from his meal. Mia followed the gesture and had a few bites before asking,

"Can I ask something else?"

"Of course." He took another bite.

"How did you know?"

"How did I know what?"

"You know. How did you *know*?" Mia sipped her drink, watching River sit back in his seat and put his hands on his thighs.

"I kind of…always knew," he said after a long pause. "The little signs growing up. Wanting my hair cut short. Wanting to fit in with my brothers and not be singled out as the baby sister. Hating everything that reminded me I was a girl. Like when they would separate the boys from the girls for class projects, or when I'd get birthday gifts that were different from my brothers'. And one day, it just all came together, and I realized who I really was."

"That's heavy stuff." Mia felt silly for saying that as it was coming out of her mouth. He probably thought she was just some creepy dude who liked to call himself 'bi-curious' only so he could get into a threesome.

"Yup, real heavy. Hey, I need to go smoke." River stood up, grabbing his leather bag.

"Oh. Can I come with?" Mia already found herself fumbling for her pack.

"Only if you don't smoke from a pipe."

Grace shook her head, smiling.

"You two go on ahead. I'm staying right here with my boba tea, thank you."

They headed out the side door to the alley beside the deli, where the wood pallets piled up. River leaned against the brick wall and pulled out a pack of Marlboro Blacks. Mia lit her menthol and glanced at him.

"I'm sorry if this question is rude, but I'm super curious, so it's going to kill me if I don't ask. Your name. How did you pick it?"

To her surprise, River laughed again. It was blissful, like she had just said a great pun.

"I actually love answering this question! So when I was a kid, I had this huge, huge crush on River Phoenix. I loved all his movies. *The Thing Called Love* and *Dogfight* are my top two if

I had to pick, and personally I think *Stand By Me* is overrated, albeit still good. But I loved everything about him. How he did his hair, his attitude, the way he dressed. And years later, I figured out that it wasn't just a crush, or maybe it wasn't at all. I don't know, sometimes it's neither or both and feelings are fucking weird. But the point is, he was exactly the kind of guy I wanted to be. He had the look and energy I wanted to embody when I transitioned. So when I wanted to pick my new name, it was my first and only choice. Haven't looked back. But it's fully my name, and it's like its own thing separate from all that now. He just really inspired it."

She chose her name at sixteen. She had combed through a list of ideas on and off for a while, not putting much thought into it because it wasn't like she could use it anytime soon. It came down to how 'Mia' sounded. The way it felt when she looked in the mirror and said it, the way it appeared when written on paper. It was small, cute, a petite sort of name. For an extra bonus, she could change the dot in the letter 'i' to a heart, for that little feminine touch.

"That's really cool. I love that story. And…oh, I can see that now that you mentioned it." Mia looked him up and down, feeling like a whole other layer of him had been peeled back. Her English teacher in freshman year showed them *My Own Private Idaho*, so she had an idea of what he was talking about. She made a note to pirate the other two online when she got the chance. "One more question, and then I'm done, I swear." She paused. "Is it…hard? I mean, of course it's hard, but…what's it like being out? Especially with someone like you who's open about it. You don't even hide that you're trans. You told me flat-out, and I was a stranger. Wouldn't you be worried if I was some transphobic asshole who would try to get you fired or try to hurt you or worse?"

River took a couple of drags on his cigarette and tousled his hair before answering.

"Well, it has its good and its bad. There's always a risk when you put yourself out there. But if I wasn't open, I wouldn't have made as many friends. And it's not something I want to hide. I'm proud of who I am. And for me, part of that is not hiding that from anyone, even if it's risky. Not everybody has the chance to be open about it. But it's what I chose for myself."

"I see. Makes sense." She focused on her cigarette and could not hide the bitter edge to her tone this time. "I grew up in the middle of nowhere. Very conservative. Like Confederate flags everywhere conservative. If you were different at all, you didn't tell anyone, or you might as well paint a big red target on your back. And I guess that's why I'm still having trouble figuring it out. I didn't have anyone to talk to. I didn't trust anyone."

"Damn. I'm sorry." River winced.

"Yeah. I have a lot of catching up to do with the outside world."

"This isn't a bad place to start. Catching up, I mean."

"You grew up here?"

"Nah, out east. My family is from Greenwich. It's just out of New York City."

"Lucky bastard," she said, trying to sound as playful as possible. But deep down, jealousy was turning everything the color of bile. Here was a guy like River who had been living as his true self for over a decade and looked gorgeous, got to have a mostly open-minded family from a wealthy city, which probably meant he had had all sorts of connections to get him a good start on his career and transition. Meanwhile, she spent her whole childhood far away from any support or resources and just focused on getting through the day, much less planning her future. Not to mention how that exposure to other trans people helped him come out so much sooner. It was unfair. It made her feel cheated out of so much.

"In many ways, yes. I am. I know I have it way luckier than most."

"Let's go back inside. It's freezing out here." She ducked back in, unable to look him in the eye for a few minutes. Mia made herself smile, even as she was still processing everything River told her before, and how much she wished it would be so easy to tell him she was like him. Their conversation drifted into lighter topics, and by dessert, they ended up discussing their college majors.

"Have a preference for a science subject?" River asked.

"Mechanics, of course," Mia said. "But I'm also kind of into nuclear physics, plant genetics and horticulture, um…and I've just started reading up on marine biology."

"That's amazing." Grace beamed.

"Real amazing. See, science was never my strength. And math. Makes my brain hurt."

"Because you're a starving artist, right?" Mia said with a teasing smile as they got up from the table.

"Hey now, we got to open for a band that's been on international tours, thank you very much." He scowled, but just before Mia could worry that she had crossed a line, he gave her a smile to signal he was returning the jest.

"Yeah, well, when your first album sells a million copies, I'll take back what I said. Oh, that reminds me. Last question for real this time. Being famous, or I guess at least being a performer…is that hard with being…?"

River shrugged.

"I mean, we always get that one person or two who makes a big stink about it. But we all just embrace that part of ourselves. We're all very open, and that's drawn in a bit of a crowd. Lots of our fans are also part of the queer community."

"Wait, 'we'?" Mia felt her head begin to spin.

"Oh, yeah. No one in the band is cisgender." River grinned, and she could tell he had been hoping to tell her this fun little trivia too. "So I'm lead singer and keyboard. Cat's nonbinary and on the drums. The bassist and rhythm guitars are both trans girls, and then the other trans guy is on lead guitar."

"Okay, well, now I really have to hear what kind of music you guys do." She glanced at the time and winced, hoping she would get to her next class on time. "Shoot, well…I should get going. Thank you both. This was great."

"Anytime! This was really lovely, and I'd love to hang out more." Grace smiled.

"See you around?" asked River.

"Yeah. See you around."

Chapter Six

River always got nervous before his band performed.

Even though The History of the Disillusioned had done dozens of gigs for the past three years, he never ceased to get anxiety attacks before going on stage. He hunched over the small bathroom sink at the back of the bar, holding his bottle of medication and studying how much he had left. After a brief pause, he took his pill and washed it down with a handful of water from the sink. Then he went back to putting more black eyeliner on. Tonight, River wore a black long-sleeved shirt with some tears and gashes around the ribs, arms, and back, skinny black jeans, and his favorite pair of large black boots. To finish off the costume he had a torn black scarf hanging down over his shoulders and down his back. His hair hung in a mess over his eyes.

The bar on Eighteenth and Lincoln was not packed tonight, but a lot of the local fans showed up, always a good sign. It was small, decorated with posters of cult classic films and old metal signs rescued from the scrap pile, and it had about half a dozen unique cocktails on the menu. River had always liked the atmosphere here. Once he stepped up on stage, the fans in front clapped and cheered. Everyone else just applauded the bare minimum and clutched their drinks, staring at the group like they were about to summon a demon. He couldn't complain. The band's social media pages each had several hundred likes. People from all over the United States and even some in Europe and Canada knew about them.

The lead guitarist, Oliver, introduced the band. Oliver was someone with the energy and strength of a six-foot-seven basketball player trapped in a five-foot-one ninety-pounds-soaking-wet body, a little powerhouse who didn't know how to give anything short of 110% when performing onstage. To further the point, Oliver kept his curly hair long and unkempt, and since his top surgery last year, he never wore a shirt unless socially or legally required. He and River met through a mutual friend years ago, bonded over their love of music, and started the band once they found a few others in their circle who were interested.

River adjusted the mic, eyes focused on the floor, shifting his feet from side to side. When Oliver finished explaining that the band was debuting a new song tonight, the lights went dim save for a red spotlight on River. Then he gripped the mic stand and began to sing.

At the beginning of the song, River started with a slow, haunting, but otherwise sweet melody, pulling from his years in middle school when Amy Lee's voice got him through every bad day. But the closer he got to the bridge, the more his voice dropped into a more guttural tone, building in intensity and rage and pulling the listeners into a much darker place than they started. River took a deep breath, squeezing the mic, his chest heaving. The Ativan was helping, but he still felt his heart pounding. By the chorus, he wasn't singing anymore so much as growling, almost screaming into the mic. That was something the fans adored about the band, saying it even scared them sometimes, how animalistic River's singing could sound.

It had been bad enough when he wrote the lyrics with his band, as the song channeled much of all their fears and memories. From the bullying, both from his brothers and kids at school, to the accident, to the violence and abuse he had had to survive over the years. Friendships gone ugly, exes he never should have dated, lines he had been forced to cross, images and smells tattooed onto his brain. His bad temper and tendency to let out his anger in unhealthy ways, like the fights he used to start all the time in high school and early college days, even though he was working so hard not to do that anymore. To say nothing of the lyrics contributed by other band members, which meant that when he performed, he carried not just his own pain through the words but theirs too, all their stories swimming together in words that could only be sung, not spoken. Tears rushed to his eyes, and he lost himself in the moment. He let himself scream out his rage, his horror, his revulsion at those years that would always feel like they happened mere minutes ago. The fans, thinking it was all part of the act, cheered even louder.

After the show, River didn't stay with the band to mingle with the fans. He just couldn't. Not this time. Instead, he rushed back to the bathroom, shaking like someone had rattled him, the neon lights swirling above. Inside, he clutched at the counter and realized that sooner or later he was going to throw up. Rather than wait, he opted to just get it over with and shoved his fingers down his throat until he could empty his stomach contents in the toilet. Waves of feverish heat crashed over him when it was over and done. It felt good.

Victoria, the bassist and backup vocals, found him a couple of minutes later. She didn't look shocked. This would not be the first time she saw their lead singer like this, but her eyes got big as she approached him. He felt her fingertips graze his spine. He had no control over the flinch in his body. Victoria pulled her hand away like he had burned her.

"Christ, River…you okay?"

He shook his head and fumbled for his bottle of pills.

"I'll be alright." He coughed. "I just need a few minutes."

"I told you we shouldn't have done that song live. It was too much. You weren't ready."

"I had to." He spat into the toilet and flushed it, then stood up. "Mind ordering me a drink?"

"Yeah. Sure thing." She left him alone to go get his order: rum, coke, orange juice, and whipped cream, with a cherry garnish. One of the bar's specialties.

River ducked his head in the sink and ran cold water over the back of his neck. The stars in his vision slowly subsided. Then, when he felt a little more grounded, a bit more present in the here and now, he left to rejoin the band.

Victoria may have had a point, though. It was one thing to write down lyrics that expressed some of the worst moments of your life. Yet another to have to sing those in front of an audience that needed the show to go on.

River had texted Mia the invitation a few days ago. Now and then, Mia read the text over again, just to make sure she got it right.

River: hey so the band's drummer is having a birthday this week, so we're throwing a party for her. Sunday the 18th, 7:30 PM to whenever the fuck we want which will probably be like 2 or 3 AM lol. it's at my apartment on 110 Falcon Drive, Apt 3. If you're down to come i'd love to see you there!!

Mia hadn't been the kid in high school who got invited to parties. Crashed a few, though. Got high with the other outcasts and swam in the pool fully clothed before they got kicked out. So, all things considered, the idea of someone wanting her to actually show up and just be there was something she had to take a little while to reckon with. But she had already told River she would be there (she texted him back ten seconds after he messaged her), and it felt wrong to go back on her word, especially to her new friend. She re-read their conversation from earlier that week, hoping she hadn't seemed too desperate.

Carlos: ok, but only if you'll have food there that isn't just one bowl of chips. Because that would just be sad

River: just for that, i'm going to make four pans of lasagna. Now you have no excuses

Carlos: you got me! i'll be there!:)

At seven, she took stock of her appearance and opted for slim-fitting jeans, converse shoes, and a large graphic tee from the bargain section. She tucked the shirt into her jeans, enjoying how the shirt's shape made her frame look smaller. Made her appear to take up less space.

The party was already starting up when she got there. She parked on the street and walked up the steps to the brownstone building, soon finding River's apartment. To her disappointment, he wasn't at the door greeting the guests. Just by glancing inside, Mia saw dozens and dozens of people. It was a spacious apartment, but it had crowded up fast. Although with someone like River, she shouldn't be surprised that he was the type of person who had a ton of friends, especially the partying type. He probably didn't even think twice about the weird kid he had lunch with the other week. She saw a lot of young adults with tattoos, colored hair, piercings, and alternative clothes. Exactly River's type of people, or at least his band's type. But there were also many dressed more casually and 'basic', like her. She also spotted quite a handful of kids who seemed to be more Grace's crowd, preppy and bubbly, wearing clothes in pastel colors or thrift store finds with new life breathed into them. Mia's heart sank. Was there anyone here she could talk to? No, that wasn't even wording the question right. Was there anyone here who would want to talk to her?

Shoving her hands in her pockets, she shuffled through the living room until she found the table with bowls and trays of food laid out. She didn't see River anywhere, which made her shoulders sag. A guy as tall as him couldn't be hard to find, right? To pass the time, Mia filled a paper plate with some snacks and wolfed them down. Because, after all, free food is free food is free food. After wandering around the apartment some more, she finally found him in the corner chatting with two other guys. Mia inched closer and closer towards him. Everyone else at the party acted like she wasn't even there, passing by or bumping into her. In part she would prefer it to getting lots of attention, but at the same time, being invisible stung.

River finally looked up, seeing her at last. He wrapped up his conversation and walked up to her.

"Hey, thanks for coming. How are you?" He had to shout over the music. Luckily, he was used to speaking louder than normal, so it wasn't a huge change for him.

"I'm alright. Midterms are a bitch, but I'm surviving."

"You making friends on campus?"

"Eh? Kind of. I got a study group. They're alright. A bunch of nerds, but they're nice."

He shifted his weight, like there was too much height and strength to him he didn't know what to do with. She noticed he had touched up his black nail polish for the occasion.

"Sorry for the big crowd. I was going to have this be a small thing but one thing after another and, well...here we are. Would you like to meet the band?"

"I'd love to!" Mia said before thinking. But as he led her over to a group of several young adults all dressed in a similar dark gothic fashion, she found herself blushing.

"Hey, guys, this is Carlos! Here we have Oliver, lead guitar. Victoria, bassist and vocals. Cat, our drummer. And Emily on rhythm guitar."

Cat, who was even taller than River, with a shaved head and black lipstick, pointed at Carlos' shirt.

"I...am...*obsessed* with that shirt. Where did you get it?"

"Oh, this?" Mia glanced down at the 80s cartoon villain with the caption that could be interpreted as inappropriate. "I've had it for years. I couldn't tell you where I got it."

"Well, I'm jealous. I would *literally* buy it from you if I wasn't broke."

Mia pinned her shyness to the ground, despite the feisty struggle she put up with, and chatted with the band for a few more minutes. As soon as they started talking to her, Mia realized they were all just as sweet and funny as River. And nerdy, too. Real fucking nerdy. In less than twenty seconds, two of them started a deep discussion on which of the two latest video game adaptations of said 80s cartoon was better, and just how bad the live-action adaptation from twenty years ago was. River rolled his eyes, and they exchanged some more 'nice to meet yous' before River slinked away. Mia followed him closely. When it was just them again, River held up his bottle of beer. It was a brand she didn't recognize, but it had an illustration of a trilby on the logo, which told her enough.

"Have a drink with me?"

"Sure," she said, neglecting to mention she would prefer something non-alcoholic until he offered her a beer from the fridge. She blushed. "Actually…just a soda or something. I don't like drinking too much."

"No problem. I'm sorry. I didn't know." He grabbed her a can of Pepsi instead.

"It's okay. I just shouldn't drink in big crowds or tight spaces. Fewer walls and fewer people, the better." She rubbed her palms on her jeans to erase the sweat, thinking of the night she went out with her coworkers. Just because she knew her own boundaries did not mean she always reinforced them, but she had to start somewhere, right?

"Too much noise?" River asked as he put ice cubes in a glass and poured her soda.

As Mia took it, she made a small shrug.

"I think alcohol in enclosed spaces makes me anxious. I had some foster parents who were alcoholics, so it brings up bad memories and fucks with my head. It's stupid, I know. It's silly. Sorry for dumping that on you. That was bad. I'm going to shut up now."

He twitched a bit. She could see the guilt hit him like a punch to the gut. Which made her feel just as guilty for dropping a bomb on him like that. *Way to time the epic tragic backstory reveal, idiot.*

"Oh…*fuck*, I'm sorry, man. If I had known…" He looked like he was going to be sick.

"No, no! It's okay! No worries. I'm okay. I promise." She smiled at him before sipping at her Pepsi. "Don't let me ruin your party."

He stared down at his half-empty bottle before setting it on a nearby shelf.

"Nah, I'm good. This stuff is awful. I don't know who brought it, but it tastes like worms. Fucking hipster craft bull-shit shit. If you're going to drink shit, at least save your money and get fucking Hamm's or something. Let's go smoke."

That she could do. They walked out to the small porch out back. She noted the empty flowerpot on the windowsill and a rickety chair in the corner. He pulled out his pack and offered her one, which she did not turn down. One of these days she really was going to quit. Pinky swear. But cigarettes got her through high school and had become a source of comfort, a security, a morbid company. The world could always knock you down, but that first cigarette at the end of a long shift or class would always be there for you. Don't tell Freud, but Mia sometimes wondered if cigarettes were not unlike pacifiers for adults.

They shared a few minutes of silence, staring out at the downtown area of the city. Mia couldn't complain right now. The party in the background, the cool fresh air. The solidarity that came with sharing something as simple as a cigarette with a person who was a lot like you, even if that person did not know it. Then, River started jotting something down on a piece of paper he had retrieved from his pocket.

"What's that?" she asked.

"Working on something new for the band."

"And you're not going to show me? Rude."

She meant it as a joke, but next thing she knew, River handed it to her so she could read it.

"Still working on it, but what do you think? Is it bad?"

Reading the lyrics, she found herself more moved than she had expected. It was a song about loss, pain, regret, about trying to make peace with horrible things that had happened, about falling into an abyss and having to figure out how to live inside it without climbing out. At least that was how she understood it. She didn't flunk creative writing class, anyway.

"Dark stuff," was all she found herself able to say.

"Not too dark?"

"Not at all. I like it. It's real. It's honest. Life isn't all rainbows and ice cream. Especially when you aren't allowed to talk about the bad stuff."

"I don't know if I could ever write about rainbows and ice cream." He smoked his cigarette while staring out at the city skyline. "Anyway, I like to get different opinions on the lyrics before we start working on it."

"So that's why you invited me here. I see how it is. You're just using me. You wound me, River." She put out her cigarette.

"Rude." He handed her another one, along with his lighter.

"Is it okay if I ask what this song is about? Is it about, you know, being...?" Mia glanced up at him, only to see him shake his head. But he didn't jump on that question, not like the others she had asked, which made her fear she had crossed a line she didn't know had been there. The world seemed to be full of lines like that.

"No, it's…" River's voice trailed, and he leaned against the railing. "I guess it's only fair since I showed it to you. It's about my last relationship."

"Oh…dude. That bad, huh?"

"Uh-huh. I was able to leave her a few months ago, but it got pretty bad. I knew it wasn't normal, and that she was really fucked up and unhealthy and controlling. But she made you feel like she was the only one who ever loved you and you'd be nothing without her. She made you feel like it was all just so normal, or if it wasn't normal, you did something to deserve it. Felt so good to finally get away, but it messed with my head."

Yep. Definitely crossed a line. See, this is why we don't go to parties.

"I think I know what you mean. I've never dated someone like that, but I can imagine." She hated the idea of someone doing that to him. Of getting to date someone as cool and wonderful and amazing and handsome as River and using it to cause him so much pain.

He sighed and rolled his head back, staring up at the stars. Then he let out a loud, angry groan that made his whole body give a shudder.

"Sorry. I think I had too much to drink, and I never know when to shut the fuck up when I drink. You don't need to hear this."

"It's okay! I don't mind. It's my fault for bringing it up, anyway."

And then he said something that was like a dagger to her heart.

"I'm not dating anybody. At least not for a long time. I need to figure a bunch of stuff out before I can even touch that again."

"Makes sense." Mia nodded. She understood that; she really did. But it would not have felt any different if he said she was sentenced to the gallows. Those words felt like a death sentence, and the fact that she could feel herself making this about her only tripled the heavy weight building in her body. He wasn't even hers to claim. All she had was a stupid crush she was too awkward to act on, so why should she be upset that he wasn't interested in dating? Why should she feel rejection when she hadn't given him anything to reject?

Who was she kidding? It's not like he would say 'yes' if she asked him out. She'd exhaust him, or worse, bore him. She probably wasn't even his type. If nothing else, he deserved far better.

"We should probably go back inside." He put out his cigarette. "You like karaoke?"

"Oh, no thank you. I don't sing." She could sense River was rushing back in, wanting to not think about what he had just brought up. Which she found odd, considering he had shown her those lyrics. Maybe he thought he wanted to talk about it and then regretted it.

"I'll go first, I swear. Karaoke is fun!"

"Easy for you to say. You're in a band!"

"You sure?"

"I'm sure. But thanks." Not even her crush on River stood a chance against the odds of her standing in front of a room of strangers and singing. Fuck. That.

River shrugged, pouting, when they both heard someone call out his name from the other end of the room. He started to head over. Mia began to follow him but stopped, figuring it wouldn't be fair to him to follow him along like a lost puppy for the entire party. So she let him go instead, wishing she hadn't made him bring up his shitty ex.

Just like her, she mused. She tried to do a simple, fun thing by showing up at this party. And now she had probably upset one of the few friends she had. All she could do was make things worse just by being there.

Mia went back to the kitchen to find something to eat, but any appetite she may have had was gone. Neither River nor Grace were anywhere to be seen, so she found a spot where she could lean against the wall and wait for them. But whenever she saw a passing glance of one of them, they always seemed busy. Chatting or playing a game with someone. She watched them break out the karaoke machine and watched River get up there, singing party songs from the 80s and 90s, working the crowd up and getting them cheering for him. By then, several people were noticeably drunk, beer bottles and cans filling the trash bags. Had she not known the words he had been writing just minutes ago, she would have looked at him and seen someone who had no idea what it was like to be unhappy. He looked so content, so in his element, while she hid in the shadows. Only those moments shared with the cigarettes revealed that this person, this guy who lit up the party and didn't seem to have an anxious bone in his body, had tasted the darker underbelly of the world too.

It wasn't even half-past nine when she finally gave up. She was too awkward, too quiet, too weird, too boring…too everything. She shuffled out of there without even finding River or Grace to say goodbye. Once in her car, Mia huddled there, hating the burning sensation building up behind her eyes, and she was not even sure why the tears wanted to come. As if she had a good reason for them.

Just as she arrived back on campus, Mia felt her phone buzz. A rush of both butterflies and needles filled her at the name on her notifications.

River: where'd ya go??

Carlos: Sorry, I had to hurry home to study. Thank you for inviting me though! I had fun!

She put her phone on 'do not disturb', not wanting to worry about when he'd respond. Once she was inside her dorm, she tore her clothes off and sat down on the bathroom floor, where it was cold and soothing. But this didn't help her feel better.

After a few minutes she put on some loose-fitting pants and went to her bathroom to disassemble her shaving razor. The more she thought about the party, the more she wished she had never gone in the first place. Now she felt ill, and the world felt out of place, like everything was off by a few degrees.

Then, as she stared down at the razor, it hit her. Of course. Smelling all that alcohol and seeing people drink so much must have done it. However subconsciously, she had to bring back all those wonderful memories. Their favorites had been gin, wine, and vodka, but she remembered they would choke down just about anything that got the job done. They would forget to feed her or help her clean up, resulting in a hazy few months of rashes and stomachaches. She remembered the fear most of all.

It had been years since Mia came down to this. It started when she must have been thirteen and took apart the razor given to her when her facial hair started coming in. She only stopped when someone at school noticed and she got into trouble, and so she found other vices like cigarettes and vandalism.

But now, no one could tattle on her. She could hide it with so much more ease. Not to mention how it was going to be long sleeve season for several months, and that made it even more difficult to stop herself from going back. Of course. How had that never occurred to her when she got here? College wasn't high school at all. Here, she could find solace in this form of release whenever she wanted. No one could stop her. And as soon as she realized that, it was like hitting the point of no return.

She pressed the razor down to her skin, then snapped her hand back. She waited until she saw the small red droplets appear before she did it again.

Tears welled up in her eyes, but not quite enough to fall down her cheeks.

Meanwhile, River felt equally as bad about how his conversation with Carlos went, but for different reasons.

He shouldn't have brought it up. Shouldn't have even written down those ideas for a new lyric, and just saved it for later. It wasn't like Carlos asked him to dump his problems on him. They were supposed to be having fun. Typical River fashion, always burdening people with all his silly problems.

But even all this time later, he still felt shaken up about those few short but dark months. He never should have dated her and thank goodness she graduated last spring and was long gone from the school. But he still heard her voice in his head a lot of the time. He still had old habits he needed to break that she had made him do.

This time, River had sworn she was the last. He wouldn't get into relationships that he knew were bad for him anymore, as some twisted means of punishing himself or trying to find love. He promised himself that the next time he dated someone, if at all, it would be to find and build on something beautiful and good that could happen between them.

Easier said than done, of course. The trick was finding someone like that and suffice it to say that his dating history didn't exactly make him optimistic about his odds of finding that someone.

River pushed those thoughts away and grabbed another drink. But it felt dirtier now, and he was ashamed he may have brought Carlos into an environment that would be triggering for him. He still felt awful for not knowing Carlos didn't like being around alcohol. But whatever he had done, it was too late to fix now. Might as well have a drink or two.

Chapter Seven

Mia wished she could say it ended the same night it started again.

She wished she could say she didn't try it again as soon as the scabs fell off, just to see if it would give her as much of a rush as she remembered it once did. That she didn't feel like she deserved not just the initial pain of making herself bleed, but the constant burning that would persist for days afterwards. That every itching, stinging, searing reminder of her cuts seemed like something she had earned in more ways than one.

If she said that, however, she would be lying.

It always starts with no plans to do it again. So does the second time. And with each time you need a little more to get the same result from the last. And eventually you stop promising yourself there will never be a 'never again', and instead, you begin to accept it. It doesn't help when you look down at your body and realize how easy it'll be to cover yourself if you're careful enough. All the little places a few can fit, and no one will ever know.

Mia liked the rush of adrenaline when the red spots appeared on her biceps and upper thighs. And she hated that she liked it. And that made her like it even more.

Winter break arrived before Mia knew what to do with herself. The weeks had flown by in that rush of her first classes, and now, she found herself with too much free time for her own good. Worse yet was the thought of having nowhere to go and nowhere to be. Sure, she didn't have a ton of close friends on campus, but she had a few friends. Guys she liked to see every day in the dorm and classmates she chatted with or worked on assignments with. Their absence, however short, would feel heavy. Everyone else was flying back to fucking Sacramento or Denver or Houston to stuff their faces with homecooked meals, while she would be stuck here eating instant oatmeal.

No, truth be told, it terrified her. Routine was a bitch, but damn if it kept you even capable of pretending to be okay.

Finals had been so stressful that her brain still hurt even after it was all done. But, good news, at least she did not fail any of her classes. Passed a couple by a hair, but passed nonetheless, thanks to her study group. They weren't in River or Grace's social circle, so Mia kept them at arm's length, a habit she fell into easily. But they were good peers, decent enough. They didn't depend on alcohol to socialize, anyway. They were more into computer games and fan conventions. Not Mia's thing, but it sure was fun to listen to them talk on and on about trading cards. One semester done, seven more to go.

Luckily, after explaining her situation to the admin office, she was allowed to stay on campus during winter break. But that also meant no cafeteria food, so in order to eat, she either had to get takeout or, worse, cook something. Cooking was quite literally the worst. Julian liked to text her recipe ideas, and he always had something to say about how important a good diet was, to the point it was starting to annoy her.

Alan and Julian stopped by at the start of winter break, right when most students were busy moving out. They stood out among the younger faces, a pair of well-dressed bachelors among kids clamoring to be the first to leave. The halls were crowded with students loading bags and tote boxes, mostly filled with dirty clothes. Mia was glad they were leaving. Most of these guys didn't know the difference between detergent and fabric softener, or hadn't even tried, and by now, the dorm's inescapable fragrance was proof that their moms' washers back home would be working overtime over the holidays. When Alan saw Mia, he grinned and gave her a playful smack on the shoulder.

"Hey, man! Good to see you."

Mia wished now, more than she ever had before, that big, tight hugs were more socially acceptable for men. She would love to get one of Alan's, even if she still wasn't sure how to reciprocate them.

"Good to see you too. It's been a while." She glanced between the two men as they shuffled into her dorm for some privacy. "And what the hell are you two doing here?"

"Wondering if you want to crash at our place now that it's winter break. We have plenty of room. You can sleep in the guest room, even though technically it's an office right now but I'm actually trying to merge the office into the living room space and make it more of an open concept," Julian said. The look in his eyes indicated he really, really hoped she'd agree. "Anyway, not the point. Point is, you interested?"

"No." *Shit. Too blunt. Fix it!* Both men blinked at her before she added with haste, "I mean, thanks, but no thanks. I'm staying here for winter break."

Julian gave her a funny look and glanced around the room.

"You sure you want to stay cooped up here when you could be hanging out with us?"

"Why do I get the feeling you just want me in a threesome?"

"Come on, I'm serious. Please? You'll get to eat my world-famous spinach quiche every morning for breakfast," Julian said with a wink.

"I promise we're not boring. We're not like those old boring gays who just sit around all day playing Scrabble and drinking the most disgusting mimosas," Alan said, with an eye roll in Julian's direction that indicated that sentence was pulled from a deeply traumatizing experience. "And we have three game consoles. We don't do a lot for the holidays, but we'd be happy to host you."

"I can visit, but I'd really rather stay here. The admissions office had to pull a few strings so I could live here because of my situation and all, so I'd feel awful if I told them I changed my mind. We'll hang out for sure, though."

"Yes! We do. There's so much to do around here we haven't shown you yet." Julian smiled.

She smiled and nodded, wondering what she possibly could have done to deserve them.

Mia headed into the coffee shop the next day. River was there, writing something on the large chalkboard. It turned out to be the shop's holiday specialty drink. She skimmed the name but caught the words 'pumpkin' and 'delight.' When he saw her, he headed over with a small smile.

"Same as always?"

"Yes please." She searched all her pockets until she found enough coins to put in the tip jar. "Got any plans for winter break?"

"I'm staying here another week. Then I'm going on a short trip." He turned away to work on making her drink.

"Ooh, where to?"

"London. My mom is there for a business trip so I'm going to meet up with her for a few days."

"Oh. Wow. Nice." Sadly, that sentence, at least to Mia, made River start to sound like a spoiled brat. But that wasn't fair of her. He didn't ask to have wealthy parents, after all. "London's far away. You should bring me back a souvenir."

"Do you want a surprise, or what do you like?"

"Jesus! I was kidding, man," she laughed, amused at how he jumped on that. It embarrassed her, but also warmed a small part of her that River would want to buy her something without question. It felt like he really cared.

"Well, I wasn't. And what are you doing for winter break?"

"Work. Chill. Not much." Deep down she hoped maybe, just maybe, he might invite her to hang out again. Not for a big party where half the city showed up, but just them and maybe one other friend. Were they close enough for that? Did he think of her as a 'friend,' or just the awkward kid who always bugged him at the coffee shop?

"That's cool. Hope you have fun."

Fuck my life.

What should have been a pleasant break from school became Mia's hell. A living hell of nothingness.

When you're shut in a small room with eggshell walls, no decor, no roommate, and no electronics like a TV or a radio for background noise, and you stay in there for days on end, only leaving to buy a sandwich or a bag of chips from the nearest gas station, or drag your ass to work, and you ignore the very few friends you made here…it starts to mess with your head.

Really mess with your head.

Growing up, she had never seen snow before. And when she moved here, she had been looking forward to seeing it for the first time. But when she woke up to the world blanketed in white, nothing in her wanted to run outside and dance and laugh, just like she had imagined she would. Instead, she just stared at it, thinking that snow made the world look like a blank canvas. An empty place with no color or creativity. In a sense, it made the world look exactly how she felt.

All Mia had to pass the time was her laptop and phone. She would wake up around noon and finish off the energy drink she had left beside the bed the previous night. Then she might scroll through social media a few hours before she couldn't take the hunger pains. Her meals were almost all frozen and instant items, with little to no nutrition. She'd take forever to nibble on it, or maybe just scarf it down, then toss the paper plate on a growing pile of trash that was starting to stink up the whole place. Then she would go to work if she had a shift that day. Otherwise, she might take a nap she didn't need, scroll on the internet some more, masturbate, cut, then debate if it was worth going to the coffee shop in the small chance River had returned from his vacation yet. If she wasn't afraid of coming off as a creep she would have already texted him about when he would be back. As for the study group full of nerds, she had muted their group chat long ago, only popping in to post a random meme so they couldn't accuse her of being absent.

When she slept, Mia had nightmares. Sometimes scrambled together from the scattered memories, all the long nights unable to sleep because of commotion from elsewhere in the house. Sometimes they were from the occasions kids would gang up on her at school. And sometimes they were conjured up out of what had not happened, but she felt was bound to. One recurring dream took inspiration from a scene in the animated Disney film, *Cinderella*. Only it was people with empty faces instead of the sisters, and Mia was Cinderella, and they were ripping away her dress and hair to expose the ugly, hairy, masculine *boy* underneath it all.

But in most nightmares, she watched herself drown from the shore. And the scariest part was she could not even be bothered to save herself. She just stood there, waiting to die.

After a couple of weeks, the dorm began to smell bad. As in way, way worse than the usual kind of 'bad' that accompanies male college dorms. The sheets were unwashed. Her dirty clothes lay in a wrinkly pile. The smell worsened each day, and she noticed it most when she got off work. But then again, she didn't deserve to live in sanitary conditions. This was her life now.

Days began to overlap in her mind. She started to lose track of what day it was, what time it was. Daylight, or lack thereof, in the room was the only thing that kept her sane. And it went on like that for four weeks straight. One day, one of her coworkers even pulled her aside and asked if she was doing okay. Mia was left to wonder why until she saw her reflection later that night while brushing her teeth. Her skin looked clammy and pale, like she was sick. There were bags under her eyes.

But she didn't look nearly as bad as how she felt.

Chapter Eight

Mia woke up to the sound of her phone's text notification. She thought it might be Alan or Julian messaging her again to ask if she wanted to hang out. After lying there for several minutes, debating if she should even bother looking, she finally picked it up and glanced at her lock screen.

River: hey stranger!! how's break going?

Mia frowned. River hadn't texted her since the party.

It took her a few minutes to reply, her fingers shaking. Her mouth felt dry, and her head hurt. Definitely from dehydration and lack of nutrients. But not so intense that it drove her to get some fresh fruit or plain water.

Carlos: Going okay. Just chilling a lot. You?

River's reply arrived in less than a minute. Mia quickly ran the numbers in her head. If River was still in London, it must be around five in the afternoon there. Of course, she could have just looked that up on her phone, but that was too much work.

River: Busy haha. You didn't show up at the coffee shop for a whole week so I wondered if you went on a trip or if you were doing alright

Something stirred in Mia. Nothing too serious. But it was the fact that River had not only noticed her absence, but checked up on her because of it. She had not been in his life for a brief time, and he noticed. He noticed, and he asked her about it. He asked her about it, and he wanted to know if she was okay.

Tears rushed to her eyes. And then her throat ached.

What was wrong with her? Why did this slightest attention bring her crashing down so hard? But once it started, she realized she couldn't stop crying. River had thought of her. Maybe he was even worried for her. Was she crying because it felt so good to be recognized, or did it hurt because of how much she felt she didn't deserve it?

Finally, she texted him back.

Carlos: no, just staying on campus

She cried some more when he texted back a couple of minutes later. Two simple words that just broke her.

River: You ok?

She could just tell him she was fine. It would be so easy. She had been lying to Alan and Julian and they were basically her best friends. Hell, she had been lying for years to teachers, foster parents, classmates, guidance counselors…it had become second nature for her to lie.

But as she reached for her phone again, the sickness building in her hit a point where it refused to extend to her fingertips. It was a funny feeling. As if River would know she was lying if she did. Or that he already knew the truth and she just had to be the one to admit it out loud.

Oh my god you're really going to do it. You're really going to do it.

Carlos: Honestly, I'm not doing so great. She hesitated, then added more. *Been cooped up. Depressed.*

(Yes, she had actually typed out the dreaded d-word. She hardly believed it either.)

River: Do you want to talk about it?

Carlos: Not over text

River: Understandable. You should try to get out of the dorm then. Find someone to hang out with

She buried her face in the pillow. That was the last thing she wanted to do. A few minutes of silence, then her phone blinked with more texts from River.

River: I'm serious. If you're depressed, being cooped up will make it worse. I'd invite you to hang out if I wasn't still in London haha. But trust me, I've been there too. Don't feed your demons.

Carlos: Ok fine haha. Thanks dude

Funny enough, as soon as Mia messaged Alan and told him she was free all day, he replied in minutes.

Alan: Sweet! Come on over. We still have lots of leftovers from the New Years Eve party and could use a hand getting rid of them

She got up and forced herself into the shower, turning the knob all the way over to 'hot'. Aside from where her cuts stung, the water felt good, as if she could scrub the self-loathing off her body. For almost ten minutes she just stood there, breathing in the steam and imagined it working itself through her system, like a deep cleanse. Afterward, she put on clean clothes and even brushed her hair. Just before leaving, she texted River a quick thanks.

Once at Alan and Julian's, it didn't take many rounds of video games before Mia's second confession of the day pulled through. Like a water dam, it was like the instant she poked a hole in it by admitting that to River, the water came gushing through, and she just couldn't stop. Mia realized, with dread, that her ability to keep up this lie was dying fast. At least, the lie that she was just a normal, chill person who wasn't depressed at all.

It was humiliating. Even just saying the word 'depressed' made her want to puke. But it happened all the same, and then it kept happening.

Through her tears, she rolled up her sleeves and showed them where she had been cutting herself, all the crisscrossing lines, some still scabbed and others now resembling state roads on an atlas.

But they took the news well. There were hugs. Reassurances. Alan brought over a box of tissues and let her cry it out until she was done. Julian gave her glasses of water to rehydrate with and even checked all her newest cuts to make sure they were healing okay.

Even with her job, Mia couldn't afford to go to a therapist for treatment, so Alan set up a bunch of self-help resources for her to try. Which he explained wouldn't cure depression but would help her be able to cope with it until she could get professional help. Julian made a list of healthy, affordable meals she could start eating, and showed her a few apps to help her track things like hydration and exercise. Lastly, they had a big meal before Mia went home for the night. She still felt like shit. But at least she was a socialized, bathed, well-fed piece of shit.

At ten in the morning, River texted her again.

River: Did you get out of the dorm

She smiled a little as she texted back.

Carlos: I did, yeah. Thanks. I needed that push

River: Want to talk more after winter break?

She texted back a thumbs up and shut off her phone after that. It was the first good night's sleep she had in weeks, possibly months.

River swallowed hard as he approached where his mom's car was parked right outside the terminal. He hadn't seen her in over a year, as he spent last summer in Oregon. Plus, River wasn't the biggest fan of family reunions, and for the last one, he had found just enough excuses to get out of it. But at least he loved seeing his mom.

She smiled as they ran to each other, and she pulled him into a hug. Thanks to blockers and hormone replacement therapy, River's height sprouted overnight in high school. Now his mom only came up to his shoulders, and he had to lean down to hug her.

"Come on, let's get in the car. We can go to the hotel first and you can unpack. Then I know exactly where I'm taking you to dinner. It's a seafood place."

As they got in the car, River's mind skimmed all the inevitable conversation topics. He took a deep breath and stared out the window at the scenery. It had been some years since he was in London. His parents used to come here about every other year. Back then, he and his brothers sometimes got to tag along, and the family would make a vacation out of it. As much as he loathed some of the memories from back then due to how a couple of his brothers bullied him, he still held onto a fondness for it. For more reasons than one.

"Is it the one Dad would take you to?" he asked. "And we'd get takeout at the hotel?"

She nodded. Just at the mention of him, she reached down and rubbed at her wedding ring by habit. Six years since the accident and she still hadn't taken it off. River didn't think she ever would at this rate.

"Speaking of Dad, I've been saving some things of his I thought you might like to have. I've been holding onto them for you."

"What about the guys?" he asked.

"Oh, you know them. They took his big toys and ran off with them as soon as they were out of the house." She said with both exasperation and love. "I saved some other things for you, like Dad's old tapes and CDs. A lot of his clothes, too. Not exactly your fashion style, but…I saved some just in case. People kept telling me to donate them, you know, to give them back to the community. Maybe I was just being selfish, but every time I tried to do it, I couldn't even make it to the parking lot. Some of them still smell like his favorite cigarettes."

He remembered. USA Gold. That smell took River back in time like no other. Countless memories of sitting on Dad's lap on the back porch as Dad chain-smoked, and River watched his brothers play football in the yard, and Dad would tell him he was so grateful he finally got a sweet little baby girl in a house full of rowdy, reckless boys, and they watched the sunset together.

"I'd like those. A lot. I don't have enough of his stuff. I guess I have no choice but to come home then, huh?" He smiled a little.

"He would have wanted you to have them. But hey, they're not going anywhere. Tell me how school's going." She patted his arm.

During the drive to the hotel, River's mind wandered while he talked about school. He listed the various projects and groups he was involved in, which led to talking about his volunteer work with the student center. Then, seemingly out of nowhere, an image of Carlos popped into his head, and the last time they had seen each other. And even after the conversation moved onto other things, he kept thinking about him. Carlos, the boy who always had just enough cash for coffee. Who made awkward jokes with obscure pop culture references (River understood maybe less than half of them), who carried way too much in his backpack, and who lit up at the most unexpected times. River felt like Carlos was the kind of guy who wasn't sure where he fit in, so he tried to fit in everywhere at the same time. His heart ached for him. He hoped the guy would find his footing one day.

Carlos had also mentioned some pretty fucked up stuff at the party the other week. Stuff that made River feel terrible for inviting him to a party that involved drinking. And now, over text, he had told River he was struggling with some mental health stuff too. But even with that, Carlos seemed like he tried so hard to make the people around him laugh. Even if he looked so uncomfortable all the time. Always rubbing at his chin, adjusting his clothes, glancing almost suspiciously at anyone around him.

River suddenly had the thought of texting him again. Just to make sure Carlos was doing all right. It couldn't hurt, could it?

After dropping his luggage off at the hotel, they drove to the restaurant in question, where his mom had a reservation for them and River quickly realized he was underdressed in his Mothman sweater and shredded jeans. As they were sitting down, he pulled out his phone and found Carlos' number on his list. Before he could second-guess himself, he sent Carlos a quick text checking in on him again. And of course, his mom noticed; nothing escaped her. She shook her head as she set her cloth napkin over her lap.

"Hey, I saw that. You know the rules."

"Sorry. I'm done, I swear." He showed her he was shutting it off, then shoved his phone back in his pocket. It seemed his mom was still adamant on her 'no phones at the dinner table' rule. "It's this classmate I'm kind of worried about. Well, not a classmate. Same school, but we don't share any classes. But he's been to the support group once. He's kind of struggling."

"I see. Is he…?"

"…*like you?*" was the unspoken question. River bit his lip.

"No. Well…I don't know. He says he's questioning. Whatever he's dealing with, I just felt like I needed to let him know I was thinking about him."

He was interrupted when a waiter came over to take their order. His mom ordered them a bottle of white wine. River frowned. He couldn't stand the taste of wine, thanks to one incident in high school that ruined it for him forever. But he didn't want to be rude, especially since he hadn't seen his mom in a while. She was one of the few people in his family he preferred getting along with. When the waiter left, his mom cleared her throat.

"And you're staying out of fights? No more of that."

"Mom, I told you. I haven't done that in over two years. I'm much better."

"You know, Nate and Brandon asked me the other day how you're doing."

"What did you tell them?" he asked bluntly.

"I told them they should ask you directly and not use me to get to you."

"Good answer." Nate and Brandon, the middle ones, took it the hardest when he came out and began transitioning, and made his life more miserable for it too. At least the other two, Anthony and Dean, had come around in recent years.

"Both of them are still in town, you know. Nate's got an internship at your uncle's law firm, and Brandon is starting up another one of his self-owned businesses. I want to say he's a personal trainer or a life coach or something like that. Or maybe it's landscaping? I really feel like it's something involving plants, but I could be wrong."

"That's not a fancy way of saying he's a weed dealer, is it?" River asked, playing with his fork.

"No! Good lord, no. I think he's really going to find his footing this time. Listen..." His mom sighed. "I really think it would be nice for you to come home for a visit. I know it wasn't easy for you growing up, but your brothers really do love you. And they miss you."

"I know," he said, just to keep the peace. But in truth, he didn't miss them at all.

"So," his mom asked, "last time we talked, you were dating a girl. What was her name? Lucy, Lila?"

"Lianna." He hadn't told his mom about the darker side of that relationship, and he wasn't about to get into that. "We had to break it off. She finished college and moved away, so it wasn't going to work out."

"I'm sorry about that. But I'm sure you'll be fine. You're going to find someone one day."

"Maybe." River stared down at his appetizer. The last thing he wanted to talk about with his mom was relationships. Anthony, the oldest, even got married a few years ago. It didn't bother him, but it did feel annoying when his mom treated him like there was something to keep up with, like there was a deadline in finding the person you wanted to spend the rest of your life with.

"Speaking of which, you should see how big your nephew is getting. Anthony sent me this picture the other day." His mom, thereby bending her own rule, pulled up a photo of his oldest brother's toddler on her phone. Noah was almost three and the spitting image of his dad. River adored the kid, but he hated Anthony's wife, Britney. And her whole family, too. As if dealing with his own family wasn't bad enough, the in-laws were unbearable.

But he didn't want to think about that right now. As they talked, he caught his mom up on everything he had been doing lately with the band and in school. And soon enough, River was able to relax and just enjoy his mom's company. And he kept his word on not checking his phone at all. Which meant that he didn't see Carlos's response until he was turning in at the hotel long past midnight. He quickly sent a message back saying he'd be back from break soon and they could catch up then, and he found himself missing everyone he had left behind. His good friends Grace and Sean, the band members…and yes, Carlos too.

Chapter Nine

The next week, Mia put more effort into eating better and cleaning the dorm, thanks to daily motivational texts from Julian. Every morning he sent her a reminder to eat something healthy for breakfast, which meant she had to get some fruit and protein in her system. Right now she stuck to apples, oranges, and healthy granola bars. Very disgusting. In addition to checking in on how she was eating, Julian also texted her to make sure she had cleaned something in the dorm. Even if it just meant throwing out a few pieces of trash lying on the floor, it was better than nothing. Julian always finished off his texts with a big smiley emoji to make it seem friendlier, a reminder that he was doing it to help her, not make her feel bad about herself. Now she was starting to have a Pavlovian eye roll at that emoji, even if sent in different contexts. But she knew she needed the extra help. And she didn't accept it lightly. Mia learned two things growing up. One, generosity comes by rarely, and two, when it does come, don't take it for granted.

In truth, based on their conversations and when they hung out, it was becoming more than just two financially stable gay guys helping their poor little college friend. Julian was becoming more like a big brother to her every day. Now all she needed was to become his little sister.

River texted her once he was back from his trip. Half in jest she asked when he would be back to work so she'd know he'd be there. And because she couldn't help herself, Mia headed in to get some hot tea on his first day back. She immediately noticed that River had a new tattoo on his forearm of a gray and black penny-farthing.

"Hey!" She smiled when she walked up to the counter, teeth still chattering from the cold. These sure weren't like the winters she had had growing up.

River looked up at her and smiled back.

"Hey, Carlos! Usual for today?"

"Actually, I want to try the hot cinnamon spice tea." Mia rubbed her hands together.

"Something new for the new semester?"

"Trying to be healthier. My diet kind of went to shit over winter break." She shrugged. She saw a look of understanding skim over River's eyes as he set her mug of hot tea on the counter.

"In that case, here's to a healthier semester. Cheers."

"Yeah. Cheers." She shivered before taking a sip of her tea. She was about to say something else, but a group of four soccer moms walked in. River adjusted his apron as the women approached. While they gathered around the cash register and began arguing over who would be treating the others, Mia slinked away.

A few days later, as she was walking across campus after class, Mia noticed a group of students running around in one of the big open areas. She was shivering. The winter coat she bought from the used clothing outlet was not quite enough to warm her. In some places the coat had worn thin, so that didn't help either. Her hood was pulled as far over her head as it could, but her ears and nose had already turned red. Today was especially cold. Fifteen degrees. Insane temperatures up here. She had had to do a double-take when she saw that number on the thermostat. She knew those temperatures existed in theory, but she had imagined that only happened on the North or South pole. Not right in her new city.

Everything hurt. Her nose hurt, her fingers and toes hurt, and even her ears hurt. Mia cursed the slightest gust of wind as she walked, hands shoved deep in her pockets. The snow sure was pretty, and she did like seeing it, especially when it covered the trees. But once the initial ecstasy of seeing snow for the first time wore off, the hangover of realizing how miserable and annoying snow could be kicked in and would probably stick around until spring. Plus, snow looked a lot less pretty when it piled up on the curbs. All she wanted right now was to curl up with a blanket and hot tea and not go back outside until she could see green grass again.

Before she could tread too far down that path of negativity, however, she took another glance at one of the college students who was playing in the open area. He was tall, wearing a black coat, a dark beanie, and a gray scarf. It was River. Mia stopped walking to see what he was doing.

As she stood there, knees locked and chapped lips stinging, she watched River grab a handful of snow and packed it together. Then he chucked it at one of the other students. It hit them on the shoulder and they shouted something at River as they grabbed at more snow and threw it back at him. A snowball fight. Mia had only seen those in movies and television commercials. She had never understood the point, as being hit with snow sounded miserable.

River turned and saw her where she stood. Mia was about to hurry off, but it was too late. He grinned and waved at her.

"Carlos! Get over here! We need reinforcements!"

It took Mia a few moments to register that he was inviting her to join them. She kept her knees locked and all that came out were stammers.

"I, uh…I'm good."

The other students had paused the snowfall fight. Now that she had more time to study them, she noticed both Grace and Sean were here, too. River began walking over to her. He had snow on his coat and all over his gloves. His face was beet red, and he was grinning like a little kid.

"Come on, we're dying out here. And don't think I forgot when you told me you played varsity baseball so I know you can throw."

Mia frowned, hating that she was in the spotlight now. River's smile faded the longer she took to reply.

"I'm…really cold. Still not used to all this snow," she finally confessed.

River's eyes softened with realization. She could see the moment it clicked for him and he remembered, *Oh, right, this is his first northern winter ever. He must be miserable right now. No wonder he doesn't want to.* But even so, he stood a little straighter and held out his hand to her.

"It'll be fun. Trust me."

Mia swallowed, then nodded. After another pause, she took his hand.

"As soon as you start getting used to the cold, you'll love it," River said as he led her over to where the others were waiting for the game to resume.

"I don't know about that, but okay," Mia said with a nervous laugh.

River took a few minutes to show her how to make the perfect snowball. How to pack it just right so that it didn't fall apart when you threw it but would explode when it hit the target. When Mia had made a few for practice, River signaled to the other students they were ready. Mia aimed the snowball and threw it at Grace, missing on purpose. To her right, River was grinning as he chucked snowballs at Sean. At first the others didn't seem to aim for her much since she was taking longer. But within several minutes, as Mia got to making them faster, she found she had to actually dodge the snowballs being thrown her way. River was getting really into it, shouting with frustration whenever he took a hit and laughing at anyone he managed to hit.

Mia kept watching him, how his dirty blonde hair glistened with half melted snowflakes. His nose was red and his cheeks were flushed, and he was breathing hard. He looked so beautiful.

Mia went to her knees to scoop up some more snow and pack it. This time she wanted to see how big of a snowball she could make. While she was doing that, Grace saw Mia was distracted and got her good. It hit her right in the middle of her chest. Snow sprayed up, sprinkling Mia's neck, her cheeks, her mouth, and her eyes. Mia smiled and threw one right back at Grace, getting her good on the shoulder. As the game went on, Mia realized that all this exertion was warming her up, and she was sweating under the coat. Now it was starting to make sense why northerners played in the snow all this time. Who would have thought that a snowball fight would be such a culturally enlightening experience?

By the time they had all grown too tired to throw anymore, Mia was laughing. Her body was now in a strange place where it inhabited cold and warmth at the same time. She wanted to peel off her coat and yet she still couldn't feel her nose or fingers or toes. But it felt good. A bit like the feeling she got when she used the razor, but more refreshing. Almost like a cold shower. And it was all over her, quieting down the constant anxiety and dysphoria, which both took a back burner on account of all this energy.

Damn. Maybe I need to take up sports or something. Because this feels fucking amazing. Do they do professional snowball fights up here? No, Mia, you idiot, of course they don't. Maybe hockey or skiing?

"Hey, Carlos! You deaf?" River shouted.

Shit, how long was she yelling at me?! Focus, Mia! She hurried to catch up to him as he was leaving. When he saw her beside him, he beamed.

"So? What did you think?"

"That was...so much fun. Way more fun than I thought it would be."

"See? All you had to do was give it a try." River shrugged. "Now we just need to get you to learn how to skate so you can play hockey with us. You'd be really good, and I love hockey."

"One cherry at a time." She laughed. "I really got to get back to my dorm. I'm soaked."

"Get dry and warm as soon as you can. Don't want to catch a cold."

Mia shrugged that off with a snort and made the peace sign with both hands.

"I don't get sick, man. My immune system is in tip-top shape. I've never even had the flu!"

Well, Mia thought the next morning, *I spoke too soon there.*

Sure enough, she woke up and immediately felt like she had been hit by a truck. Her throat was dry and hurting, and her nose was all clogged up. And on top of all that, her head pounded. Thanks for nothing, immune system.

Mia grabbed her phone and texted River a joke about their snowball fight making her sick. After that she put in her boss' phone number. Mia didn't even want to get out of bed, much less go to work. Luckily, she must have sounded *really* sick because her boss told her,

"Hey, it's okay. You haven't missed a single day the past several months you've been here, so I trust you. If you're really too sick to work, then don't work. You sound like you swallowed a frog."

"I feel like I swallowed a horse," she said, trying to laugh, then once she thanked him again for understanding, she hung up. For a little while Mia just lay there only thinking about how much her body hurt all over when her phone went off, indicating a text from River.

River: Shit dude i'm sorry. Can I grab you anything?

Mia had to read the text again to be sure she got it right. The thought of being 'nursed to health' sounded even more humiliating than saying the d-word aloud. It was her own fault she got sick. On the other hand, this meant she got to see River today. Even if he saw her sick, was that better than nothing? It had to be, right?

Carlos: Yeah sure. Cold medicine and something for my throat and headache would be great. thanks!

River: I'm almost done with homework, then I'll run to the store. I can bring you tea and chicken soup too. Do you have enough tissues?

Carlos: I don't know, anything else you know is a good cure-all for a nasty cold I guess

River: Be there within the hour!

About forty minutes later, River arrived at Carlos' dorm and knocked on the door, holding the bag of goodies under his arm.

"Door's unlocked," he heard Carlos croak from inside.

River opened the door. Carlos sat up a bit, a halo of crumpled tissues surrounding him on the bed. The poor guy looked miserable.

"I got your stuff." River walked in and set the bag on the small table. "Pain and fever relief, both daytime and PM, congestion relief, lotion, chicken soup, ginger tea, cough drops, honey, and lemon juice."

"What are the honey and juice for?"

"Boil water or make tea, then add both in. I always do that when I get sick. It'll feel really good on your throat." River opened the medicine packs and removed a few pills. "While I'm here I can heat you up some tea and soup if you want."

Carlos blinked up at him, like he had been struck upside the head.

"Why are you being so nice to me? It's just a cold. I'm not dying or anything."

River found a clean mug, filled it with water, and put it in the microwave. River was an avid supporter of only heating water on the stove, but these dorms didn't have one, so he had no real choice. You had to pay a lot more to get an actual kitchen.

"I kind of feel like it's my fault you're sick. Since I dragged you into that snowball fight yesterday." *And,* he mentally added, *I just have the feeling that you don't have a lot of people in your life to help you when you need it. And if you do have them, you'd never ask for it.*

"Oh. But it was fun!" Carlos sneezed into his hands, then groaned with pain. "Fuck, my sinuses are on fire…"

"When was the last time you even got sick?" While the water heated up, River poured some soup into a bowl.

Carlos reached for his water bottle and took a big gulp to wash down his medicine.

"I don't know. I must have been really little. I never get fucking sick." Carlos sulked.

"Then I should probably remind you that you need to drink a lot of fluids and avoid caffeine."

"Okay, *Mom.*" Carlos laughed. Then he coughed hoarsely, wincing again. When they were ready River brought over the tea and soup. Carlos smiled a bit before he took a sip from the mug, then closed his eyes. "Oh, shit. You're right. That does feel so good on my throat."

"Just keep your icky sick ass in bed until you're better." River lightly kicked the foot of the bed in jest. "So, got a good watchlist of stuff to binge while you're resting up?"

Carlos shook his head. With his permission, River booted up Carlos' old laptop and started browsing for shows and movies Carlos might like.

"Any preference?"

"Good question. I'd say nothing too smart or fast-paced. Nothing you have to, you know, pay attention to. None of that Christopher Nolan or David Fincher shit."

"I know exactly what you mean." River ended up finding a few things for him. A couple of sitcoms and cartoons as well as a handful of movies, a range of comedies with a side helping of action and fantasy. "There. You're all set."

"I hope I don't get you sick." Carlos looked so small and helpless, curled up in bed like that. And yeah, it was because he was really sick. But River had a small thought that maybe he should stay and chat if Carlos wasn't ready to fall asleep yet. Maybe he could use some company.

"I'll be fine. Hey, by the way…how's the…other stuff?"

"I'm okay. Couple friends helping out."

"Good. That's good. Friends are good." *Ugh, and I brought this up for what? It was just a conversation over text. Yeah, it was about something pretty serious, but it's not like we're super close and he's told me about everything that's going on. He probably feels like I'm pushing him.*

"Yeah. Alan and Julian have been helping me. They're the couple I told you about. Make sure I eat well and can talk to them if I'm having a bad day. It'd be nice if I could…" Carlos paused to blow his nose. "…it'd be nice if I could get a doctor or some pills to help. But you got to do what you got to do."

"Your job won't help cover medical expenses?"

"Nope. I'm part time."

"Just do what you can. Friends aren't therapists, but it's better than being alone."

Carlos looked up at him at that, his expression concealed by the tissue being held to his nose. There was an awkward pause in the conversation before Carlos finally spoke up.

"I guess you're right. I'm going to try to rest."

He's pushing you away. Should have known better than to ask questions like that out of nowhere, River thought.

"Text me if you need anything else." River headed for the door.

"Thanks again." Carlos smiled shyly.

River had a stuffy nose and dry throat the next day but that did not really surprise him. Colds were almost impossible not to catch. He took some medicine to power through the day, as he didn't feel sick enough to skip classes or work. Between lectures, he texted Carlos but didn't get a reply until a couple hours later while he was trying to focus on his paper, sipping on hot tea to soothe his throat.

Carlos: I don't feel any better today. Snot is pouring from my nose and my sinuses are on fire.

River: Liquids and sleep, dude

Carlos: I know, Mom, lmao. Shortly after Carlos added, *I'm out of chicken soup:(*

River couldn't help but smile at that text and sent him one back, saying he'd bring some over soon. Once the second draft of his paper was done, he got up and headed to the local grocery store. At the checkout he grabbed a bottle of iced tea and a protein bar, which were both gone by the time he was back at Carlos's dorm.

Inside, Carlos still looked awful. River took off his coat.

"Want me to heat it up for you?" he asked, almost calling Carlos 'buddy' but that seemed a bit too much of…something.

Couldn't put his finger on it. Maybe they weren't there yet with their friendship.

Carlos nodded.

"There's always the one day it gets really bad before it clears up," River said, trying to cheer him up as he fixed Carlos his soup. Before he could hold it in, River sneezed.

"Did I get you sick?" Carlos demanded. When River didn't answer at first that seemed to say enough. "I'm sorry. It's all my fault. I shouldn't have let you come here."

"Nothing to be sorry about. Trying not to get a cold is like…trying not to see a political ad during campaign season."

"Serves you right for being nice to me," Carlos said, then laughed.

River had no idea if he was supposed to laugh along with that joke or not, so he compromised by smiling a bit as he handed Carlos his bowl of hot soup.

"You know what? Just for that, fuck you for getting me sick," he said with a teasing smile. River remembered when he first started his transition, what it was like suddenly having to learn the codes cishet boys had with their friends. For most of middle school he thought all the other boys hated him, until he finally figured out that many guys bonded by insulting each other and poking fun. It was a code he learned to adapt to but never felt that he spoke with complete fluency, like he was putting on an act instead of just going with the flow. Frankly, it annoyed him sometimes that men couldn't just exchange genuine compliments without it being seen as odd. But at least he got to drop the act around his queer male friends.

Carlos smiled, then looked down at his steaming bowl. His fingers tapped around it lightly as he sniffled.

"When we're both better, maybe we could…you know…"

"Hang out?" River guessed.

"Yeah, sure. To talk about stuff."

Shit. Getting a little awkward. Just go with the flow.

"Well, now that you mention that, there is something I should probably tell you," River said, figuring he might as well bring this up now that he was here. He had been meaning to tell Carlos before he got a cold. But the longer he put it off, the more uncomfortable it was going to be. "I signed up for a program to study abroad and I'll be gone for a couple months."

Carlos looked up in surprise.

"Woah, nice. Where the hell are you going?"

"Tour of Italy. Mostly Rome and Venice."

"Well, good luck. And yeah, we should hang out before you leave. If you want to."

"Of course I want to! Once our colds clear up, I'll text you, okay?"

Carlos nodded and seemed almost relieved to hear that. River plugged in his dying laptop before leaving.

The next day, while River was walking through one of the main buildings, he noticed a familiar face standing just outside the cafeteria area. Today Carlos looked a lot better, like his cold was finally behind him.

River would not learn until much later that it had not been a coincidence after all. Carlos, in due time, would admit he had been hanging out there knowing that River would walk by to get to class, in the hopes that they could chat a bit.

"Hey, River! Off to class?" Carlos blew his nose into a soggy tissue.

"Just heading that way. You?"

"My class is that way, too."

"Feeling better?" River moved a little to the right so Carlos could walk beside him.

"Much better. Cold's gone. Just got to get rid of all this junk in my nose."

"Mine's almost gone too." Right on cue, River sneezed.

"Which class do you have next?"

"Italian Ancient Classics. It's for the trip that's coming up."

"Oh, right, duh. You must be excited." Carlos beamed. "You haven't told me much about this trip. Mind filling a guy in?"

In the next ninety seconds while they walked to class, River filled him in on a general idea of what his trip would be like. Where he would be staying, what his studies would be focused on, the whole itinerary they had planned, and what he hoped to get out of it. Luckily, he was able to provide enough of a summary by the time they arrived outside Carlos's class.

"That sounds so cool. Maybe I should study abroad someday, but I don't know if I could do Italy. I didn't even know you could speak Italian."

"Believe me, I only know the bare minimum so I can survive the trip, and that's it," River laughed. "Okay, better let you get into class. I'll see you around."

Carlos gave a tiny wave before slipping inside.

Mia was still beating herself up as she walked into class. She had told herself today would be the day that she would come out to River. Or at least, tell him, "Hey, there's something important I want to tell you. Can we meet up later?" Something in the direction of telling him about her gender identity. At least before he went off to Italy because of course he had to.

She had planned it perfectly. Their classes started at the same time on Thursday afternoons. If she got there a good half hour early, there would be no way of missing him. So she waited, listening to Ariana Grande for a good fifteen minutes or so before River could finally be seen walking down the hall. And for one little second there, she felt ready to finally say, for the first time, "Hey, I'm Mia, and I'm a girl!" Or something to that effect. Just *something*.

But nope. That did not fucking happen at all. She had been so close, but at the last second, she chickened out yet again.

Was she ever going to tell them, or was this going to be the rest of her life?

Chapter Ten

Second semester came with new challenges for Mia. For one, River's support group had a couple events, the biggest one being an on-campus screening of some cult classic LGBT+ films, and the group had invited her to participate if she was interested. For another matter, her boss at the auto repair had started to give her longer shifts because of her good performance record. Good in the long run, because no one can complain about a fatter paycheck. Not so good if she wanted to stay ahead in her classes.

She enjoyed her job, and she was happy to be in school. She had her study group, the support group, and Julian and Alan. That was a lot to speak of. Mia would never trade this life for the one she left behind. But burnout-phobia lingered in the back of her mind. The last thing Mia wanted was to end up like the people from her hometown, where their only escape from the constant grind were drugs and hard liquor. Those were the kind of people who stole her childhood from her. And many years ago, Mia had promised herself she would never end up like them. That was what inspired and preserved her dream of getting into a state university, after all.

One morning, when Mia only had one class from noon to three, Grace texted her, asking if she wanted to hang out one more time before River left for Italy. This time, Mia didn't wait at all to reply. She finally agreed to meet up with them again. This time at River's apartment instead of a public setting.

As she got ready to go, the truth slowly sank in. She wouldn't see River for months. He was leaving in a week. No more free pastries and espresso shots. No more having someone like him to talk to and make her day a little brighter. No more of his weird laugh or gross jokes or the stink of his sweat and cheap body spray.

But it would be fine. It had to be fine. It wasn't like they were best friends or needed each other or anything. It wasn't like she would die without around him.

Of course, this all led up to another problem. If she didn't tell him now, she wouldn't get the chance to come out to him in person for months, and she hated the idea of telling him over text or video call. And worse yet, she didn't know if she could stand to hide it that long.

In other words, all things considered, it was now or never. Or at least, in her dramatic, albeit self-aware brain, it felt like it.

Before she drove to River's apartment, Mia stopped at the grocery store to grab snacks. She actually felt proud of herself today. She had showered, washed her hair, put on clean clothes, and even ate breakfast. That was a lot for one day. But it wasn't until she got in the car and started the engine that it started to hit her what was about to happen. What she was about to do. Mia clenched her jaw, fear turning into loathing which turned into anger, and she smacked the steering wheel.

I have to tell them. I can't hold it from them anymore. Somebody has to know.

Her heart was already pounding. Sweat beaded her forehead. Mia gripped the steering wheel and tried to focus on her breathing before she would have a panic attack.

I can't tell them, the same voice suddenly shifted into. *If I tell them, that means I'm out to the world and I'll never be able to take it back. No one can ever know. Think of the risks. Think of everything you could lose. That's got to be worse than what this life is, isn't it? Isn't it? Isn't hiding better than being hated?*

She didn't even realize it was raining until a loud crash of lightning made her jump so hard she hit her head on the roof of the car. Still shaking, she started the engine and drove down the street toward River's apartment. When she arrived, River answered the door.

"Carlos! Get in here, you. I ordered takeout, so help yourself. Grace and me were just finishing up some last-minute stuff."

Mia took a deep breath as she sat in the armchair across from the sofa. Now that she was here when there wasn't a party going on she got a much better look around the place. River's apartment was cluttered, not dirty, and there was a big difference. He had a lot of stuff that all seemed to have their own proper place. Dozens and dozens of books filled up three tall shelves along the living room wall, and for the extra books, these formed stacks all around the main seating areas. She couldn't get a sense of any commonality in his books, as she saw everything from Neil Gaiman, Bohumil Hrabal, and Edgar Allen Poe, to Chinua Achebe, Judith Butler, and Robert Cantwell, all in varying condition from like-new to being held together by rubber bands and duct tape. He also seemed to have an impressive collection of coffee mugs, all hanging on rusty hooks and handles on the kitchen wall; at least twenty, maybe more.

Mia's lungs still hurt from her little episode in the car. She took a deep breath.

Stay calm. You can do this. He's literally like you. You can tell him this.

River sat on the end of the couch and was already helping himself to the food laid out on the coffee table. On the other end of the couch, Grace had several books and notebooks laid out, filled with sticky notes. Just by a quick glance Mia caught on to the fact that it had to do with the support group.

"So, Carlos, what have you been up to?" Grace asked, fiddling with a gel pen.

"School and work?" Mia shrugged, not sure how she should answer the question. What was she supposed to say? That she wasted winter break cooped up and depressed and scarring her body? That the weight on her shoulders had gotten heavier and heavier the more she got to know her friends here?

"Yeah, no kidding. I've been busy too. We all are. Especially now that River will be gone a few months, so I'm going to be taking over the support group and planning our upcoming events at the student center. Which I'm fine with! Don't get me wrong." She held up her hands. "It's just going to be a pretty crazy. For all of us."

"What about your music?" Mia asked River.

"We're still going to meet over video chat. Still work on our songs and stuff while I'm gone. So I'll have plenty to do when I have down time over there," River managed to say between monstrous bites.

"I can't imagine. I've been meaning to go to one of your shows. I just…don't have the time." Mia looked down at her hands. Was she a bad friend that she hadn't listened to any of his music yet? She probably was. Definitely was. "I'm sorry."

"Don't be sorry. I get it. First year of college is the fucking worst. I'm so close to the end and it can't get here soon enough," River said.

She smiled sadly at him.

"Yeah…I guess." There was a bowl of tortilla chips on the coffee table between Grace's pile of study books and River's laptop. Mia grabbed one and munched on it. What she said next came out more cynical than she intended, but she was at her limit of holding back things that were plaguing her mind. They were slipping out more and more, it seemed. "Sometimes I just wonder if it's worth it, you know?"

Grace frowned and set down her gel pen, inching a bit closer to her.

"What do you mean, Carlos? Is…everything okay?"

This is what she wanted to say.

No, it's not. It's never been fucking okay. I haven't been okay since I was three years old and my first memories are being screamed at, beaten, and mocked by the people who were supposed to protect me, and I never felt safe since. I have always been aware of the space I take up in this world and how small that space is supposed to be, and now that space is the tiniest little box and I can barely fit into it but at least it protects me from them. I haven't been okay since I realized I was trans in a world where I am despised and hated just because I exist. Not for saying or doing anything, but just the fact that I breathe is enough to make people want me dead. I haven't been okay since I saw the way everyone in my life talked about girls like me and the things they think are okay to say about them, and they had no fucking idea I was there the whole time, and they can never know, and I had no one to talk to for all those years about it, and now I do, and you all are the best people I've ever met and I cannot stand it because I don't know what to do with it, and that's why I know you're going to hate me if I tell the truth because everything I touch gets ruined. I've never felt okay about the space I take up or the person people see when they look at me. Nothing has ever been remotely okay about my entire fucking life.

This is what she actually said.

"I don't know. I mean…I don't know."

Now it was River's turn to inch a bit closer to her. He finished chewing his huge mouthful of food and swallowed.

"You sure you're okay, dude?"

"I mean, there's a lot going on. Kind of what I mentioned in that meeting and when we talked last time. I just…" God, she could hear herself and did it ever sound grating. Her random hints at the truth without just outright saying it. She was starting to sympathize with everyone who had put up with her in the past for more than one conversation. This always fucking happened.

"If you need someone to talk to, we're here for you," Grace said softly.

Mia munched on another chip.

"The thing is…I've never told anyone this. Ever. But I think I have to tell someone or I won't be able to go any further."

Nothing is okay about me. I don't want to say it and if I do, I can never take it back.

Before she realized it, Mia had burst into tears.

Few things are more embarrassing than that, and this was coming from the girl who peed herself on stage at the spelling bee. But the realization of what she was actually about to say, for the first time in her entire life, hit her like the weight of the world on her heart.

She felt a hand on her shoulder. River. The touch was so unexpected she almost wanted to smack his hand away. She wanted to snap at him, *Don't fucking touch me. I'm disgusting and I don't deserve to be touched like that.* But she swallowed it down instead.

"Hey. Hey…" he heard him whisper above the heavy sobs wracking her body. The warm sensation of his hand gently rubbing her shoulder was the only thing keeping Mia grounded in reality. Other than that, all she could feel was terror and fear and repulsion and disgust. Terror at the world she was going to walk into the moment she told them the truth. Fear of how the world would turn on her when it knew who she was and all the things that could happen to her. Repulsion at her body, her voice, her mannerisms, and everything else. And disgust that she couldn't even be honest with someone as loud and proud as River or as accepting and supportive as Grace.

"It's okay, Carlos," he said softly.

"I'm sorry. I'm just so scared and it hurts so much," she managed to choke out, hating that all the attention was on her now, but she could not stop crying. The dam didn't just have holes in it; it had been washed away in one sweeping blow. Mia thought of all the times she had wanted this moment more than anything. A person she could safely talk to and a place where she could finally come out. And now that it was here, she was doing whatever it could to throw it away, as if it had taken at last getting what she had needed the most all those years to realize she did not feel she deserved it, and that she must get rid of it before she ruined what little good she had going for her life right now. She struggled to say the words as her throat hurt. "I always knew something was inside me that made me different from everyone around me. I knew that since I was a little kid."

River kept rubbing her shoulder. Grace put a box of tissues in her lap, and Mia grabbed one and blew her nose. After she wiped away her tears, she continued slowly,

"I don't think I can keep ignoring it or pretending this isn't me, and I think moving here and meeting all of you has made me realize that. It's forced me to realize what I have to do. And I'm so, so scared. Because I cannot fucking hide it this from the world anymore. I don't think I could hide it anymore if I tried." Mia looked up at both of them, knowing she must be a sight.

River's eyes were glassy. He swallowed hard.

"It's okay," he said so softly she almost couldn't hear him.

She had to take another deep breath and could not look at him when she spoke next.

"I...I'm...I'm trans." She paused, and she said it again, just to be sure they heard her. "I am a transgender girl."

River reached up and gave her shoulder a gentle squeeze, as if encouraging her to continue, so she did.

"I've known for a long time. I just...haven't told anyone because I didn't know what to do." Mia began shaking again as she realized what she had finally released into the world.

Oh my god...I did it. I said it.

She gasped for air. And it felt like, for the first time, she was finally able to breathe.

Suddenly, she felt River pull her into a hug. She pulled him in tighter and began sobbing all over again. Now that the words were out, everything felt so much different. It was like a whole weight had been taken off her chest. Like the world had more color and vibrancy, and everything felt so much clearer and brighter. And most of all, that she had been stirred awake after years in a coma. She was the princess awoken from her cursed slumber, returned to the land of the living after so many years in purgatory.

"Hey, hey. I'm here. I'm here," River said. They slowly let go of each other and he looked her up and down. "You know, um…I kind of had a feeling you'd tell me something like that."

"Oh, god." She rubbed her eyes and laughed a little. "What gave it away? My coffee order?" she said sarcastically, still wiping away tears.

"A lot of little things, to be honest. Call it a sixth sense or something. I just had a feeling."

Grace got up and hugged her, too. She squeezed Mia tight, and Mia rested her head on Grace's shoulder, still struggling to stop herself from crying.

"Do you know what name you want us to call you?" Grace asked when she pulled away.

She paused, thinking it over. 'Mia' had always been such a private, intimate thing for herself. There was almost a morbid sacredness in her invisibility. The idea of making her name a public thing, even just between friends, felt like too much all at once.

"I'm not there yet. You guys can still call me Carlos and use male pronouns as far as it goes in public, but…I just felt that I could trust you with this." She looked down at her hands and sighed. "I don't have the means to even think about transitioning right now, so I just want to fly under the radar, you know? At least until I figure out how I'm going to do this."

"Of course." River's hand was on her biceps now. "We won't tell anyone unless you say it's okay."

"Thank you…" was all she could manage to respond, and she gave him a weak smile. Her body and her brain were exhausted. She felt like she had just run a marathon. But it was a good feeling, like she had finally ascended a massive mountain that had been looming in front of her for years. And the air at the top was so crisp, clean, and restorative.

He smiled sadly.

"It gets easier," said River. "Trust me on that. It really does. It won't be like this forever. I know right now that sounds real fucking corny to hear, and I know when I used to hear it back in the day I thought it was bullshit. But I mean it. It *does* get easier."

Mia couldn't even fathom the idea. But the words did give her a sense of comfort, especially coming from someone years farther down that road. Besides, River was not the kind of person to say things he didn't mean.

"Telling us today was a big step already. That takes a lot of guts. I don't know how else to tell you just how brave that is."

"Anything we can do to help, anything you need, just let us know, okay? And yes, I mean *anything*. You have our numbers. Text, call, anytime," Grace added.

Mia nodded. Maybe she was going to make it after all.

"Are you going to be okay?" River asked, looking her over.

"Yeah…I think so." She took a deep breath and realized she actually meant it. Another sensation that felt odd in a good way. "I mean, I've survived this long, haven't I?"

"There you go. Look how far you've come already. You're on your way." He smiled reassuringly.

"Do you…want to stay here and hang out longer? We could watch some fun movies or something," Grace offered.

"I'd like that a lot actually. What do you recommend? What are your favorites?" Mia asked.

"We have a little of everything, really. River says his favorite movie is *The Crow,* but it's really *Beauty and the Beast.*"

"Hey!"

"What's yours?" Mia asked Grace.

"Oh, mine changes every week, but right now it's *Joy Ride.*"

"You're going to roll your eyes at this, but mine is *The Matrix,*" said Mia.

"I love that. That's a good one," River said with a small smile. "I actually think we might have a copy of it, hang on." He rummaged through two whole bins and a shelf of DVDs and CDs until he found it.

Mia snuggled with a pillow as the screen lit up with all the visual comforts she knew so well by now. The muted greens, trench coats, sunglasses, and special effects that blew her mind when she first saw it so many years ago. Before the ending, Grace fell asleep.

"I swear she does this for every movie we watch. She always promises she'll stay up, but she never does." River checked his phone for the time, then groaned. "Shoot, forgot to charge it again. I'm dead. You got a charger?"

"I always carry one. If I get under thirty percent, I'm panicking. How the fuck do you forget to charge your phone, dude? That's like, a basic survival skill for the twenty-first century." Mia threw her cable at him and he caught it.

"Yeah, well, why should I have to remember that if you'll always have a charger?"

"Hm. Yeah, good point." She shook her head. Only River would let his phone drain until it literally died. She couldn't imagine even looking at a single digit number in the corner of her screen.

"Hey," River said as he plugged in his dead phone, "do you want to camp out here for the night? I have tons of blankets and pillows."

"Oh…yeah, sure!" The idea sounded fun. Camping out with River, surrounded by the little things he filled his life with. Plus, she wasn't a huge fan of the idea of spending the night alone after all they had talked about today.

He smiled. Grace woke up just enough to say goodnight to both of them and head back to her own place for the night. Once she had left, Mia settled in on the couch, which River set up with pillows and blankets for her, and he made sure she had enough to make her comfortable. There were more than enough blankets, so many that Mia gave a few back to him.

"Does your heater not work or something?" she teased.

"Sorry. I figured you get cold more easily. I don't know why I thought that." The poor guy looked so embarrassed. Mia just smiled again.

"It's fine. I like a lot of blankets," she said.

"I don't know about you, but I'm still wide awake. I'm a bit of a night owl."

Usually, Mia would agree, but they never tell you how exhausting coming out is, on both the brain and body. But she humored him all the same.

"What do you usually like to do this late?"

"Watch TV while doing some writing and some home-work," he said while tousling his hair.

"Me too. I usually need it as white noise to help me sleep. Usually some dumb sitcom or something." He hunched over in the recliner, curled up with his notebook where he wrote his song lyrics. The sound of the pencil on paper as well as his presence in the room was soothing, and it lulled her into a deep, comfortable sleep.

After strange, restless dreams, Mia woke up to the smell of pancakes and bacon. Grease was sizzling and the batter was browning. Mia rubbed her eyes and sat up, realizing that she felt more well rested than she had in weeks.

"Good morning," River said from where he was in the kitchen standing in front of the stove. Sometime in the night he had gotten out more notebooks and now they were all over the coffee table. Mia glanced at the mess before getting up. Of course, just her luck, River was only wearing a loose-fitting tank top that gave her a perfect view of his shoulder muscles, stomach, and hips. He was also only wearing boxers, so she could also see his strong thighs and calves. All in all, way too much on display before morning coffee.

"Morning..." She pulled her shirt down to soften out the wrinkles and hastily looked away. Either he knew she had a crush on him and was teasing her, which seemed very unlike the River she knew, or he still had no idea how much she liked him. She took that to be a good thing, as it meant she was doing a good job of hiding it. So far, that is.

"Sleep okay?" he asked. He tossed a blueberry towards his mouth and missed, so he quickly picked it up off the floor and ate it.

"Good. Real good, actually. You didn't have to cook me breakfast, you know."

"That's part of the contract for a sleepover. Juice is in the fridge. Help yourself."

She pulled up the stool in front of the kitchen counter, then poured herself a generous amount of syrup before she dug in. The ensuing groan that came out of her at the first taste sounded like something out of a bad porno, but she didn't even care. The blueberries were so soft they melted right into sweet goodness in her mouth and the pancake had been cooked to buttery, fluffy perfection.

"Jesus Christ, River. I think this is the best pancake I've ever had. And I'm not just talking shit."

"Thanks! It's an age-old recipe, handed down from generations."

"Bullshit."

"Yeah, you got me. But it *is* exactly how my dad used to cook us pancakes when we were kids, and maybe he got it from his parents. So I might not be wrong." He shrugged, feigning innocence.

Mia rolled her eyes and snatched another pancake.

Ugh, I'm going to miss him and his stupid jokes. Why did he have to go to Italy, anyway? Meanwhile, River dished up his own plate and leaned on the counter across from her. She kept her eyes locked on her pancakes, knowing that if she looked up, she would be able to see down his entire tank top. *Look. Away. NOW.*

"You want to stay a bit longer after we eat? I don't really have much to do except pack up a little. And it's going to be a while before I see you again," he said before taking a huge bite.

Mia debated it for a moment, only to realize she didn't have to. Although if he didn't change into some more decent clothing soon, it was going to be a long, frustrating morning.

"Yeah. I'd like that, a lot."

Chapter Eleven

In the way that only a kindred spirit could, River had always had a feeling about the girl named Carlos.

Even when she first walked into the coffee shop he worked at, constantly adjusting her clothes and glancing at everyone around her, River had sensed something was going on. The way certain words and phrases came out of her like something inside had to shove them off her tongue. Like she was always trying to hide herself and avoid exposure. The weird 'sameness' feeling he got around her now made so much sense in light of everything she told him.

In truth, when she told them she was trans, River had to take a minute to hide his own tears. For many reasons, some good and some less than good. He would have let himself cry if Carlos didn't need him to hold himself together. He remembered the reaction from his own family, and the things that would have been really nice to have said to him back then, and he tried to give as much of that to his friend as he could.

She stayed for the rest of the morning after breakfast, playing a couple of video games with him, then even helping him sort through his things he was taking with him to Italy. Before noon, she had to leave to get ready for an afternoon class and they said goodbye.

Once he was alone in the apartment again, River lay on the couch thinking over their conversation from last night. He should be working on his assignments. But he couldn't get her out of his head. The little fragments he knew about her rough childhood, her experiences at school, and now the fact that she had just come out as transgender…it all fit together to form a person River wanted to get to know more. Carlos deserved the world. She just needed to see it.

He had to work up the courage to send her a text message the following day.

River: Not to pry but I really think you'd get a lot out of coming back to one of our meetings

Carlos: Sure you're not just desperate for more members? Lmao

River: maybe lol. I am serious tho. You don't have to tell them at all but if you do they'll support you.

He sort of regretted sending that one right as he hit the 'send' button. All he wanted was for Carlos to be happy, to be able to be herself. He wanted to see her wear the clothes she wanted and put on makeup if she wanted to, and he wanted to see her face light up when a total stranger said, "Have a good day, miss," or "Enjoy your meal, ma'am!" Everything he had fought for and slowly built for himself over the years…she needed that too. This awkward, sweet but blunt kid who loved iced coffee and old cars and hid her scars so carefully…she was in there, waiting to be let out. Just like how the brooding, tattooed musician in him had been let out years ago.

But there he went again, trying to push his own transition onto someone else. And that wasn't fair to her. He knew that. Carlos had to do this her way, at her own pace. If she never came out publicly and she was okay with that, River had to be okay with that too. Even so, it hurt to see her still closeted to the world, showing all the telltale signs of that hellish dysphoria he could relate to so deeply.

Carlos: Thanks River :) that means a lot, you're really sweet

He was relieved by her response, but still worried that it was forced. That he had pushed her too hard.

Couldn't worry about that now. River had a lot to do. The next day was his last day working at the coffee shop before he left. He distracted himself from his thoughts by focusing on his work. Even when it was slow, he could always find something to do. Something to organize or clean. Or if there *really* was nothing to do, he could just jot down song lyric ideas in the little notebook he always kept with him. But in the back of his mind, he wondered if he should have accepted the offer to study abroad in the first place. The support group would do fine without him for a while, and he had helped coordinate leadership responsibilities so Grace wouldn't be too overwhelmed. But he still had plenty to worry about between the band and being far away from all his friends for that long.

Carlos walked into the coffee shop, interrupting River's train of thought. He was about to call her 'Ms. Reyes' then stopped himself, remembering she wasn't publicly out yet.

"Hey, stranger," he said.

She smiled at him. Today she had not bothered brushing her hair, and her cowlicks were more visible. The top of her ears were starting to be covered by her locks and her bangs almost reached her eyebrows now. She wore a retro-themed shirt with the caption 'Elton John; the bitch is back.'

"Hey yourself. I think I'll have the jasmine white tea with…oh, fuck it. Large iced blended Oreo mocha. Extra whipped cream. I've earned a treat." She adjusted her backpack strap. Judging by how deeply it dug into her shoulder, Carlos had brought at least three books for reading material, plus her laptop.

"I like your thinking." When he handed over her beverage, his hand lingered a bit on the cup. Carlos noticed and looked up at him.

"So…leaving tomorrow?" she asked.

He nodded silently.

"I'm going to miss you. These don't taste the same when you don't make them." She took the cup and licked at a bit of the whipped cream where it got on her finger. There were no other customers waiting in line, so Carlos didn't walk away as she sipped her beverage.

"Must be my masculine touch." He waved his fingers.

"What's first on your trip to Italy again? I know you told me before, but I forgot. Sorry."

"Let me think. An excursion to Pompeii and Naples. Capri Island too, I think. Lots of history and literature. Some culinary stuff, too. Oh, I know what I didn't tell you before. I've been talking with the band and we hope to implement some of my research into our songs."

"You don't say? So now you're *Italian* indie gothic rock. That's a mouthful."

"You say that, but we hope to have this high-concept album centered around a Roman gladiator who is reincarnated throughout the ages…I know, it sounds dumb when I say it out loud. But maybe if I do enough research—"

"Are you kidding? That sounds fucking amazing! You have to do it." She took a big slurp from her drink. "Also, if you don't try to seduce anyone by cooking authentic Italian dishes when you get back, I'll be sorely disappointed."

River turned beet red, and he looked away. He fiddled idly with the corners of the towel in his hands. He wasn't even sure why he felt shy around Carlos all of a sudden, especially when she poked fun at him. Perhaps the fact that she was transgender like him made her words carry more weight for him.

"I'll do my best," he said.

"I'm kidding, man. I meant it when I said I'd miss you, though." Carlos turned around to go see if her usual spot in the coffee shop was vacant.

River asked the question before he could change his mind.

"Would you like to video call or something while I'm away?"

Carlos looked over her shoulder at him and it was like she lit up inside.

"I would love that."

"That way we can talk more about...you know..."

"Yeah. The stuff." They exchanged smiles. "Good stuff to talk about."

"I'll text you when I get to the airport."

"Thanks. Have a good trip..."

"You too. I mean..." He blushed again.

"I know what you meant." Carlos smiled again, then curled up in her usual spot on the corner couch to work on her reading. River had to look away as he resumed his work.

Just when Mia thought she could hold it together, she started crying all over again as she came out of the closet a second time. She sat across from Alan and Julian in the armchair facing their television while they shared the sofa. They had known she had some 'big news' to tell them over dinner, but they probably had no idea this had been coming.

To her surprise, both men gave her a warm hug almost the instant the words were out of her mouth. Her body began shaking as she realized how much physical affection she had been missing out on all these years, and that she had spent all but the last few months of her life without regular positive contact with other people. She felt like she had been starving to death for years and now had the first taste of the most incredible thing that made her feel waves of overwhelming happiness. Now she just wanted to give and receive hugs nonstop. When they pulled away from the tight embrace, Alan was the first to speak, smiling at her.

"Thank you for telling us." Alan squeezed her arm. "We got your back, always."

"Does anyone else know?" Julian asked gently.

"You remember River from the coffee shop?"

Julian frowned and looked away, deep in thought.

"River…is that…Curtain bangs, tattoos? Giving mall goth who stopped following fashion trends after 2010?" He smiled when she nodded. "Oh, he's so adorable. If only I were fifteen years younger…"

"Yep. That's the one. And another mutual friend of ours. That's it."

"Anything we can do to help you? What do you need right now?" Julian asked.

"Honestly, just letting me tell you. Just being here as friends. That means way more than I can say." She smiled and wiped her eyes. She may have been unlucky before, but damned if she didn't consider herself lucky for the friends she had made here.

Later that night, while Julian was cleaning up dinner and the other two relaxed on the back porch, Alan nudged Mia with his foot to get her attention. Tonight, he was wearing his favorite black hoodie under the brown leather jacket he 'borrowed' from Julian. In fact, he wore that jacket so much that Mia had thought it was his for a long time until Julian made a passing remark about Alan always stealing his clothes.

"Sorry about Julian, by the way. He can get pretty excited about this sort of thing. He's like a Golden Retriever," he laughed. Mia had not even been out to them for five minutes when Julian began listing off all the clubs and hangout places that were popular in the local queer community, plus all the drag shows in the area, ranked by his preference of course.

Mia just laughed again.

"It's fine. I get it. It's going to be a long time before I can go to any of those places, but I know Julian means well. He's a great guy." She glanced over her shoulder where Julian was singing to himself as he did the dishes. Mia could have teared up all over again, recalling how Julian had grabbed her hand and said, with a smile so warm she could bake cookies with it, that he had always wanted a little sister. Alan sipped his drink and glanced at her.

"Yeah. He is. He may be a lot sometimes, but he's my Prince Charming."

"Hey, Alan, you don't have to answer this if you don't want to, but…what was it like when you came out?"

He sat up a bit straighter, indicating this probably wasn't going to be a happy tale. Mia steadied herself and watched him close.

"If you don't want to talk about it…"

"No, it's okay." He smiled softly. "It wasn't easy for me either. I grew up in two very different worlds. I'd spend the school year with my parents up north in the city. Then, during the summer, I'd live with my grandparents down south. And I always knew I was different. I wasn't going to be the kid they wanted me to be. But in the city, I got to meet some other kids like me and there were some friends and neighbors who, looking back, probably knew I was different and accepted me for that. The town my grandparents lived in was the opposite. Everyone saw the world a certain way and didn't like anything that didn't fit it. They were shocked when I came out as gay, but only because I learned how to hide it every summer. They stopped wanting me to come to their house, and I wasn't invited to family outings anymore."

"Oh, Alan..." Mia's face fell, and she reached for his hand. She had heard bits and pieces about his story before, but not this much. "What happened after you came out?"

"A lot of my family hated it. Pushed me away. And of course, kids at school and even some friends turned on me. I had to learn how to defend myself because I certainly couldn't count on anyone else to watch my back. So..." Alan's face fell and he let out a deep sigh. "I had to toughen up. And I didn't trust people. I became angry. It was a dark few years there. But then I kind of got what you're starting to get right now. Meeting new people who accept you just for who you are. Especially when I moved away from my hometown and came out here. I started engaging more in the gay community here, and I met Julian through a couple of mutual friends. That changed my world. And for the past few years, I've really been working on healing from those bad times. Letting myself let my guard down. Not feeling like I always have to be on the defensive. Julian has helped me so much with that." He began to smile a little as he looked at her. "And as for my family, I actually got to visit my parents recently. They're doing much better about it now. Can't speak for the rest of the family yet, but…it's a start."

Mia bit her lip, biting back tears.

"Thank you for telling me that, Alan," she said with all sincerity.

"I guess what I'm trying to get at is, I hope you know there's no shame in being closeted for this long. With the circumstances you grew up in, it makes total sense. You've always been you. And whether everyone else knew doesn't make a difference in who you are."

Mia took a long gulp from her drink and smiled. Her cheeks were aching. She had smiled so much tonight.

"Jesus, Alan, you know how to make a girl cry."

Alan returned the smile and squeezed her shoulder.

"Someday I'll tell you guys the whole story. But I probably need to be drunk in order to get all that out," Mia said.

"Yeah, it definitely takes a certain level of booze to unlock a tragic backstory." He grinned. "But not tonight. Too heavy for tonight."

River and Mia had agreed to video chat today. Sadly, because of both of their schedules, they would only have a few minutes and wouldn't be able to sit down for a nice, long conversation. It was noon for Mia's time, nine in the evening for River's. Her city had just been hit by heavy snowfall and it fell in droves outside her dorm. But today was the kind of day where she loved the snow again. It looked gorgeous and better yet, she didn't have to worry about driving anywhere for the next couple of days, so that was a bonus.

When his video came up on her laptop, she saw that River was starting to grow out his facial hair. He had also gotten a new tattoo, this time on his ribcage, only apparent when he lifted his shirt to show it to her. It was a fine line of the Roman Colosseum. Mia had recently cut her hair, which deep down she didn't like having to do, but she didn't have much other choice for the moment. She crossed her legs and sat in front of her laptop, which she had set at the foot of her bed.

"What do you think?"

"I love it! Was it painful?"

"Nah, didn't feel a thing," he said, but she could tell he was kidding. She didn't think she could ever get a tattoo. It looked terrifying.

"How's the Roman life treating you?" Mia beamed, looking him over. The facial hair had thrown her off at first, but the more she studied it the more she decided he rocked the look.

"Good! Real good. Definitely worth studying the language for a year before coming here." River was wearing a dark gray wool cardigan sweater and kept idly playing with the ends of the sleeves.

"I'm sure they love you over there. Make any friends?"

"Yeah, a few. Learning a lot too. Tomorrow is the start of the Battle of the Oranges, and we're going to participate. Well, a couple are just going to watch and take photos. But I'm doing it."

"The Battle of the what now?"

"It is what it sounds like. Three days of a full out war with citrus weapons. I can't wait." He grinned.

"Sounds fun! Are you adjusting okay to the time difference?"

"I've traveled before, so it's nothing new," River said with a shrug.

Oh right, I forgot. His mom gets to travel the world for work. Once again, that pang of jealousy hit that she despised about herself. They chatted a bit longer about what they had planned next and what they had been up to, but twenty minutes went by before Mia even realized it. River glanced at the time and sighed sadly.

"Shoot, I'm sorry, but I need to take off. I have to get up really early tomorrow."

"That's okay. You'd better stay safe, big guy." She waved at the camera.

"Yeah, thanks. Talk to you later." He pressed the 'end call' button and Mia watched his face vanish, leaving her staring at a blank screen.

God, she missed him. This crush was being real fucking stubborn.

Chapter Twelve

As it had a bad habit of doing, Mia's mind had plenty to dwell on as she worked at the shop for another long shift. To be fair, she had all kinds of things to think about. School. Teachers. Classmates. When to buy groceries. Her transition. One topic in particular, though, she decided to stick with today. While her hands were busy, she wondered if it was time to share her true name with the people she was out to. It still felt like such a private part of her own story for herself, especially with how much time and care she took into deciding what name she wanted to use.

Then again, now that her closest friends knew she was a girl, she had noticed they all seemed to stumble with what name to call her now. And the biggest part was already out.

By the end of her shift, she had made her decision. It was time to officially make 'Mia' known to the world.

As always, she left the auto repair shop covered in filth—dirt, grease, engine oil, and general grime from fingertips to elbows as well as on her face. She didn't mind it at all, and in fact loved a job where she was able to get dirty from working on cars as opposed to, say, being stuck in a cubicle all day, but it always felt nice to get clean again.

Alan and Julian had invited her over for dinner tonight. And even though her brain preferred to curl up in her dorm with her laptop and do nothing, she knew she had to fight that urge to self-isolate. Julian was making homemade tacos and claimed that Mia would rather die than miss out on these. So, naturally, that left her little choice.

When she arrived, she greeted Alan with a big hug, as was their new normal. Ever since she came out, the barrier that held her back from hugging friends or even just being close to them had broken down. She hadn't seen that coming on the other side of the closet door, but she loved it. Today he was wearing a very nice basketball jersey that did not leave much to the imagination in regards to his strong arms and back muscles. Poor Mia felt herself flush a little, even though Alan was just a friend.

"How have you been doing?" was his first question.

"I'm okay. As okay as I've always been."

"Food's just about ready." Alan led her inside. "You keeping up with classes well, little sis?"

"I'm managing. I've been studying by myself more these days instead of with the study group, but it's fine. It's like…pushing myself out of the nest." As they entered the kitchen area, she crossed her arms and leaned on the counter, where all the taco ingredients had been set out. Julian was humming some song as he finished browning the meat. Mia shifted her weight from one foot to the other, waiting for her chance to say it until she couldn't take it anymore. "Hey guys. I got some news. Sort of," she managed to spill out.

Julian and Alan both looked up at her.

"I know what I want you all to call me. Instead of Carlos, I mean." She took a deep breath. "It's Mia. I want to be called Mia." *Oh my god,* she thought, *now that. Felt. Good.*

A small smile warmed Alan's face.

"Mia. I like that. It's a pretty name. Mia Reyes."

She twisted a lock of hair around her finger, her chest bursting with butterflies at being described as 'pretty.' So much so that that nasty part of her brain that immediately rejected any compliments and would accuse Alan of being a liar didn't even know what to say. The buzzy feeling in her body was apparently that good. She wanted to jump up and dance around like a kid in an arcade.

'Pretty.' Oh my god, no one can tell me anything anymore. I have a pretty name. FUCK YES.

"Thank you! I think so too. Well, I picked that name out a while ago. I just was afraid to tell anybody."

"I like it too." Julian beamed. "Makes me want to make you a cake with your new name on it or something."

"Cut it out!" She could feel her face turning the color of strawberries. "But I'm still not out publicly, just so you know. So still male pronouns when we're with anyone else."

"Of course, of course. I got you. Soon as you're ready, let me know and I got a lot of folks who would love to meet you. But we should make tonight's dinner a celebration," said Alan.

"To Mia Reyes, our little sister." Julian looked right at her. "Mia? Welcome to the world."

She clutched at her chest, as if afraid her heart was going to explode right out of her like the Xenomorph. Tears ran down her cheeks. And all Mia could think about, in this moment, in this little snippet of childlike magic, was how she had started the school year. She began with nothing but the backpack on her shoulders and a secret hidden from the entire world. She had been terrified, alone, and lost. Now she was here, being called by the name she had chosen for herself. She had good food in her stomach. She had friends who knew her as a woman and knew her name. She felt like she could finally breathe and understand what it meant to be human. To be happy and have a life worth living.

This was one of those moments she wanted her brain to capture like a photograph, tape to her fridge, and never, ever forget.

Mia found herself changing into a clean shirt just before their video call started, fussing over herself and hoping she looked decent.

River warned her beforehand that he had a couple of minor injuries from participating in the Battle of the Oranges and that she had no cause for concern. Nevertheless, when they connected online, Mia jumped when she saw stitches over his right eyebrow and a large, dark bruise still healing on his left biceps.

She took a deep breath. She had decided to tell him about her new name today and had felt like she was on the verge of bursting for days. That was the problem about starting to share a secret. It's addictive. Once you get started, you just have to keep passing it around like those annoying sales associates in the mall.

"Oh, god. You weren't kidding. I hope those were worth it." She frowned.

"Of course it was! It was so much fun. I need to tell you all about it."

"Please do. I need all the details. But first, River? I kind of got something I need to tell you."

River leaned in closer to the camera.

"I'm going to tell you my name for myself. I'm Mia."

"Mia. I love it." He beamed and got up for a second. He came back with a notebook and a marker and wrote something on it. When he held it up for the laptop camera, Mia read the words 'nice to meet you Mia, I'm River!'

"River, stop!" Mia laughed, covering her face and hoping she would not start crying all over again. How she managed to stay hydrated these past few days with all this damn crying was anyone's guess.

"New name day is such a good feeling. Who else have you shared it with?"

"Alan and Julian, and I'm going to tell Grace next." She scratched the back of her head. "I would have told you sooner, but I didn't want to tell you over text."

"Understandable. It's a lot more fun to say your new name out loud for the first time. Oh shit, that reminds me, I'd better go in and change your name in my contacts list before I forget." He grabbed his phone. She watched him, still smiling. "Mind if I put a sun emoji next to it? I always put one after a friend's name. One that makes me think of them, anyway."

"What was my old emoji?"

"One of the car emojis. Because you're so good at mechanics and you love cars."

"Hey, that works too." Mia bit her lip, loving this new little tidbit she had just learned about River. "But hey, how did the citrus war go?"

"It was fucking awesome." River looked so proud of himself. "One of my classmates took pictures of the whole thing. Want to see?"

"Of course I do!" River started sharing his screen for her. Mia looked over the photos which were many depictions, varying in angle, of the locals either throwing fruit into the air or being pummeled by them. She quickly picked up that the different patterned jerseys represented each team participating. Spectators were also photographed standing behind nets, watching the battle from a safe distance. Finally, there were pictures of River, some capturing him in the action of throwing oranges at the other teams. Another showed him later on, with a bit of blood on his forehead and some bad bruising on his arm and neck. He was dripping with orange juice and laughing, looking like he was having the time of his life. In the final photos, the streets were coated in orange peels and stickiness.

"Messy! And scary," she said, wincing again at the healing cut on his eyebrow. "I'm glad you didn't get seriously hurt."

"Just bumps and bruises. Couple stitches and an ice pack and I was fine. You remember I'm the youngest of four brothers, right? With all the roughhousing I had to deal with as a kid, this was just a walk in the park. And it was so much fun." He smiled, feeling his bruise. "I wonder if we could pull something off like this on campus."

"Ha-ha. Fun idea, but I'll pass." Mia shook her head, thinking that there was no way in hell she'd voluntarily throw non-snowy stuff at people, much less have stuff thrown at her that could cause her to get hurt. Maybe that was River's idea of fun, but not hers. She was more of a 'take a day trip to Coney

Island and eat a hot dog while riding the Ferris wheel' sort of fun.

"Speaking of which, have you come out to anyone else yet?" She sighed loudly.

"No, not yet. I want to tell more of my friends, but it's scary. I feel like I should wait a little longer. I keep thinking maybe I can just 'magically' make everyone just know. Just like how I wish I could just snap my fingers and magically transition all at once."

"Yeah, I get that. Anything I can do to help?"

"Honestly? This." She laughed, but she meant it in all sincerity. "Just being able to be out to you and talk to you. You were a big reason I was able to come out at all. I saw you so out and happy and so *you* and…it helped me realize I wanted that for myself, too. And I thank you for that. So much. I knew other trans people were out there, but you're just so sweet and…I can't thank you enough. Especially when everyone else thinks I'm a man."

She could see her words had stunned him, and there were tears in his eyes.

"But that's just basic human decency. Treating someone as their true self. I mean, if you want my help finding a doctor who can get you on hormones or talk to others about transitioning…" He stopped and looked away, rubbing at his bruise again. "Sorry. I don't mean to push you. I just want you to be happy."

Mia crossed her legs in front of her laptop and hugged herself.

"Believe me, if it were just up to me, I would've done that by now. But money's tight and I'm not in the best place to be thinking about this right now. And then there's my job, and college, and just..." Her gaze turned empty. She thought of her job and the career in engineering she wanted to pursue with her degree, and how all of that would become so fragile the moment she exposed her gender to the world. So much she had built for herself from the ground up could fall apart at a moment's notice, all because of who she was.

Fuck. This was not how the conversation was supposed to go at all. This was supposed to be happy.

But now all Mia could think about was how the world just saw her as a hairy, gangly, awkward boy, how there was no way she could afford hormones and therapy with her current job, how her boss would respond if he found out. And how even in the best-case scenario, the world would still never see her as completely herself. There would always be someone out there who refused to accept her and would try to make her life harder. There would always be someone who didn't want her to exist. As she blinked away her tears she saw River fumbling to try to cheer her up.

"Shit, I'm sorry, Mia. I didn't mean to...I just...hey, want to see a souvenir I got you?"

"Not your fault," she reassured him, then smiled big despite herself. "And yes, show me. Please?"

He held up what looked like the coziest hoodie Mia had ever seen. It was eggshell white and had a bunch of cute cartoons of Italian foods on it in shades of black, red, and green. It looked like the kind of hoodie she could live in all fall and winter. The kind you could freely wear in any casual public setting but could also wear around the dorm all weekend. Her favorite kind of hoodie.

"It's perfect!" She yelped. Her face flushed again. "Oh my god, that's so cute. I love it! It looks so soft."

He smiled big.

"I'm going to mail it to you next week. International shipping costs be damned."

"No-no-no, you don't have to. Just bring it with you when you get back."

"But you need it! I won't be back until late spring and by then it'll be too warm for you to wear it."

"Fine. Only if it's okay with you."

"It is! You can't stop me." He grinned. "By the way, my other friends are saying I should keep my facial hair. What do you think?"

Mia considered it. It did give him a sort of edgy 'don't fuck with me' look, but she did prefer clean shaven guys. Then again, what did that matter?

"Try shaving it. Let's see what you look like."

"But you already know what that looks like," he laughed.

"Hmm, can't recall," Mia joked. "But you're in a new country. You should, I don't know, reinvent yourself. Try new things." She glanced at the time and her eyes widened. "I'm sure it's getting late over there, so I won't hold you up, but we miss you a lot back here." She paused for a moment. "I miss you. "

"Miss you too." he rubbed his eyes. "Take care of yourself, okay?"

"You too."

"Hey. You'll be okay," he said.

"I'll do my best." She held eye contact as she pressed the 'end call' button and sat in silence.

River was glad to be with the band again, even if they were jamming together via video call instead of in person. Today, they had no exact agenda. But they did need to get some ideas rolling of what their next song was going to be about. Their concept album about the gladiator was slowly coming together in the form of online documents and scattered note-taking. River sat in front of his laptop, watching the band on their respective screens. He pulled out his new leather notebook, which he had been using to jot down song lyric ideas exclusively for while he was in Italy.

"What do you have there?" Victoria asked him.

"Some ideas." River glazed over his notes. At first he had thought little of them, but now some of them began to form together. "I might have something."

"What is it?" Cat stared at it, chewing on their black eyeliner pencil.

"I'll send it to group chat. One sec." His fingers flew over the keys as he typed bits and pieces of what he had written, etching them into the form of something that just might take the form of a verse or a chorus of a song. "Some stuff I've been writing."

A couple minutes of silence passed as each band member took the time to read them over.

"Who is this about?" Oliver asked.

"Now you know that's never important."

Emily and Cat each took a moment to re-read some of the lyrics. Emily started scratching behind her ear, which she only did when she was deep in thought.

"This line here. Is that…?"

"It means exactly what you think it means. This is about a girl."

A couple of band members made wide eyes of realization.

"Ohhhh. So that's what the song is about." Victoria nodded. "I like it. Very on-brand. It's not about one of us, is it?"

"No, no. The girl in this song is actually that friend I was telling you about." With Mia's permission, he had told them about her shortly after she came out. It had been too exciting not to tell them that there was yet another trans girl in their friend circle.

"Oh, you mean the girl you have a crush on?" Cat asked with a small grin.

River frowned. Then had to blink a few times.

"Wait...what? No!" Heat rushed to his ears. The thought of having a 'crush' was humiliating, like being back in middle school all over again. Besides, a crush on Mia? No way. That's not what this was. They were good friends, and he thought she was a cool person. God, he hated when people did this, equating having somewhat positive feelings for someone else as inherently romantic. He'd give Cat a piece of his mind if they didn't have so much work to get done.

"Uh-huh," said Emily.

"I *don't* have a crush. The song is a metaphor. It's got nothing to do with anything like that."

"All right, all right, let's just get to work on this song then," Cat laughed.

"Oookay, moving on," Oliver said, rolling his eyes.

"Right. Moving on. Thank you!" River grabbed his small keyboard and started working on a tune, still shaking his head. *A crush on Mia. Jesus Christ. More like History of the Delusional.*

Chapter Thirteen

Mia was scared to death.

An unusually cold morning in early March was the day she decided to come out to the support group. But now the second thoughts were starting up. Flooding in and saying that it was too soon or they wouldn't believe her and a bunch of other crap she knew in theory wasn't true but sounded more and more convincing as the day went on.

"Are you sure they'll take it well? I mean, I haven't even started transitioning yet." She stopped walking alongside Grace as they approached Williams Hall. Even her hoodie from Italy couldn't stop the shivers. Her cutting habit had become much less prevalent in recent weeks, but now and then, when things were too much, she still reached for her razor. She still needed her hoodie sleeves to cover up the latest scars and bandages, thinking she'd rather die than have everyone know she was a cutter.

"Of course they'll take it well! This is a safe place, trust me," Grace said. "Do you want to do this later? There's no pressure, you know."

"No, I want to do it now. I'm ready. I'm just scared." Mia hated the nervous laughter that came out of her after that. This was the other part she hadn't really thought about until she started telling people. You don't just 'come out' one time and then you're over and done and everyone knows. Coming out wasn't so much like a one-time performance and more like a long-running play you had to put on every night, over and over, to a new audience every time.

"It's okay to be scared." Grace grabbed her hand and gave it a gentle squeeze. "If anyone even thinks of giving you a hard time, they'll have to get through me."

"Thanks." Mia beamed.

They began the meeting with a couple of quick announcements about some upcoming events around campus. They all also took turns venting about classes and professors and projects. Then, once things quieted down a bit, Mia took her chance by telling the group she had a small announcement to make. And here she went again.

"I'm…I'm transgender. I'm a girl. I want to be called Mia. But I'm not ready to go out in public yet."

Turns out, Grace had been absolutely right. Mia didn't see the ensuing round of applause coming, and it startled her a little. But she did go through a lot of exchanged hugs and reassurances and congratulations, as if she had announced she had gotten her doctorate degree or she was getting married. Maybe it was just her brain doing its thing again, or maybe she was onto something, but either way, Mia felt the unanswered question hang in the air of *why* she didn't dress like a girl yet, or come out publicly. Why she wasn't throwing out all her boy clothes for dresses and why she still kept her hair short. But River had told her repeatedly that she did not have to explain herself to anybody, so she didn't bother bringing that up. And luckily, they didn't either. If it was on their minds, they weren't going to say it.

Warm weather was finally returning, much to Mia's relief. The Oregon air smelled sweet, and the school was humming with the sounds of spring. That, and students in agony from finals, of course.

She walked across campus after meeting up with her study group, headed to a local fast-food place to meet up with Grace. Today, Mia was wearing a big hoodie the color of coffee with a lot of creamer, navy blue slim fit jeans, and red converse shoes. One of her go-to 'comfort' outfits. Clothes that weren't quite as feminine as she wanted to dress, but were as close as she could get without feeling like she had a target on her back.

River had come back from Italy just two days ago, but Mia had not messaged him yet. Surely he had enough on his plate with resting up from the trip and graduation coming up. It would be rude to bug him now. So every time she pulled out her phone and saw his name, Mia resisted the urge to text him. He deserved his space while adjusting to life back home, and she didn't want to become that clingy, needy friend who depended on him to make her happy. That was the last thing River deserved.

However, seeing him again in person was all that was on her mind for the time being. Mia had every intention of introducing River to Julian and Alan sooner or later, figuring those three would get along well together. And she selfishly wanted to witness the chaotic conversations that unfolded as soon as Julian, with his refined taste in music, got to sample River's creations. But for now, Mia put that aside and let herself take a small break from finals and general stress factors.

She saw Grace waiting for her just outside and hurried up to her to say hello. As she always did, Grace greeted her with a big hug. In the past couple of months since coming out to the group, Grace had become one of Mia's best friends. She loved helping Mia with little tips to help her feel more feminine until she could fully transition. Things like practicing on her voice pitch, or using floral-scented skin care and moisturizer. Conversations with Grace were Mia's first real 'girl talk' sessions. Just girls being girls together. At first it had overwhelmed her, but as soon as she got over the initial shock, Mia held onto it fast. Now their one-on-time was her favorite part of the week. She certainly didn't get that from the girls in her support group. Then again, as nice as that group was, she didn't trust them near enough to come out to them.

Mia dunked her chicken fries in a hearty supply of barbeque sauce. They had grabbed a small booth towards the back of the fast-food place next to a window. Per Mia's request, Grace still used male pronouns and her government name in public. As they were chatting about the latest news on final exams and work, Mia's phone went off. Normally she didn't bother to check it while she was busy eating or hanging out, but this time she saw River's name on her notifications.

"Sorry…" Mia said as she pulled it up.

"It's okay. Something urgent?"

"River is asking if I can come over in a couple hours to hang out." Mia set her phone back down. "I'm going to say yes. When we're done here, of course."

"So…text him back?"

"I need to wait a few minutes. He literally just messaged me."

"Ah. Don't want to appear too needy and all. Otherwise he might figure it out."

Mia stared at her, hoping she didn't just hear what she thought she heard.

"What are you implying, exactly?"

Grace paused mid-fry and smiled.

"It's okay. I've known you had a crush on him for a while now."

It took Grace's sentence a few seconds to kick in. Then Mia slumped in her chair, staring down at her nuggets and wishing she could turn into one.

Oh. My. God. Oh my god.

Mia hid her face in her hands. Grace grabbed her hand.

"It's okay! Your secret is safe with me."

"What dumb thing did I do to give it away?"

"Oh, you know, the usual stuff. The way you blush when you say his name. The way you always ask if he's going to be there when we invite you to a party or whatnot."

"Shut up! Oh my god, I'm so embarrassed…are you serious?" Scratch the nugget idea. Mia wanted to turn into that puddle of lukewarm orange soda drying up beside her feet. Get mopped up and thrown out with all the wrappers and plastic cups and half-eaten sandwiches.

"Don't worry about it."

"Does everyone know? I mean, how obvious is it?"

"I know that Sean knows. Hailey, too. Actually, most of the group knows." As Mia let out a long groan, Grace shrugged. "Hey, you asked."

"I did, didn't I? Do you think River knows too?"

"Are you kidding? Please. I love that guy, but bless his heart, these things always fly over his head. It's like he used up all his brain cells on getting his master's degree and forgot to leave some extra for basic social cues. He's not going to know unless you tell him straight. Guarantee it. You didn't hear this from me, but with his last relationship, she had to sit in his lap and make out with him for him to realize that she was attracted to him."

"Okay, good. The less he knows, the better. I heard she was bad, by the way." Mia paused, not realizing she had said it for a second. "The ex, I mean."

Grace's smile faded at that.

"She was."

"I'm sorry…it's not my business." *But you brought it up and now you're just realizing how much you've been wanting to know about the ex who was apparently so awful she put Oregon's Most Eligible Bachelor off the market and ruled out any chance you have at him, so…here we are. I guess I really do want to know.*

"No, it's okay. It's not like it's a secret what happened. River just has a tough time talking about it." Grace sighed, rubbing her forehead. "She was horrible to a lot of us. She loved making me feel terrible about my height, weight, my accent, even the foods I ate. She just always had something awful to say to cut me down. But she'd only do it when River wasn't around, so that later, she could accuse us of lying when we told him. But when River was there? She was all smiles and everybody's best friend. And that's not half of it. I saw it for myself. She'd try to coerce him into stuff he was not comfortable with, like going to certain parties or trying drugs or calling him pet names he hated. She wouldn't let him be in a room alone with anybody else and would lose her mind if he so much as talked to another girl. *And* she hacked into his accounts to get all his passwords, so she could always monitor what he was doing. We were all happy when she finally moved away. He was the one who broke it off, for the record, but she liked to act like she did it. One day she just decided he didn't matter to her anymore, and she left him like dirt. On to the next one or whatever. Lucky for her because by that point, I would have strangled her. I'm not even kidding."

Mia nearly lost her appetite after hearing that story. This ex-girlfriend reminded her of some of the kids who bullied her in high school. Nothing better than someone making you feel like you want to die, only to pretend they're your best friend a split second later, just to confuse you.

"Geez Louise. Sounds like a real peach," she muttered, licking ranch dressing off her fingers. "I can understand why he says he doesn't want to date anyone after all that."

"It sucks. But, hey. He'll be okay. I've known him since I started school here three years ago. He dated her for about half a year, and since they broke up, he's been doing way better. Someday he'll want to try again, and when he does…" She gave Mia a cheeky smile and Mia shook her chicken wing at her.

"Not going to happen. My crush will wear off one of these days and then we can just be normal friends."

When she arrived, she found River still with a bit of jet lag. His suitcases were scattered, still unpacked, the apartment full of laundry in various states of cleanliness and lack thereof. Even with the exhaustion from the trip, he still gave Mia a smile when he answered the door. He was wearing a basketball jersey and sweatpants, and no socks or shoes.

"Mia! Get in here!" he said in that typical slightly-too-loud voice she had missed so much, and he pulled her in for a hug. She found herself burying her face in his shoulder, just happy to hear his heartbeat again. "I missed you, buddy."

And right then, of all the times and places, Mia felt herself getting an erection. With the way he was hugging her and the smell of his sweat and body spray, there was no way he could not feel it against his leg right now. The underworld could not sweep in and take away her soul fast enough. She cursed herself for ruining their reunion.

But whether River felt her girl boner or not, he pulled away from the hug as if nothing awkward had just happened. Mia played along and smiled up at him, fixing her hair a bit.

"You've been growing it out since I last saw you," he said, reaching down to tousle her hair.

"Yeah." She laughed. "Rocking that Zac Efron *High School Musical* look."

"Fuck yeah. Bring it back." He pulled out a chair for her. "Well, I'm starving. Let's fucking eat." He had mentioned he ordered takeout for when she would get here. And even though Mia had eaten fast food with Grace just a couple of hours ago, she still had plenty of room for more.

Right. Food. Eat the food.

She sat across from him and they dished up their plates. Neither of them were shy about stuffing their plates. That was one thing Mia liked about eating with River. She could eat a ton, without any manners, and he never cared at all. No judgment or passing remarks.

"How is your semester going? I mean, really going?" He poured sweet and sour sauce all over his rice and chicken.

"So close to the end I can taste it. Well, of the first year. But still. I was so sure I wouldn't even survive the first month, and here we are. So when are you going to tell me all about Italy?"

He swallowed a couple mouthfuls of beef and broccoli before he started into a long story about everything he got to see, do, and learn on his trip. Typical of River's stories, he went off on one energetic rabbit trail after another as he kept remembering things he wanted to share with her. Mia was content to just sit and listen to him as she ate, keeping up as best she could even as he seemed to talk at a million miles an hour.

She took a deep breath. This was all fine. Nothing unusual to see her. Just a conversation between two friends who hadn't seen each other in months, eating takeout and complaining about finals. Why should it have to be any more than that at all?

Chapter Fourteen

After they finished dinner, they sat on his couch under cozy blankets and talked for hours. They talked about school, as he was just about to graduate, and she had another three years to go. They talked about how Mia was still adjusting to life up north, all the similarities and differences she had discovered over the past several months, and all the things that had begun to really grow on her. He showed her the photos he took, along with all the things he bought. And, of course, as was inevitable, they talked about her transition. What it was like to be called 'Mia' by her close friends now as opposed to 'Carlos.' Her feelings about starting to grow her hair longer, and the mixture of jubilance and terror that came with that. Her own apprehensions about, someday, looking for a local doctor who would hopefully prescribe her hormones. And how that might affect her status at her job and her future prospects in her career.

"This is going to sound like weird advice, but don't rush getting on hormones." River sat up a little straighter and relaxed his arm along the back of the couch. "It feels like something you want as soon as possible, like a drug you've just got to have right now or you'll die. And that's kind of true. But it really, *really* changes your body in ways you won't expect. And you have to be mentally prepared for how much it'll change not just your body but, well, your whole life. I had to go see a therapist for a while before we both knew I was ready to get started."

Mia hugged her knees and rested her chin on one of them. It was her favorite position when sitting.

"How did it change your life?"

"Strangers treat you different. Your emotional reaction to things changes. Clothes start to fit different. You even *smell* different. And then there's the stuff it does to your appetite and your sex drive. Like you thought the first puberty is bad? Second puberty does not play around."

Mia blushed at that.

"All I'm saying is you don't have to be in a huge hurry to rush onto estrogen. You are who you are, regardless of what chemicals are in your body. And there's no rule that says as soon as you're out to the world you need to physically transition as soon as possible. It's not a race. You do it at your own pace. Go for what you want, however you want to."

"Thanks, River. That really helps to hear that. I'm just not sure how I would even start to live as a girl on campus. Then again, it's not like I have many friends here. Not anymore. I don't know."

"What do you mean?"

"I mean…" She shrugged. "It's probably on me, but things have been a bit off lately with the study group. They don't talk to me as much as they used to."

"Still…I'm sorry. That's not a fun feeling."

"It's fine. Really. I'm used to it." She bit her lip as she smiled at him. As she moved to stretch her legs, their bare feet brushed under the blankets. A shiver went up her body at the skin-to-skin contact. Was she too close to him? Probably.

Maybe? But River did not move away. In fact, as she dared to inch a bit more, until her toes were touching the leg hairs on his lower shin, he didn't move away at all, as if encouraging her to move closer. It was such a small form of contact, but she saw stars from it.

My toes touched his leg hair. Oh my god. My toes are touching his leg hair! And he seems comfortable with it! Does that mean...does he...or what...

It could mean a lot of things. For one, River had always been physically affectionate, so maybe it meant nothing to him. It could mean, based on what Grace told him, that it flew right over his head and he had not a clue what it meant to Mia. Not like Mia could say anything to him about it. For that matter, how do you properly ask someone, *Hey, if I wasn't such a mess of self-loathing and dysphoria and mental illness and had no reason to believe you'd ever find me attractive, do you think we could be a cute couple? Would you say yes if I asked you out? Would you even think to ask me out first? Would you ever look at me and see someone you could fall for?*

"Want to watch something or play a video game?" River finally asked her.

"I'd love to." For some reason, that question gave her a sense of relief. If he had tried to make a move just now, she definitely would have ruined it. "I'll kick your ass just like last time."

"Oh, I'd love to see you try," he laughed and started up the console. And just like that, the physical contact was broken as he sat up straight and planted his feet on the floor. But Mia didn't forget it. She didn't think she could if she tried.

Hours later, before she headed back to campus, River pulled her in for another hug. She let the hug linger as long as he wanted, just content that he was back home and she could see him almost every day again. Unable to stop it, her mind wandered back to that haunting question.

The words began to press against her tongue. She needed to know. Just a hypothetical question. Just to know if River would even consider going on a date with her and maybe even trying a relationship with her. Because if he was never going to see her as more than a friend, she needed to know sooner or later so she could work on getting over him.

In the end, she could not bring herself to do it.

It was supposed to be a good day.

The grass was green. The sun was shining. The air was warm. The snow had all completely melted, and finals were almost over. It was supposed to be the kind of day you treated yourself to an extra-fancy coffee, and maybe even a breakfast sandwich or a muffin because you know what, you deserved it and it was the perfect day to enjoy tasty food.

And it *was* a good day. At first.

Mia had just gotten her grade back from one of her finals. Ninety-four out of a hundred. Ninety. Four. She was practically floating beside herself with giddiness. So many little things that had been bothering her lately didn't even matter anymore, not with how perfect today was. She didn't even care that the study group hadn't said hello or congrats to her today. Was this what prodigies felt like all the time? Even bits of laughter escaped her as she headed down the hall to the elevator to head downstairs. Despite everything going on, she had passed one of her toughest classes with a score she never saw coming. A breakfast sandwich kind of day for sure.

For a few moments she stood there, almost forgetting to push the button. Another student walked in the elevator, but Mia did not pay him attention until she realized he was staring at her. She had seen him around her dorm before as he lived right down the hall, but they had never spoken to each other.

"Have I run into you before?" he asked.

"Sorry. Don't remember." She shrugged apologetically.

"You're Carlos, right?"

"Yeah...?" She frowned.

"You're the Carlos that wants to turn into a girl?" He looked her up and down, like he was trying to figure her out.

The elevator might as well have cut loose and sent them both plummeting.

Mia couldn't breathe. Cold rushed over her body. A knot formed in her stomach, and then her throat closed up like she was being choked. Then, suddenly, she tried her hardest to laugh.

"I...what?! *No*...that's not me. Must be someone else."

"Are you sure?" he asked, frowning.

"Pretty sure! You got me confused with a different Carlos."

He seemed to either accept her statement or stop caring whether she was lying. Either way, he gave her another weird look as the elevator doors opened.

She didn't move. There was no other floor to go to. He stared at her until she finally got off the elevator and forced herself to keep walking in the opposite direction from him. Once he had finally turned a corner and was out of sight, she collapsed against the wall. All the air had been sucked out of her lungs.

How did he know? How the fuck did he know...?

And suddenly the little things from before did not seem so little anymore. Mia thought back. The study group had been acting a little more cold to her these past few weeks. Initially she thought it was just stress from finals, but now she thought otherwise. Maybe word got around campus and they found out she was 'the Carlos that wants to turn into a girl.' And maybe the scratches on her car weren't from her careless driving, as she had assumed. Maybe someone vandalized her car to send a message.

How did they find out? Was it an overheard comment, a friend of a friend accidentally outing her? Maybe someone found one of her social media accounts and saw a post where she got too comfortable about mentioning being a girl. Many things could have happened.

It was the first night in a while she locked her door. The first night in about a month that she put the razor blades to her skin again, leaving a trail of sloppy, crisscrossing cuts up the underside of both her forearms. She just let the blood dry on top and went to bed in her clothes, not even granting herself the comfort of sleeping in her pajamas.

Sleep did not bring relief. The next day, she only felt like the darkness was closing in around her. Her arms hurt so much from the cuts every time she moved, but at least they helped remind her that everything was real, and that this wasn't some bad dream like the ones she had for years in high school.

After classes, she knocked on the next door down the hall. Her neighbor, Rhett, answered. They only knew each other on a first name basis, but as neighbors, they had developed a sort of exchange over the past year. He could stop by if he needed coins for laundry, and she could stop by if she needed some plastic silverware. It was a peculiar little relationship, but one that Mia valued for what it was worth.

"Hey, you got some Band-Aids? Or maybe gauze?"

Mia prayed up and down he wouldn't ask her why. But at least some good luck was on her side today and he didn't say anything, just a small mention of he'd probably be asking her for some microwave dinners tomorrow. She nodded and thanked him and hurried back to her dorm. In the small bathroom, Mia filled the tub with hot water and sat in, holding her arms underwater until she worked up the courage to scrub at the dried blood. Several cuts re-opened. When that was done, she put on bandages on each arm until the worst of them were covered, and she sat in the water until it went lukewarm and her toes pruned, and even then it took more willpower to climb out and look at her flat chest and hairy limbs in the mirror.

They know who you are, a dark and familiar voice told her in her head. *There's no more hiding it from them. They know what you really are, and they hate you for it.*

It felt like the world had taken one look at her when she finally had a small shred of happiness, was finally able to show her true self to the world in just the slightest form, and had decided even that much had to be punished. And everything was going to slowly turn against her and wrap her up in it like a cocoon.

You knew this was going to happen. You knew it, and you did it anyway, like an idiot. Great job.

When she went to her class the next morning, her fears were confirmed. She went out of her way to try to say hello to the two girls who were in her study group. But today, yet again, they had their backs turned to her, trying to act like she wasn't there.

Mia worked up the nerve to clear her throat and approach them. She tried to wave at them when a morbid thought hit her.

Was that a girly wave? Was it too feminine? What if I just outed myself to the entire classroom by doing that? Is that why they're ignoring me?

Then she stopped herself. What was she thinking? This is what she wanted when she came out, wasn't it? Didn't she want the world to know that she was a girl, and that she was happy to be herself for a change? Why wasn't she happy?

They glanced at her and nodded to acknowledge her, but didn't say much, besides one muttering a small, "Hey."

"Going to miss you all when classes are over," Mia said, then fought back a wince. *Ugh. That sounded better in my head.*

A couple of them grunted, but otherwise they didn't make much of a response. Mia's heart sank. These people had been more than happy to chat with her before and after class earlier this year, even have a couple of deep conversations as they went to the cafeteria together. They knew her favorite music artists and which foods she was allergic to and how many times she did her laundry in a month. Now she was nothing to them.

She tried not to cry during class, but that was easier said than done. By the end of it she caved in and texted both River and Alan the same message. She summarized the incident in the elevator, as well as how her classmates were treating her. Then she curled up on her bed, feeling just as miserable as she did before she came out, if not more.

"Hey," Alan said to his husband, "check out this text from Mia."

Julian put down the meal prep he was working on in the kitchen, wiped his hands on the towel which he threw over his shoulder, and leaned over to look at Alan's phone screen.

"Fuck," was all he said. "You know, the guest room is all done. We should offer to let her stay there a night or two. I think she'd like that."

"Yeah? You think so?" Alan sighed. "I'll ask her. Can't hurt."

As he waited for her reply, Alan laid back on the sofa, feeling a little ill. He had been worried for her when she started coming out to others. This city advertised itself as being openly progressive and diverse, but you could host all the pride events you wanted and it didn't erase the backwards part of the population. As early as last year, someone had vandalized the pride flag sticker on Julian's car. Before that, a customer had tried to get Julian fired from his job at the restaurant when they found out he was married to a man.

But deep down, Alan realized he had been hoping that wouldn't happen to Mia. Maybe he had held out too much hope for her wellbeing. But how could he not? How could you not want the next generation to not suffer like you did? Guess things never really changed after all.

Alan exhaled with relief when Mia accepted his invitation, albeit after a long wait. It had all been Julian's idea. He proposed renovating the office into a guest room and using it as a place any of their friends or friends' friends could go if they needed a place to crash, for whatever reason that may be. Julian never wanted anyone in their community to feel like they had nowhere to turn to, and he followed through with that as best he could. That was Julian. The guy who'd cook you a hot meal and bring it over if he heard you were hungry, no questions asked. The guy who would drive you to the airport or help you move into your new place and never once hold it against you like a social currency of favors. It was one of the many reasons Alan fell in love with him, even though it also drove him crazy. He liked to think that he helped keep Julian's big altruistic ideas at least slightly grounded in reality, and that he helped keep a close eye out for anyone looking to take advantage of Julian's generosity. But as much as it stressed him out sometimes, Alan wouldn't change it for anything.

Two hours later, Mia parked her car a little way up the street. When Alan saw her, she was a wreck. Her hair, now at the length where she could make a very tiny ponytail if she pulled enough back, was messy and unkempt. Her clothes had wrinkles like they had been slept in. She looked like she had been crying a lot. But worst of all, her arms were striped with dark lines and bandages.

He didn't say anything. He just ran to her and hugged her. Mia buried her face in his shoulder, and he felt her begin trembling.

"I'm so dumb."

"You're not dumb, Mia," he said soothingly, rubbing her back.

"I should have figured they'd find out. They know."

"It's going to be okay."

"You don't know that." Her voice sounded hollow.

"Trust me. We'll make sure nothing bad happens to you."

"Alan, that's just it. The bad things have already happened." She pulled away, her eyes red and puffy. "I don't feel safe."

"Well, you're safe as long as you're with us. Not a single bad thing has happened here and never will. And hey, Julian is making us Mission burritos and artichoke dip. And I know how much his cooking lifts your mood."

Mia only smiled a little at that, but he decided to take it as a victory, anyway.

Chapter Fifteen

One week before the end of the school year, Julian invited Mia and several of her friends from the support group over to their house for a party. As he put it, it was nothing more than a little get-together for the local community to relax, have a good time, and have a quick send-off before everyone parted ways for summer. The party was not advertised as openly 'just for us queers,' but it wasn't hard to get that message.

That was not what Mia had a problem with.

She didn't want anyone else finding out she'd be there, and she hated herself even more for that. She could only imagine what certain classmates and teachers would think if they knew she'd been seen at the 'gay couple's house party.' By now, she felt convinced everyone on campus had heard about her little secret. If her study group knew, then everyone they knew would have found out, and so on and so on, like the worst chaotic ripple effect.

Mia didn't even read the text message notifying her of it until the day before the party, and she quickly RSVP'd. She didn't want to go. But she had to, lest she wanted her friends asking her where the hell she was. Plus, Julian and Alan reassured her there would be plenty of nonalcoholic options at the party, so if she didn't go she'd feel guilty they went to all that trouble just for her. They knew she avoided alcohol, but she didn't have the heart to tell them that the smell alone could ruin her day. She saw how that took away River's fun, and she would hate to do the same to them.

On the day of the party, she barely made it through studying and her work shift. Not even a hot shower made her feel better. Her whole body ached, pushing her closer to the ground. She felt like a deflated balloon, sculpted out of concrete. Like her head was being bloated and squeezed at the same time. All she could think about was how she was the last sort of person who should be going to a damn party. She was going to be a downer there and ruin everything and make everyone around her miserable, like she always did. But that's the trick about RSVP'ing. Too late now. You're committed. You told one of your only close friends 'yes.'

She pictured herself showing up to the party in a cute dress. Maybe something black, or maybe even a bold blue or yellow. Lots of makeup and even some jewelry. She'd spend an hour getting ready like other girls do. But in reality, that couldn't happen yet. Her friends would support her, but friends of friends were always up in the air. Not to mention outing herself to her whole little corner of the world.

In the end, Mia put on her mustard hoodie and slim-fit black pants. Close enough.

This will do, she told herself as she looked in the mirror. *This will do just fine for a while.*

The party was pretty much what Mia expected, but at least it made for an interesting ruckus. Julian and Alan had a lot of friendships within the city's queer community, plus all their coworkers, which meant you mixed queer chefs with queer

computer nerds with a bunch of older gay couples and poly-
cules. Then you throw in the younger crowd like her, River,
Grace, and all their mutual friends, and the end result was a mix
of the most chill people you've ever met running into the most
stressed-out people you've ever met. She didn't think she'd seen
so much diversity in fashion in one place all at once. It was a
feast for the eyes.

She watched everyone around her, simultaneously wanting
attention and wanting to be left alone. Julian and Alan both
got to say hello, but they were so busy keeping the party going
that she didn't get to follow them around. Grace was here, but
needed to say hello to everyone, as always. No time to let her
poor little friend tail after her. Still. Mia would give anything
to have another girl walk up to her and clasp her hands the
way cisgender girls seem to do and say, "You look so pretty!"
And no, not in a way that actually said, "You look like a gross
crossdresser but I'm going to lie and say you look pretty, so I
feel like I'm being a good friend." In other words, she wanted to
be able to talk to people without constantly thinking of her five
o'clock shadow. But that would never happen. Not anytime
soon.

She grabbed a cup and poured some soda in it, sipping at it
as she wandered around the house. Easier said than done to act
like she felt like she fit in. She didn't recognize many of the
songs as she was more of an oldies rock sort of girl, not Julian's
pop and dance hits. Mostly Mia found it comfortable to find a
quieter corner of the apartment and not do much of anything.

Of course, just her luck, River showed up at the party about
half an hour into it. Mia waited until his eyes happened to meet
hers and she waved to him from the other end of the room.

When River saw her, he waved back and walked up to her. He had a twelve pack of some sort of IPA under his arm. Mia blushed and waved back, even though he was only a couple of feet away from her. The music had gotten a bit loud at that point, so he had to lean in so she could hear him. Not that Mia cared, of course. He had a nice cologne tonight. Not the cheap body spray he always wore. Mia's nostrils thanked him dearly for that.

"How are you?" he asked.

"Oh, you know." Mia shrugged. "Doing the best I can."

"Want to go somewhere you don't have to be around alcohol?" he asked.

Mia felt a pang in her that he remembered one of her triggers. But tonight, she wanted something different. Even if it would end up hurting her in the long run.

"Actually, tonight I want to drink."

"Are you sure?" River frowned.

"I'm sure. Come on. Let's have fun." She forced a smile, praying that getting drunk would help her feel a little better.

"Well, only if you're sure. In that case, I'll have one with you."

It had been a while since Mia had had a couple of drinks.

But she had a few things working in her favor right now. Julian and Alan's home was a safe place. River was drinking too and every sip she saw him take was her own inward excuse to take one with him. And on top of that, Alan was working hard at the kitchen bar, making delicious cocktails and mocktails.

She had had no idea there were so many delicious ways to get plastered.

Within a couple hours, Mia's head was in that perfect space where she was aware of her surroundings and what she was doing, but she also had a light buzz that helped her care a lot less about all of it. During most of the party she stuck close to River. But the more she drank, the less she cared about the idea of being alone. Eventually, Mia grabbed a chair in the front entryway that split into the living room on the left and the dining area on the right. She sat there, tapping her toes to the music playing on the sound system and holding onto her cup of Red Bull and vodka.

River wandered back into the room after having a cigarette outside. Mia could tell he had had quite a few drinks too, judging by the way he walked. She hollered his name and invited him to her. A bit spilled on her shoes, but she didn't care. River looked up at her, a goofy grin on his face as he walked back over to her. He carried a plate stuffed with crackers and cheese slices.

"Hey again!" Mia said, beaming. "Having fun?"

"Yeah, I guess so. Julian has the coolest kitchen I've ever seen. His cutlery collection is fucking insane. Almost makes up for him being such a coffee snob." River sat next to her. "You doing okay?"

Mia took a few moments to realize what his question meant. She remembered the last time they both hung out at a party.

"Yeah, I'm actually okay. I think? The smell was starting to make me anxious earlier, but ironically, the more I've been drinking the less it bothers me."

"I guess so. Just be careful." He laughed with her before stuffing his face with cheese and crackers. "You look really nice tonight, by the way."

Mia rolled her eyes and stole a slice of cheddar from his plate.

"You're just saying that because I look hideous and you want to cheer me up."

"No, I really mean it. You look very pretty."

Mia found herself covering her face, fearing she might begin to tear up if she wasn't careful. She wanted to believe him so much. And deep down, she knew he wasn't saying it out of pity. But as always, her body rejected compliments like a poison, an allergy where she reacted by hating herself even more.

"No, I don't look pretty. You don't have to say that, River. I *know* what I look like."

"Sometimes you don't, though."

She stared at him, blinking in confusion.

"Come again?"

"I mean, I look in the mirror sometimes and I still see that little girl. The baby sister of the family. I thought I wanted to be my daddy's little princess because I wanted to make him happy."

"But that's not you. That was who they wanted you to be."

"Exactly. That stupid little monster in your head is going to lie to you all the time. 'Oh, why even bother wearing this outfit or doing your hair like that? Everyone's going to see right through it anyway' and all that crap. You've got to let yourself have imperfections. Let yourself have bad days and bad angles and bad pictures of yourself saved on your phone. Every cisgender fucker on the planet gets to have it all and still be pretty, so why can't we? And if they don't have to dress in a way that exactly matches who they are every day, we don't have to either. We don't have to be perfect."

Mia stared at him, wanting to burst into tears. She wanted his confidence. His ability to just be himself and not give a shit what anyone thought. His courage to express the masculinity he wasn't born with, but had to fight for and spend thousands of dollars and hundreds of hours in doctor's offices for, the masculinity he had to prove to the world time and time again. Maybe one day her femininity could be the same, but for now, that seemed like a far-off dream. A wistful, aimless hope.

"What I'm trying to say is…you *are* beautiful, Mia. And I know it's hard to see. I get it, I do."

Mia put down her drink, cursing the hot tears clouding her vision as she spoke.

"I want to believe you. I wish I could be a happy drunk. Well, I was up until now."

"I see you. Not just your beautiful eyes and smile, but your heart and sense of humor, all of those things."

Don't do this to me, she wanted to scream at him. *Don't you dare do this to me.*

"Thanks. You're really too nice to me, you know?" she said with a small smile.

River put his arm over her shoulders and pulled her into a sideways hug. She still had enough soberness to be aware that they looked like two over-emotional, sappy friends who had had too much booze and were hugging it out. And Mia felt enough self-consciousness to know they must look pretty silly and pathetic to the rest of the people at Julian's party, but not quite enough that she wanted it to stop.

"Hey, River? Does it get better?" She swallowed the painful lump in her throat. "Just, promise me all of this gets better. Even if it's not true, I need to hear you say it, anyway."

She felt him squeeze her biceps and she sighed against his shoulder.

"It does, Mia. You're still you, with all your imperfections. But someday you get to look back at it all and you think, 'Fuck, I'm real glad I didn't give up. I'm glad I survived it and got to see where I am now.' So...yes. It does get better."

It sounded so beautiful that Mia became certain she would never get there. She didn't deserve any of this, and she wanted to laugh at the idea that she had considered otherwise.

"That sounds really nice," she said, her throat still aching.

"Oh, Mia..." River started rubbing her arm again. "You're going to be okay."

She nodded, wishing with all her heart he was right.

Chapter Sixteen

That night, even after sobering up and drinking enough water before bed, Mia barely slept. There were lots of nightmares. The dirty clothes and the pain of her first broken bone. Apparently, the alcohol had triggered her after all, albeit a few hours late. And then she had a particularly nasty dream in which shadowy figures surrounded her and forced her to cut her hair and scrub her face until her skin broke. She woke up exhausted from crying and wishing the world would end.

Normal people don't feel this way, she thought as she forced herself to pull on clean clothes. *Normal people don't wake up and pray for the apocalypse so all of this can just be over with.*

Per her morning routine, Mia checked her phone for any missed text messages during the night. There was one from Alan, which was a viral video he said was guaranteed to make her smile, and there was a text from River asking how she was doing, complete with a few emojis she could only guess represented poor River's hangover.

Mia wondered if he would be done with her if she told him the truth. If she complained about how much her life sucked until River got tired of it and blocked her number. Maybe she could do the same to Julian and Alan if only so they stopped wasting so much money and kindness on her. She headed out the door to drive to work, knowing that it would be pointless to call in because then she'd have nothing to distract her. The warm weather was starting to remind her of her old home. Her car had gotten a bit of rust over the winter season but of course Mia couldn't care less. Her mind went back to the way her old study group had looked at her when she ran into them, the way their tones were different when she said hello or asked a question. She wanted to cry.

Listen to yourself. You're acting like a spoiled brat who thinks everything is going to go your way and that life isn't worth living if it isn't perfect. Who do you think you are, expecting that as soon as you're out of the closet everyone is going to dote on you and treat you like a princess? What makes you think you deserve that?

She slammed her car door shut, watching her air freshener wobble as a result. Before heading to work she finally texted River back.

Mia: I'm okay

River was starting to worry about Mia. He knew something had been off since she came out and people around campus started finding out about her. But he had noticed a real change when they hung out at Alan and Julian's party yesterday.

She didn't open up as much as she used to a couple of months ago. Didn't give him a corny pun or joke to laugh at. She didn't even attempt a fake smile these days. And worst of all, she had a lot to drink at the party, even though the smell of alcohol was a trigger for her. That alone had red flags all over it.

It killed him inside, knowing the kind of hurt she felt and how hard it was. He just wanted her to be happy.

One afternoon, Mia came over to the coffee shop to hang out during his shift. As he wiped down a couple tables, she pointed up at a poster of the History of the Disillusioned on the wall, surrounded by other ads for local venues and events.

"Nice poster," she said, gesturing with her free hand as the other cupped her drink. It was from a photoshoot the band took at an abandoned cemetery about an hour out of the city. River was crouched on the ground, hands folded in front of him with a deathly glare, showing off his dark locks and big black boots.

"Thank you." River got an idea and was saying it before he could think twice. "We actually got a gig at the craft festival next weekend. Do you want to come watch us play?"

"How much are tickets?" she asked bluntly.

"Fuck that. I can get you in for free," River answered, trying not to let himself get pissed off that she was acting like she didn't care about his music. He was reading into her tone too much. She was depressed, for fuck's sake. Didn't mean she had stopped caring. "It'll be a lot of fun. I can get you coupons for food, too."

Mia looked up at him. If only he could read her mind right now.

"Sure. I'll come. I'd like to watch you play."

"Good! We got a lineup I think you'll enjoy."

"Okay." Finally, Mia perked up a bit. "What should I wear? Is there a dress code?"

"The only dress code is wear whatever the fuck you want." Mia gave him a knowing look, and when he remembered Mia still wasn't able to dress as feminine as she wanted, quickly added, "Well, you know what I mean."

"Okay. Thanks." She gave him a small, tired smile.

Two days later, River was warming up backstage with the band before the show. It was a beautiful early evening at the city's annual craft festival, and they could not have asked for better weather, plus the turnout this year was decent, too. The band had been booked to play for a solid hour at one of the park pavilions, a bit away from the main traffic of the festival, but he still saw lots of people around who were excited to get some live music. Today, he wore a black mesh tank top and black jeans with rips, zippers, and extra belts.

Just a few minutes before they were set to go onstage, he finally saw Mia walk into the pavilion. She was wearing the hoodie he got her as a gift while he was in Italy. She also wore a baseball cap and cargo shorts.

Today would be the first time they'd perform their new song in front of an audience. The song that River had written about Mia. Now that it was really happening, he felt the anxiety kicking in as it always did when he was about to show his latest song to the world. Mia noticed him and waved until he gave her a small wave back.

Shortly enough, the History of the Disillusioned were ready to go. River put just a bit more gel in his hair before they stepped out onto the stage to the opening round of applause. To start off, they did a few of their favorite song covers and then started doing songs they had written together. Every now and then he glanced at Mia. She seemed to enjoy the show, clapping and cheering with everyone else, only sitting down to eat something or take a sip of water.

But the band was saving the best one for last. As the audience clapped at the end of the most recent song, River grabbed the towel he had set on a nearby stool and wiped the sweat from his brow. His hair was drenched, and he had soaked through his mesh shirt. He leaned into the mic and glanced down at Mia.

"This song is about a girl who is invisible to the world but is determined to make herself known whatever it takes. This is our first time playing it for an audience, so…hope you like it."

He saw the light in Mia's eyes as they began the song intro. The song's first verse was about a girl standing on the edge, looking out to the sea, then about her burning a new name for herself with cigarette cherries. He was especially proud of the line 'some angels must crawl from hell to find their wings.'

He never held back any energy when he sang, but this time he really pushed himself to the max. Screaming his heart out into the mic and pushing through his exhaustion as he sang for her. The second part of the verse sang out the girl wanting to feel something real, and waiting for the world to see her fly away. River pushed harder than he had in a long time. Soon he got the crowd singing the one-line chorus with him. He moved back and forth on the stage, pouring out all his rage and terror and regret and grief into his singing.

When the song came to a close, River looked down and saw he was sweating so much he was dripping onto the stage. The whole performance felt like a haze, but he had never felt so alive before, so electrified.

After the show, Mia walked up to him, her cheeks flushed and her hair a little messy. He was pretty sure he had seen her getting into the song along with the crowd, even though it wasn't normal for her to sing songs loudly in public.

"So that song…"

River nodded, biting his lip.

"Yeah. It was a little inspired by you." He looked away, still wiping at his forehead and neck. "Sorry if—"

"No, I thought it was cool." It was then he noticed her eyes were bloodshot, like she had been crying a lot. "I loved it. It was psychedelic and badass at the same time. I'd hug you if you weren't all gross and sweaty."

River smiled and grabbed the water bottle Jimmy offered him. He took a couple gulps, then poured the rest over his head and the back of his neck to cool himself off, completely oblivious to the titillating show he was putting on for Mia.

"Rain check on that hug after I've taken a shower and changed?"

"Yeah, okay." Mia nodded. He felt a bit of guilt. Maybe Cat had had a point earlier and he should have given her a warning or something, anything at all. But he had wanted it to be a nice surprise. Maybe those were healing tears. "Have you recorded that song yet?"

"We hope to as soon as we can afford to rent a studio long enough. Trust me, as soon as it's recorded, you'll be the first to listen to it."

Chapter Seventeen

Two days later, River got a voicemail from Mia that turned his stomach cold.

He paused it, took a few deep breaths, then had to play it again just to be sure he heard it right.

"Hey, River, so…if you can call me back as soon as you get this, if you can. I just got fired from my job. They didn't say it but I know why they did. I just left there without grabbing my lunchbox or jacket or anything. Just call me or text me? Thanks…"

He texted her immediately and asked if she wanted him to come over. Instead, Mia asked if he wouldn't mind picking her up instead.

River grabbed his extra motorcycle helmet and was at her dorm in minutes. He knocked on her door and when she answered she seemed more held together than he had expected.

"What the fuck happened?" he immediately asked.

She made a 'shushing' motion.

"Let's get out of here first. I hate it here. It fucking reeks."

"Right, sure. Jesus, it does stink. Where do you want to go?" He handed over his extra helmet.

Mia shook her head as she put it on. River thought fast.

"Let's go to that restaurant on South Morrison, the Italian place. My treat."

"River, you don't have to." Her voice was hoarse. She had been crying a lot.

This is so unfair, he thought. He had half a mind to storm into her former workplace and give a new eyehole to whoever did this to her, but he had to restrain that part of himself.

"Takeout at my place instead, then?" he suggested.

Right on cue, Mia's stomach growled, and he remembered that she had left her lunchbox behind. When she couldn't argue with him, he drove them to the nearest place that served hot meals and put in their order. Later, at his apartment, Mia curled up on the couch, hugging herself. He sat beside her and put his arm around her shoulders, waiting patiently for her to tell him what happened.

"So last Thursday, one of my coworkers was chatting with me in the break room and he started talking about trans people and cross-dressing and things like that. How he's read on the news that a guy pretended to be a trans woman so he could sneak into the girls' bathroom. And of course, I know he made that up since I asked him where he heard that and he said he didn't remember, but one of his Facebook friends told him, so…you know. It was really weird. Almost like he *knew,* but didn't want to tell me he knew. But I thought maybe it was just a coincidence and ignored it." Mia swallowed hard and rubbed at her eyes again. "And on Saturday, I know for sure someone else overheard me on the phone with Grace, and I know I said something to her that would have outed myself to anyone listening in. Maybe I said 'I'm a big girl, I can handle it' or mentioned something about coming out or buying new clothes. You know…like a fucking idiot! Why did I say that so loudly?" She smacked her forehead.

"Mia..." He grabbed her hand to stop her from hitting herself.

She took a deep breath, clenching her jaw.

"Then this morning, my boss called me in his office, and he said he'd gotten reports that I was disturbing the workplace, being inappropriate with coworkers. And none of it's true! I didn't do anything! But I didn't know how to explain it. Oh, and he mentioned my attendance was an issue too, which is funny because I've only called off twice and I've been late once, and it was never an issue before. So double bullshit. Anyway, he said that he had to put me on suspension because of it. And it's pretty obvious at this point I'm not going to get my job back."

River pulled her into a hug. He was shaking.

"Fuck. That's so wrong."

She sobbed into his shoulder.

"What am I going to do?"

"We'll help you find a new job. A better one. One where you can get good health insurance and you won't be afraid to be you."

"You don't have to cheer me up, River. It's not as easy as 'oh, we'll find you a job and everything will work out.' Don't you get it? It's *not* working out. It's never going to work. I don't know why I thought I could even get a degree here, anyway. Or come out and think everything was going to be sunshine and puppies. And if I have to hear another 'you have to survive the rain before you can see the rainbow' I'm going to..." She looked like she wanted to say something else, but stopped herself at the last minute and instead said, "I'm going to scream my head off. I feel so alone."

River squeezed her hand again, still shaking a bit. He knew what it was like to be this low.

"But you're not alone, Mia. You never have been since you got here, and you'll never have to be alone again."

She let out a sigh that seemed to be one of defeat.

"Okay, River. If you insist," she said quietly.

"I do fucking insist. You remember Bridget, from the student center? She has a list of jobs around here with health insurance that will cover HRT. I can message her right now."

She nodded again, but he could already tell she had stopped listening.

Mia went back to her dorm later that night feeling emptier than she had in a long time, numb from the day's events. River's words filled her mind. All Mia could think was how nice it must be to believe, even just one of them. And she wanted to. She tried to think of what she knew about what River had been through and how much better he was doing now. Surely that had to be a sign of hope for her.

Yet she kept coming back to how a happy story was not meant for her. That not everyone survives. That some get lost and left behind in the trenches, and she could not see herself ending up in any other place.

Damn. I'm really bad off, aren't I?

As she drifted off to sleep, she could not help but think how nice it would be to not worry about waking up. That she could just sleep forever with no worries about anything. In a way, just the realization that she was getting this bad, thinking these thoughts, made her scared of herself and what she might end up doing. But at the same time she found herself unable to care. If anything, it felt like a sign that the world was making more sense and she had more clarity than ever of how pointless this all was. That there was no light at the end of this tunnel. It would just keep going, deeper and deeper into the dark.

When she woke up that morning the feelings had not gone away, and she knew what she had to do.

The thought of it did not even sound that extreme anymore. No longer horrifying or absolute. It was just another decision, like what to get from the vending machine or what shirt to wear. Most of all, no one could know what she intended. The less people knew, the happier everybody would be afterward when they realized they didn't have to worry about her anymore or dread her next needy text message. So she made up her mind. And it felt peaceful. Now that it was almost all over, all the years of pain and emptiness, it was good to know that the end was in sight at last.

To appear normal on this day, Mia went to classes with all her notebooks and even hung out in the library to study and listen to music for a while. Afterward, she went to the coffee shop and ordered her usual. River took her order. His gaze lingered as he stuck a straw in her drink for her.

"You okay?" River asked in a soft whisper.

She nodded.

"Doing a little better." A lie. "Just tired." Also a lie. Maybe he wouldn't press her for more information, though.

"I can come over soon as I get off work. How does that sound?"

Great. He wasn't falling for it. Of course, the one time he saw through her.

"Only if you want, but honestly, no worries. I have things to do, and I'm sure you do, too."

"Fuck that." River looked up at her, handing over her blended iced mint chocolate chip mocha. "Doesn't matter. We always have another day to get stuff done."

She smiled a little, noting the irony. Their fingers brushed as she took it from him.

"Maybe, yeah. I just need to finish one thing." Another customer walked in, and River had to tear himself away from her. Mia took a couple of sips and then walked outside. She threw the rest of the drink in the garbage can as she headed back to campus, while all the streetlamps began to flicker on and the sun went down behind the city's downtown, and everything darkened.

Back in her dorm building, Mia knocked on the next door down.

"Hey. What's up?" Rhett asked, sipping from a mug of some hot beverage.

"I need some liquor. Do you have a little extra?" she asked, rubbing her arms, hoping the dim light in the hallway concealed how raw and red her eyes were.

"I got you, dude. What's your poison of choice? Whiskey, vodka, tequila, rum?"

"Whichever is the strongest, I guess."

Rhett smirked and handed Mia a pint of strawberry-flavored vodka.

"Here. This stuff tastes like candy, but don't let that fool you. Shit's ninety-proof."

"Yeah, perfect. Help yourself to anything you want in my fridge. Whatever you want, it's yours." It was all going to go to waste, anyway. Rhett might as well get something out of all this.

"Wait, really?"

"Yeah. As a thank you."

"Cool. Thanks, Carlos. Have fun!"

"I will. Goodnight." She left and returned to her dorm. Inside, she locked the door behind her.

Mia walked to the little bathroom and grabbed her bag from the store, where she pulled out the bottle of strong OTC medicine she had purchased. Just by reading a little online earlier today, she learned how life-threatening an overdose on this stuff could be, and that danger tripled when combined with liquor. Almost scary how easy that was to find out. Her hands shook as she poured a handful of the pills onto the table, then counted. More than enough to be a lethal amount, plus a little extra, just in case. She found herself laughing at the fact that both the pills and the vodka were pink. How terribly fitting. She grabbed the heaviest item close by, which turned out to be one of her school textbooks. She pounded on the pills until they resembled powder, or as close to powder as she could properly get them. Then she scooped it all into a cup.

She spent a solid ten minutes staring down at the cup. Thinking of how wonderful it would be to sleep forever. Thinking of her corpse having its organs pumped out by the funeral director or whoever before she was laid in a coffin and left to the worms. Or perhaps she would be cremated. Save everyone the trouble of having to look at her at the funeral. Yeah. Actually, that would be much better. She'd like that instead. Everyone was going to get over her quickly. Just like she knew everyone in her hometown either had no idea when she left or hadn't even bothered to call her, text her, or reach out to her when they found out, so these people would do the same.

The study group hated her, so that had taken care of itself. The support group would keep growing and thriving without her. Julian and Alan had literally thousands of other needy queer kids in the city they could dote over and easily replace her with. As for River and Grace, they had enough friends that they wouldn't feel much of a difference without her. Her existence would just be a small blip, a little hiccup, here one moment and gone the next, and it felt comforting to know that none of it had amounted to anything. Eased the pressure off of any notion that you had to make something of your life or whatever.

At the last second, Mia grabbed her phone and texted the first person she thought of. River. He had given her so much. He had poured his heart out to her. What a waste of time.

Mia: can I ask you something?

Five minutes. Then ten. Ten minutes of hellish silence. Maybe he had finally given up on her. She filled the cup with vodka, then stirred the pills in until they dissolved. It was such a pretty shade of pink. The exact sort of color she could have seen herself wearing all the time, pink skirts and stockings and bows and all the things that would be inherently tarnished if she dared put them on. Pretty like she wanted to be. Pretty like she never would be.

Mia grabbed the glass. She gave it one last good look before choking it all down. The liquor burned her throat like purifying fire, but she kept going until it was empty. Then she curled up on the bed and waited for sleep. For a while she felt nothing, and then the familiar drowsiness of alcohol began to kick in. She felt dizzy, and her mouth felt dry. She reached out to hold on to something when her phone went off, and by habit, she picked it up.

River: What is it? Sorry my phones at like 1% and could die any sec lmao

Mia: cremate me

River: What??? What are you talking about??

Mia: I don't know. don't feel good. I want to sleep.

Mia had to hit the "send" button several times before it worked. River would be so much happier when she went away. He didn't need this. He deserved better than her. So did Grace, of course. Alan and Julian too, because surely they could find someone more lively and confident to have in their home without constantly killing the mood.

River: Are you alone right now?

Mia: Yes

River: I'm coming over

Mia: Dobnn bbothrer

Her phone went off with an incoming call from River. Against her better wishes, she answered.

"Mia, what's going on? Are you okay?" He was literally shouting into the phone. She could hear the sound of his motorcycle engine in the background.

"I'm fine. I just took something to help me fall asleep because I'm very tired." Mia closed her eyes as the room began to spin. Talking was more difficult than usual. It was like her lips and her tongue had been stung by a bee or something.

She heard River cursing. Heard him say something about calling 9-1-1. Then, an abrupt cut to silence. His phone must have died.

The sickness in her stomach started. She could feel her body slowing down. Her brain felt foggy.

It was terrifying.

River's phone had died in the middle of calling her. He screamed out in rage, but focused on driving. Served him right for forgetting to charge it yet again. Now that he had no way to call 9-1-1, his best hope was to hurry to Mia's apartment and either drive her to the emergency room himself or use her phone. Pulling over and asking a random passerby for their phone would take too much time. In his head, the last words she said over the phone played over and over. He was going thirty miles over the speed limit by now. It did not feel near enough fast enough.

Something to help me fall asleep. I want to sleep. Cremate me.

Not Mia. Not the kid he looked forward to seeing every day at work, who struggled so much with loving who she was and being herself. She had already been through so much hell just to get where she was now. *Not Mia.*

By sheer luck, he did not get pulled over. He didn't bother to park properly and just ran as fast as he could to Mia's dorm, shaking as he used his student ID to get in. Breathless, on the verge of a panic attack, River banged on her door.

"If you can hear me, open the door!" He paused. No movement inside. Couldn't even hear her crying. He screamed again, then looked up and down the hall, but there was no one.

There was no time for this. River backed up, not even stopping to think of what he was doing. He just knew he was running out of time. A few moments later he rammed his body against the door. The impact broke the lock, and he stumbled in. It only took him a second to see Mia lying on the bed. She was still breathing, but otherwise motionless. River grabbed her phone, still cursing himself that his bad habit finally caught up to him, and dialed 9-1-1.

"H–hello? Yes, hello, she overdosed and she's unconscious." He quickly scanned the room, trying to find the source of what Mia had taken. He soon saw the vodka and medicine. "I think she took a lot of liquor and a lot of pills. She's breathing but doesn't seem awake…okay. Okay." After he gave the address, he grabbed Mia's hand, squeezing it, trying to wake her up. Her eyelids fluttered. "Oh god, Mia, what the fuck did you do?"

"I think I fucked up…" She started to cry.

River did his best to keep talking to both the dispatcher and to Mia, praying to every god and goddess he could think of that she wouldn't die in his arms.

Mia had a lovely dream of someone picking her up. They felt big and strong and safe. Whoever it was carried her out of rushing cold waters, icy waves that crashed around her and filled her mouth with the taste of seaweed. Her face was pressed against a firm chest. Someone kept telling her it was going to be all right. Then she heard the waves on the shore. The sound of birds crying overhead. She heard her rescuer walking through wet sand, and she felt the salty breeze through her hair. And she knew she had someone with her. She wasn't alone anymore. She never had been.

Then she blinked and saw strange lights above her.

She smelled something. Disinfectant. Clean sheets. That icky hospital smell. She heard a machine beeping about every other second. No, two machines. One by her right side, and one several feet away.

Mia looked down. And that's when she saw the IV in her arm and the white paper bracelet. Slowly, as if they had all the time in the world, the pieces formed in her mind.

I'm alive. I'm in the hospital. I survived.

The reality of what she had done sank in, but she couldn't cry. She could only lie there and think of how close she had come, how the abyss had seemed so kind and inviting until she finally dipped down into it, and it almost swallowed her whole.

Chapter Eighteen

When he headed to the waiting area, River messaged the only two people he could trust to know about this. As they hurried over, he wandered to the nearest vending machine and ended up staring at all the options for a solid five minutes before walking back to the waiting room empty-handed.

Alan, Julian, and Grace arrived in minutes, all visibly shaken by River's simple but ominous message about what had happened. As for Grace, she just sat next to River and hugged him. Let him sob against her shoulder as the two older men ran up to him, eyes wide with fright. Grace began rubbing River's back to help him calm down.

"River. Is she…?"

River stopped crying enough to choke out an answer.

"She's okay. They pumped her stomach. They're keeping her until morning to monitor her, but she's okay. They're letting me stay so I can take her home."

Alan covered his mouth, leaning against his husband.

"If she hadn't messaged you…"

River looked away. He had not attempted it since age twenty. That had been his third time. One of those three left him in the psych ward for several days. He had been doing much better in recent years, but the shadows never really left you. They always kept their mark, one way or another. Seeing Mia like that had brought back a lot of things he had promised himself he would not dwell on.

"Can I get you anything?" Alan asked, sounding far away. "Phone charger? Water? Something to eat?"

River found himself laughing a bit. Food was the last thing on his mind right now.

"No, but thanks." He glanced back down the hall to where Mia's room was. "I'm calling into work tomorrow. Fuck this."

Alan nodded, as Julian squeezed his husband's shoulder. River realized that Julian hadn't said a word since they got there, very unlike him. In fact, he was eerily quiet, almost catatonic, just staring down the hall where Mia's room was.

"I don't blame you, and your manager shouldn't either. Are you holding up?" Grace asked.

"Honestly, no," River said, returning her gaze. "But I'll be okay. I just…"

"I know." She squeezed his hand, and he didn't stop her. "I'm guessing visiting hours are over so we can't go in and see her."

"Yeah, but I'm sure she'd like to see you all tomorrow morning."

"You need fuel if you're going to be here for her, you know." Alan rubbed his shoulder again. "We'll go get you something. We'll be back soon. Come on, Julian."

"Thanks," River said quietly. More hugs were exchanged before they left, and returned about a half hour later with burgers, fries, and a milkshake. He mumbled out a thanks and went back to Mia's room, where he found her still awake but pretty out of it. "How are you feeling?"

"Like crap."

"Do you want to watch TV? They've got HBO here. Very fancy."

"Sure...okay." Within a few minutes they found some random movie Mia had seen a while ago but enjoyed. She barely paid attention to it and kept glancing at River while he ate as quietly as he could. "River...I'm so sorry."

"No," he cut her off. "You have nothing to apologize for. We're going to get you help. It's going to be okay."

"But how am I going to pay the hospital bill?"

"Don't worry about that right now. We can figure that out later." He held her hand, careful not to disturb the pulse oximeter on her finger. "I've got you, okay?"

"I...I just felt so lost. I just wanted to sleep. I'm so tired. It wasn't stopping. I just..." She looked like she wanted to cry again, but was too tired to shed a single tear. "My memory's all fucked up."

"See if you can try to get some rest. It'll help."

Mia looked up at him, looking so helpless and small.

"Okay, but hold my hand until I'm asleep, okay?"

"Of course." He took her hand in his. She was out in minutes. As he curled up in the hospital chair, watching as Mia dozed, River's mind drifted to places he had not been to in a while. He looked down at the long pale scar beginning from his left wrist and ending right at the base of the forearm, which was now mostly covered up with tattoos, but not quite.

Mia would later have trouble remembering the details of her hospital stay.

She knew nurses came in and out of her room. Bringing her water, adjusting her pillows, checking her vitals. She remembered a therapist coming in and asking her questions, and she tried to answer as best she could. Questions were asked about health insurance, which she did not have. Questions were asked about her family history, and Mia vaguely mentioned things about her childhood she thought were what they needed to know. Other than that, the rest of her stay was a blur. All she knew was that she wanted to leave. Later she would begin to remember that River was there too and helped answer many questions, as well as fill out some paperwork for her. She also remembered he never left her hospital room and held her hand a lot of the time.

The following day, she was released. They directed her to the pharmacy to pick up some medication a psychiatrist prescribed to her. When she explained she didn't have a job, they gave her numbers to call for financial assistance regarding that lovely itty-bitty medical bill that would be on its way soon. She left the hospital with a folder full of paperwork. Later Mia would joke to herself she had no idea that surviving a suicide attempt meant signing your name so many times.

Alan and Julian let her crash at their place for the rest of that day and the next until she felt ready to go back to her dorm. They practically smothered her with care, more than the usual amount. Julian made her favorite foods, Alan helped her study for her last exams, and save for trips to the bathroom, they never left her alone for a second. At first, she had to admit, it was a little nice to be treated like one of those forlorn sickly Victorian women whose doctor prescribed a summer by the seaside to fall in love with the ghost of a drowned sailor, but it got old fast. In truth, Mia just wanted things to feel normal again. Being handled like she was a fragile doll irritated her. Alan even hid the contents of their medicine cabinet for her, just in case; that was plain embarrassing.

By some sheer miracle, Mia survived her last finals exam the following week. Even so, it was a hollow, empty few days following her hospital release in which nothing felt fully formed, like she was always half-awake.

To Mia's knowledge, word about her brief stay at the hospital stayed between River, Alan, Julian, and Grace. Nobody else mentioned it to her. And all four of them made sure to stop by and say hello if they could, or at least send her a text message or a quick phone call. And she never knew what to reply with. Never knew how to talk to them when she knew why they were doing this.

For the next few days, she went through the motions, feeling numb all over. A state of blank nothingness in which she still had not fully comprehended it.

Graduation day came and went. Mia couldn't believe it. She had finished her first year of college.

Her grades could have been better, especially towards the end of the semester. Nevertheless, she had done it.

As she joined the other students in congratulating all the graduates, she thought back to the girl she had been exactly one year ago. Alone in her beat-up car with nothing but a few days' worth of clothes and the money she had scrimped and saved for years, leaving her hometown behind and taking a lonely road trip up north to go to college. All those people who told her she'd never make it and she didn't have it in her to fulfill her dream.

But she had done it anyway, in spite of all the odds against her.

Mia waited until after the graduation ceremony and things had died down a bit around campus. Then she went to find River. She had texted him asking where he was, assuming he joined most of his other graduating friends to a bar or restaurant to celebrate. But instead, he said he was relaxing at the coffee shop and she should come on over.

As she walked into the coffee shop and ordered her usual, Mia noticed him sitting on the corner sofa towards the back. He was sipping some tea. Nothing about his demeanor gave the impression of someone who had just finished getting his degree.

This was the first time she had seen him in person since that night. They had texted a bit since then, but only small conversations limited to asking how the other was doing and him making sure she was doing okay. To be fair, this was the worst time of year to expect college students to text back paragraphs, or text back promptly at all, so she did not hold it against him. But she did have some pretty big news to tell him she had been holding in.

Mia looked at him. No words came to mind. What do you say to the person who took you to the emergency room, to the person who literally saved your life? Where was the fucking script for that kind of conversation? So, naturally, Mia did what she did best and cracked a joke to break the ice.

"Hey, mister graduate." She grinned at him.

River returned her gaze, hesitating. Then she was relieved when he finally smiled back.

"Hey, Mia. Are you doing alright?"

"Well, the hospital is helping with finances. The meds seem to be helping a little bit but they said it'll take time to get results, so who knows, it must be a placebo effect or something. I told them about my, you know, gender stuff. And they referred me to a therapist in the area. So…yeah. I'm on a waitlist to see her now." It felt good to tell him. A waitlist, of course, could mean weeks or months before even seeing someone, much less starting hormones. But it was a start. And she would take it.

River jolted up like he had been electrocuted by the sofa, his smile growing.

"Holy shit! That's great, Mia. And hey, look at you. One year of college done."

"Yeah! Look at me, a real sophomore. Going to miss everybody, though." She hesitated, looking at him. "What are you doing for the summer?"

"Work. Band stuff. We might get a studio rented out soon so we can start recording the album. So if that works out, I'm going to be very busy."

"Me too. Oh, I just found out about this one on my way here over a phone call, so you're the first to know. But I got a job! It's temporary, working at a science camp in Washington state. Up in the mountains. Only a couple months, but it's supposed to be good money and it'll look nice on my resume anyway."

"So things are looking up. That's good. Fuck, I'm happy for you. I mean that." He tousled his hair. And she realized the conversation was about to enter rough territory. "I'll miss you a lot, you know."

"Hey, you're the one who spent months in Italy." She playfully punched his arm and he smiled at her.

"I'm serious, though. We need to stay in touch until you get back. I plan to keep living here so I'll be close by."

"Good. You'd better." To her horror, Mia ran out of words to say after that. She had almost lost her life, and now all her friends would leave for the summer. The future was supposed to be full of hope and promise. And it was, but not without its own terrors and uncertainties.

Within a span of forty-eight hours, all of Mia's friends from the support group had left campus. One by one, they headed out either to go back to their families or summer vacation. There were lots of hugs and tears all around. Grace promised to see her soon.

Alan and Julian were the last she said goodbye to, as they were the ones giving her a ride to her job in Washington. Typical them, all she had to do was mention she needed to get her car worked on so it would survive the journey and Julian was already reaching for his keys. Mia almost wished she hadn't taken the job. The pay was decent, even if it was only temporary. But she had no idea what would happen after that. If she would get a job with good health insurance that would cover a therapist, hormones, and medications.

But she reminded herself that no matter how bad it got, she would never be alone.

Chapter Nineteen

In June, the History of the Disillusioned rented a studio in Redding, California. They drove eight hours south and spent almost the whole month recording the new album, working long hours to make the most of their time and only stopping to eat or get a few hours' rest. As for housing, they rotated between camping illegally in public parks and crashing in cheap hotel rooms. To save on phone data, they would steal wireless internet wherever they could, whether it was a library or a cafe. It was a wild few weeks filled with long hours of playing, recording, writing, and re-writing until River was so tired he almost got sick, followed by even longer hours of looking for a place to sleep. But at the end of the month, they had done it. They had their first album recorded and ready to release in September.

River texted Mia and his other friends when he could. Redding's local library was not far from the recording studio, so they usually stopped there after a session to use the internet for a bit. He found a spot where he could charge his phone (yes, it was dead again) and sent her a message.

River: Hey, Mia! So sorry I'm almost never online. It's been crazy these days. We're getting the album finished and spending long days in the studio and we hop around places to stay so never sure when

we'll get internet again without eating up all our data. Anyway!
Hope you're doing okay. Hope we can get together and talk again
real soon. When you get this, message me back and let me know how
your summer is going!!

He was left on 'read' for almost an entire week. Which he didn't normally mind. River remembered that she was busy working too, and he didn't need an instant response. But he found himself constantly checking their messages for a response, even if he ended up burning precious data as a result. Yes, he was worried about her, but would it kill her to just tell him how her summer was going?

The longer the days went on and he was left not knowing anything about Mia, the more he thought about it. To the point that as they were in the studio, working on getting the songs right, his mind would drift back to her and he would try to steal a small glance at his phone on every bathroom and snack break, just in case.

By the fifth day of this, Emily finally had enough and snatched River's phone as soon as they were ready to start recording again.

"Whoever you're waiting to text you back, it can wait," she said sternly. "Do I have to remind you how much money we're spending just to be here? You can have your phone back when we're done for the day."

"Fine, fine…" He let her take it. And it helped a little. But he still wished Mia would text him back soon. The next school year couldn't get here fast enough.

Several days later, she finally messaged back. They were eating at a 24/7 diner, and it was after midnight. The band was scarfing down burgers and sandwiches when he finally refreshed and saw the notification. River hurried to the bathroom to read it alone.

Mia: Hi River! So I got kinda big news. I am meeting with a doctor who is going to get me started on hormones soon!! There's tests and stuff to do first, but it's going to happen!!!! I'm so excited but really scared too, like this is really happening. Oh and in a couple weeks I'm going to start seeing a therapist for my depression and anxiety and self-harm so we'll see how that goes too. Well, talk to you soon. Can't wait to hear the album! You'd better make sure my copy is autographed;)

River read it over and over and found himself unable to stop smiling. He couldn't believe it. His chest felt like it was going to explode. After debating how to respond, he ended up typing out some sort of celebration of the news with more exclamation points than actual words, then hurried back to the table. He didn't realize everyone was looking at him until he happened to glance up.

"What...?"

"What the fuck has got you all excited?" Victoria asked, slurping on her milkshake.

River started to tell them about Mia's big news. But before he could finish, Cat cut him off.

"Hang on, hang on. Is this the same girl you wrote the song about? Mia was her name, right?" they asked.

"Yeah, how did you know?" River asked.

The four of them looked at each other. Oliver just shook his head, muttered something in his first language, and resumed eating, while the other three exchanged a series of peculiar expressions. River started to frown, tensing up.

"What?! Seriously, what is it?"

"River, River…" Oliver kept shaking his head.

"You need to ask this poor girl out already. You've known her, what, almost a year?" asked Victoria.

"'Ask her out'?" River echoed. He scrunched up his nose, trying to figure out what part of the conversation he was missing, but at the same time he felt heat rushing to his face. "What do you mean? Why would I ask her out?"

"Are you playing dumb or actually being dumb?" Emily waved her pickle at River like a little wand.

"I'm seriously asking what you're talking about."

"River." Victoria braced her palms flat on the table. "You've liked this girl for months. And she's single. You should ask her out when we get back!"

Fuck. Here we go again. Seriously?!

"I don't…" River blinked, then stared down at his half-finished club sandwich. He didn't *like* Mia in that way. At least, he didn't think he did. That's not what a crush felt like. Crushes meant you didn't know how to talk around the person and your palms got sweaty and your knees knocked together. With Mia, they could go back and forth in conversation for hours and he always felt so relaxed. With Mia, he never felt awkward or scared. Clearly, then, it wasn't a crush. Why didn't they understand that? "I just like her as a friend, that's all."

"You sure? I don't know. You looked like you grew a pair of wings just now when she just texted you back." Victoria rolled her eyes.

"I'm sure. And that's the end of it, okay?!"

"I just had to say something." Victoria held up her hands, feigning innocence.

But this time, the teasing lingered long after they finished eating. They did have a small point, to be fair. He did love Mia—as a *friend*. He thought she was cool and fun to talk to and yes, it had made his entire day and gave him a spike of adrenaline when she texted him back—as a *friend*. But it wasn't a crush. Obviously.

It wasn't until he was lying awake later that night, camped out beside their van, that it finally hit him.

He had spent most of that night thinking about Mia as he fell asleep. But not just Mia as herself. He had re-read her text message over and over until it was memorized, and then he tried to picture her what she might look like when he saw her again in August. Would she dress more feminine, or would she still be wearing her torn jeans, graphic tees, engine grease under her nails and a Band-Aid or two on her chin? Would she have grown out her hair? Would she start wearing makeup, and if so, what style? But most importantly, would she be wearing what *she* wanted to wear, not what she had to because of expectations or complicity?

Then he remembered what Victoria had said at the diner. He sat up straight, like cold water had been thrown over him. He looked down at his phone, but he didn't need to read her message yet again. River glanced to his side, where Emily was up late on her tablet drawing.

"Hey," he said to get her attention. She glanced at him.

"You okay?"

"I…think so?" He frowned, holding his head. "I think…you were right."

"I mean, that's a given, but what was I right about specifically?"

"What you guys said before, at the diner. About me and…"

Emily set down her tablet pen and smiled.

"Yeah? You think so?"

"I think…oh, my, *god*." River fell back down and stared up at the stars. It was like someone had punched him upside the head. As he said the words, they hit him until they were each and all fully realized. "I have been crushing on her all these months and I think I *just* now figured that out."

"Goddammit…"

"What?!"

"I owe Oliver ten bucks. I bet you wouldn't figure it out until the end of summer."

River threw a crumpled-up gum wrapper at her forehead. Emily just scrunched up her nose in a satisfactory grin as River tried not to smile.

"You all are the fucking worst."

"I know, right?" She gave his biceps a loving squeeze. "But hey, serious question. If you're not ready to act on it or ask her out, that's okay. That's completely your call."

"I know. I thought I wouldn't be ready for a long time, but…" He looked away. It had been a while since he had thought of his ex. And not in a way where a smell or a song triggered a bad memory of her, but when his mind proactively brought it up, pondering everything that happened and how he was going to be better. It almost startled him how, for the first time, he didn't feel as scared, angry, or helpless as he used to just at the recollection of her. He didn't feel as tied down to that trained impulse to go to her, to do whatever she wanted him to do. It was as if something had been chaining him down to her, however much he hated it, and now that chain was broken. Or rather, maybe it had been broken for a long time, and it had taken all these months of healing, work, and time to realize that. He looked at Emily again, who seemed to almost see exactly what was on his mind. "I think I want to try."

"That's good, River." She smiled softly, but he didn't return it.

"But I don't know if Mia likes me or not. What do you think? I know you don't know her all that well, but…"

"I think you should just talk to her when we get back and see what happens." With that, she picked up her tablet again and resumed drawing.

The band spent July and the beginning of August doing several gigs around northern California, all to promote the album's release. When they weren't performing or on the road, there was always last-minute editing and production work to finish on the album, plus keeping up a presence on social media.

He still texted Mia on and off. There were long periods where he wouldn't get a message, and as always, he was left to assume she was busy or had no internet connection. She would send him a paragraph, and he would send one back when he got the chance. Then there would be radio silence for a week or so. And on and on it went. He did not want to tell her anything about his feelings for her until he could in person—and not just because he found it impossible to try to type out anyway.

If it were anyone but Mia, he would have been okay with it. But this…this was just torture.

The good part was that hundreds of hours of work paid off, and in the end, they raised enough funds from merchandise and sponsors. They also nearly doubled their number of followers on their social media platforms, all in anticipation for the album's big release in a month. The bad part was that by the time they were back in Oregon, everyone was exhausted and on their last legs. River headed back to his apartment and his part-time job, drained and scared and anxious, trying to readjust to his life back here after months away. Between shifts he would go practice some more with the band, where they would almost always ask how Mia was doing. In the final warmth of August, River felt like he was going to burst. Mia would be back on campus soon, but the days felt endless. All his spare time was wrapped up with the band, so at least he had busyness to occupy his mind.

Even so, he had no idea what he would say when he saw her again. What she would say if he told her he liked her. Was he even her type? Would she want to stay just friends? Or what if she had found someone over the summer, and he had missed his chance?

Quit thinking so much about her, River told himself. *You're going to see her soon and get all your answers, anyway.*

At last, the next school year began. Students arrived on campus in flocks on a beautiful late summer day. As much as it was relieving to have finally graduated last spring, River had to admit he did miss the thrill of move-in day. Some of River's friends who were still in college asked for his help moving in, and he couldn't say no. The whole day he looked around, hoping he might spot Mia in all the chaos. She had said she would be here to meet up with friends, even though she was now living in an apartment off-campus. But no such luck. She wasn't anywhere.

Don't worry about it, he told himself. *She's here. Just busy. Will be plenty of time to play catch up later.*

To celebrate the start of the school year, the LGBT+ student center decided to host a get-together. They booked one of the study rooms on campus and ordered a bunch of food for everybody, which ended up being about a couple dozen pizzas and a lot of soda. River was the only student from the group who had graduated, and two more were graduating, but this year had also introduced several new faces to the group. Even though they didn't force him to, River volunteered to stay on as an office assistant for the student center and to keep leading the support group as an alumnus.

On the day of the party, he arrived at the study hall where a few of the others were getting things ready. Between setting tables and chatting with old friends, he broke and texted Mia from his phone.

River: Will you be at the party tonight?

This time, she responded within just a few minutes. The way his heart skipped a beat at that told River all he needed to know about how he felt about her. Summer was finally over, but it had felt like years since he saw her. He hated it when others were right.

Mia: Hell yes! You??

River: yup, already here getting things ready!

Students began to file in. All the decorations, plates, and napkins were in various pride flag colors, and everyone got a custom-made pin where they could write their names and pronouns. The speakers blasted a playlist of all the usuals, a shuffle between queer artists and bands and a lot of the community's proclaimed anthems from over the decades. There were even several artists River hadn't heard of, to which one of the new kids would tell him how popular it was and had trended for weeks, which just ended up making River feel old and having to come to terms with how he was quickly outgrowing the role of 'the cool trans kid' and morphing into the 'trans elder.'

About a half hour in, Mia texted him that she was here. By then, he had volunteered to help work at the soda table and he waited impatiently to see her. He certainly expected some degree of change upon seeing her again. Even just three months on estrogen delivered some noticeable transformation, especially when you hadn't seen the person since before they started. He also assumed she might be growing her hair out, but he couldn't be sure of that.

But when she finally walked in a few minutes later, River realized nothing could have prepared him for his moment.

"River! Oh my god, hi!" She smiled brightly at him as she approached him.

And the only actual thought that crossed his mind, as his mouth ran completely dry, was,

Holy…fucking…shit.

Chapter Twenty

Mia had grown out her hair, and it now reached past her ears and bordered her face. She wore one of her favorite shirts, an old white graphic tee with the caption 'pit crew' with some racing cars on it. But the other clothes were new. She now had skinny blue jeans and yellow converse shoes. The hair on her arms and legs was all shaved off, a stark contrast to the dark hair she used to have. It was also the first time he saw her with makeup, eyeliner and mascara that made her eyes pop, the lines a bit smudged in the corners to blend. She also wore a salmon-pink lipstick to make her lips appear fuller and softer. River understood three months was not a lot of time for physical changes to take place when it came to hormone therapy. But the changes stood out to him all the same, especially since he had seen similar changes reflected in his friends Victoria, Cat, and Emily. Her face looked softer. Her cheeks were fuller and rounder. Her body was starting to change shape. Her smile was brighter, too.

This was the girl who had been in front of him all these months, and it had taken months apart for him to finally see it. He felt a warmth in his stomach and his head was swimming. Staring at the little curls in her dark hair, the scars and calluses on her hands, the dorky smile and cute teeth and soft lips...*oh god River say something you idiot!*

"Hey, stranger! You're staring," she said, bringing him out of his daze.

He swallowed. So much for not being awkward around Mia. Go figure. The moment he realized how he felt about her, now suddenly he didn't know what to say. He hated it so much.

"Sorry! It's just...it's been a while! And you've been on hormones. I can see it!" River managed to spill out, speaking even louder than usual on account of the music, which meant he was practically shouting.

"Oh, come on. It's only been three months." Mia rolled her eyes at him.

"No, I'm serious! You look..." he couldn't finish that sentence. He didn't want to.

She smiled. A big, goofy, genuine smile forming creases at the corners of her eyes that made her look so adorable he wanted to scream. How many times had he seen that smile all fall, winter, and spring and not realized what it was doing to him? God, he was an idiot.

"You know, I missed you a lot." Mia twisted a lock of hair around her index finger.

"I missed you too. And you look amazing."

"Thank you!" She smiled big at that. "Grace taught me a lot about makeup and hair stuff. But believe me, I don't dress like this all the time. Only in places like this where I feel safe. Definitely not ready to look like this in public yet." She was smiling, but he could still see the pain and fear in her eyes. Then, someone turned up the music when a popular queer

anthem that had stood the test of time came on the playlist. Mia
and River looked at each other and smiled.

"Want to catch up after the party, when it's quieter?" he
hollered over the music.

"Okay!" She smiled and waved at him before joining the
others again. "I got a lot of people to catch up with. I'm going
to come back later, okay?"

He didn't know what else to say, so he just nodded, feeling
like a fool. Inside he wanted to scream, *No please, let's hang out
the whole night and just talk. That's all I want.* But he couldn't
be greedy just because they had spent the whole summer apart.
She had other friends besides him who deserved time with her,
too.

Before Mia could get another word in, Grace ran up to her
and practically pounced on her. River backed up so the two
friends could have their moment and he watched them take off,
staying at his spot at the table. Up until now, he hadn't minded
volunteer work at these events and staying out of the action if it
meant the kids could have fun, but now he was beating himself
up for doing it the same night Mia came back. He stood there
for most of the night, only leaving to go get more ice from
the kitchen or bring out more pizza, but otherwise he didn't
engage with the party. After all, it was the younger kids' turn
to be in the spotlight.

Later, as the party was wrapping up, Mia caught River
between the last of the freshmen shuffling out.

"It's going to be late hanging out if you're okay with that,"
he told her. "I need to stay here and help clean up."

"Then I'll stay too. We can catch up right now."

"Sounds good to me." They each grabbed a trash bag and started gathering up all the paper plates, cups, and decorations that couldn't be reused. Every few seconds they would both reach for the same item and their hands would brush, making them both laugh a bit. But in a few minutes, they developed a system where they would start at opposite ends of a table and meet in the middle. River decided to start up the conversation with something simple. "So, new school year. Are you excited?"

"You have no idea. I have a really good feeling about this year. I got an apartment within walking distance of campus. It's kind of small but pretty cozy and Grace is going to be my roommate, so that's going to really help with rent. Oh, and we even have a dishwasher! I've never had a dishwasher before, you know? It's going to be so weird not washing dishes by hand for the first time. I can't wait!"

"That's great," he said, smiling, not caring that she had already told him all of that over text weeks ago. "I'm glad to be back. I missed it here."

"So did I." Mia bit her lip. "So…"

"Yes. Tell me all about how estrogen is going."

At that, Mia paused from her cleaning and blew a raspberry.

"Oh, my god. It's amazing and horrible and scary all at the same time. I cry at everything. Literally everything! See a cute puppy video or a sad post about the latest fictional bad guy I'm in love with, bam, crying. One person says something that could be taken as mean, crying. Forget what I wanted to order when it's my turn in line, whoops, crying again! Was it like that for you?"

"My first few months I just remember being hungry and horny all the time."

"Well, it's nice to know I'll be a crybaby the rest of my life," she said, winking at him.

It took him a moment to understand the double meaning of her sentence. He stared, then laughed nervously.

"I'm not *always* hungry and horny, you dick."

"Please, I've seen who you follow on Instagram. It's all basically porn."

"So you stalk me?" Now it was his turn to tease.

Mia giggled and looked away.

"No…I was bored, okay? I got curious."

"Okay, well, tell me more about how hormones are going."

"Well, like I said, horrible. I'm…okay, this is embarrassing, but I'm horny all the time too. Only I can't…you know…" She grabbed an armful of empty pizza boxes and shoved them in her garbage bag.

"Can't get it up?" he finished for her, blushing a bit. When Emily started hormone therapy two years ago, he had learned a lot about the various frustrations and complications that could accompany it.

"Yeah." She blushed too. "It's frustrating. And I know it's not a big deal, but it's hard." Before he could make a pun, she looked at him and playfully snapped, "Don't you do it. And even when I…when I *can*, it's painful." Mia winced, still appearing embarrassed at the graphic turn the conversation had taken. "Sorry if I went way overboard with the T-M-I."

"You've heard some of the lyrics I write for my band, right? I have no concept of T-M-I," he said. "And by the way, how are you doing with the other stuff? How's the old brain holding up?" He didn't know any other way to ask without being blunt, which he had been criticized for on many occasions by friends, family, and strangers. On the other hand, is there any socially acceptable way to ask someone, *Have you wanted to kill yourself lately?*

But Mia seemed to understand what he was trying to say. At least for the most part. She paused what she was doing and wiped her hands on her jeans. When she spoke again, her tone was softer, more laid back.

"You know how it is. I still have my bad days. Days when everything feels heavy and I have trouble functioning. Days when I think about doing things to myself I shouldn't. But…I think I'm getting better. I haven't cut since I was in the hospital, so that's good too. Once I finally found a therapist, I really noticed some changes. It's helped me understand why I do certain things, or why my brain tells me certain things. I've been working on how to deal with those and I'm not always that great at it, but I can already feel it's changing me. For the better, I mean. And once I started on hormones, that helped clean out a lot of the bad stuff in my head, I think. Like the storm is still raging, but the boat is stronger and the mast is fixed."

"I know what you mean. It feels like you're still you, fighting all your battles, but now you've got actual weapons to fight back with?" he asked. He paused from cleaning up and looked at her.

"Yes, exactly! That's exactly what it feels like. Except my weapons are two aching tits," she laughed as she stacked empty paper cups into a tower. "Seriously, they always hurt so much I could scream sometimes."

"But it's all worth it, isn't it?"

"I wouldn't get off this rollercoaster no matter what. It's just…changing like this a lot is kind of scary because it's not a fantasy anymore. It's not the anime magical girl transformation sequence you wish it could be in your head. There's blood tests and follow-ups and symptoms and pain and insurance claims. It's real." She took a deep breath. "Very, very real."

"Fucking right."

By then, they had done their part of cleaning up and took the garbage bags out back to the dumpster. When they were finished River gave her a quick hug. In the back of his mind, he wondered if now would be a good time to tell her how he felt. But before he could seriously consider it, he thought about how long of a day it had been for both of them. Her especially. Maybe not the best idea after all.

"I got it from here. You should go home and get some sleep. It's late," he finally told her.

"Okay. This was really nice, by the way." She slipped out of his arms, and he vaguely heard her mention texting him and seeing each other again soon before she had vanished.

Despite his exhaustion, it took him forever to fall asleep, his mind filled with images of her and the sound of her laughter.

Chapter Twenty-One

It was two weeks into the school year, and River had only been able to say hello to Mia when she came by the coffee shop.

Each time she stopped by was a nice reminder of how far she had come in only a few short months. The way her smiles no longer seemed forced, how she had more energy and even a skip in her step on her best days. Almost every day she ordered either a blended iced coffee or a hot tea, depending on her mood. Unfortunately, River wasn't always there to take her order, which was becoming a disappointment. He started to feel like his day was incomplete if he hadn't seen Mia at work. Even if it was just a quick glance while he was cleaning in the back, it was better than nothing. But even if it was slow when she came in, there was only so much conversation that could happen then.

And that meant he still hadn't gotten a chance to talk to her outside of light chat. Which made him feel like he was losing his mind.

On his next day off, he stayed in the apartment all morning. Soon he found himself staring down at the unsent text message on his phone for a good several minutes, debating whether to send it or not. It was one thing to mention getting lunch sometime, another to actually invite her out. But this wasn't a date. It wasn't a date at all. Right? Right.

River: Hey Mia. I have nothing to do this Saturday and I need to get a new jacket before it gets cold. Was wondering if you'd like to go to the mall with me? I hate going to the mall alone lol

She wouldn't read too much into it, right? Just two friends killing time on a lazy weekend afternoon. That's all it was. And if she said no, that would be fine. It wasn't like he would be lonely. He finally hit send, then put away his phone and decided to go for a motorcycle ride. He needed to clear his head.

Mia woke up that morning to the text from River. She smiled a little and texted back a big yes with lots of hearts. She couldn't pass up a chance to get together with him again.

It had been a long and crazy summer, probably one of the most memorable of Mia's life. Working at the science camp had really tested her abilities to work with people and be more open. She didn't come out to anyone there save for two coworkers, and only after she learned they were both trans too. Right after that, Mia met her new therapist for the first time and started on a low dosage of estrogen.

The rest of her summer was spent working a couple of part-time jobs. One was for doing deliveries and the other was painting houses. The hours had been long and grueling, but she pushed through and ended up making a decent chunk of change. A good amount of it went to college tuition, medical expenses, and an apartment. Mia set aside the rest to gradually add more to her wardrobe as well as her small makeup collection she had so far.

Slowly, as the weeks had gone by and she started to feel the effects of estrogen, Mia found herself being able to come out to more people. She changed her name and pronouns in her bios on social media in early August. Her therapist also talked with her a lot about the trauma from her childhood, which forced Mia to realize a lot of things about herself. Mainly that she had never let those wounds heal and she had a lot to work on.

She still had her bad days. Days when she would be misgendered or worse, given that 'look' when she used female pronouns for herself. That infamous look that said it all: "Oh, I see; you're one of *those* people." There were days Mia was tempted to cut again, days when she thought about going somewhere there would be alcohol just to trigger herself on purpose. But knowing that she had finally gotten on hormones and that she had professional help seemed to calm the worst of it. It gave her hope that she was making progress, and that it was slowly getting better. That not only did she deserve better things, but those better things were within reach.

Later that morning, she got dressed and picked River up to go to the shopping mall. As she always did when she was in public, Mia wore a simple shirt and jeans and no makeup. While she drove, she showed off the work she had done on her car over the summer.

"Once I get a few more things done, I'm hoping I can sell her at a decent price. Then I'll be able to buy a really nice car."

"I still need to take you for a ride on my bike one of these days, you know."

"Fuck that. I'm never getting on that thing," she laughed.

"Even if it cheered me up?" River teased.

Mia just rolled her eyes as she pulled into the mall's parking lot.

"Absolutely not. I'm way too terrified to do that."

"Well, when you change your mind, you'd better let me know." He walked with her inside the mall. As they started heading towards the first store he wanted to shop at, Mia began to fill him in on the events of her summer. Her therapy, her jobs, her hormones. River was happy to listen for now and Mia could tell he was soaking in every word, but she did notice he was a bit quieter than usual. A normal conversation with River had him accidentally interrupting with a crass joke, or saying something that at first seemed random but, after several minutes' explanation, actually was connected to the topic at hand. Today, he just listened and nodded along. But Mia told herself it wasn't a big deal. He might just be having an off day, and that was allowed. Nevertheless, she elbowed him as they headed into the store, trying to get a rise out of him.

"Well, that's about all I've been up to. Now it's your turn," she said.

"Who, me? Oh, fuck. This summer was a fever dream, dude." He started by sharing what he had been up to with the band, which progressed into telling her about some of the adventures they had over the summer. From strange characters he befriended in parks and truck stops, to all the drama during the band's long recording days, to the antique stories they visited that definitely had a few haunted items on sale. As he talked, he looked through the leather jackets in the store. It didn't take him long to find one he liked and less than forty minutes into their errand, he had gotten what he needed. Mia followed him out of the store as he carried his new jacket.

"That went quicker than I thought. Sorry."

"We can hang out a while longer, if you want. I'm in no hurry." Mia shrugged.

"Is there anything you need while we're here?" he asked.

"Oh, I don't know. I've been meaning to buy some more cute outfits and makeup. But I'm still nervous to dress like that around strangers, so what's the point?" Mia tucked her hair behind her ear and looked away from him.

"That's bullshit." River turned towards her. "Come on. Let's find you something nice."

"Really? You sure?"

"I don't think it would be a waste at all. What did you have in mind?"

"Well…" She blushed and looked down. "I don't have any dresses yet. J. Crew and Forever 21 have some that I think are cute, but they might not even be here."

"Want to go try? We'll be extra careful, promise. I'm an expert at this stuff."

Mia smiled and finally nodded.

"You really want to see me in a dress, huh?" she muttered in teasing. She expected River to make up some corny retort, but instead he bit his lip and looked away, shrugging.

She wasn't wrong. The one Mia had mentioned was a pastel floral-patterned summer dress with shoulder straps and a light flowing skirt. It encapsulated everything she wanted to express these days, at least, the side of her that still wasn't a dirty, grungy grease monkey at heart. Inside the store, she found the stress in less than a minute. She stared at it, nervous about taking it off the clothes rack when people could be watching. River took it for her instead and discreetly handed it to her in the dressing room.

"Is it okay if I text you a picture from inside instead of coming out?"

"Of course." He paced around outside patiently as he waited for her. A few minutes later he received several messages from her on his phone. She had taken several selfies of her posing for the mirror in the dress, holding up the 'peace' sign and twirling one of her heels.

River: You NEED that dress. You look like an angel

Mia's heart fluttered. A split second later, she saw red, and she wanted to scream at him.

For god's sake, River. You can't just text things like that to a girl if you don't have feelings for her! Maybe Grace had been right about him.

But she swallowed it down, as she was used to doing, and sent back a bunch of sparkling heart emojis. He smiled at her when she walked out.

"Seriously. Sometimes you're too much." She slugged him on the arm.

"I get that a lot. Okay, what else do you want to buy? You mentioned makeup?"

She nodded, relieved that he had remembered she wasn't out in public yet and he had managed to lower his normally loud voice at the mention of makeup.

"I kind of want some bolder lipsticks. I just have the neutral ones. A nice pink one maybe. Oh, and a blood red one. I want to be able to give off that old Hollywood glamour look when I want to." She tossed her hair back and smiled. But even then, she was still casting glances around them in case someone overheard.

"I think that's a good idea."

Her face suddenly fell, like a deflating balloon.

"I'm sorry. I'm not ready to try makeup on in public yet. It's too…you know."

"I get it." He rubbed her shoulder. Then his eyes lit up with an idea. "Why don't you try them on me? At least it'll give you a good visual."

"What? Oh, come on, River. I can't do that to you."

"I'm serious. If you want makeup bad enough, let's just do it."

"But they'll think you're—"

"Oh, let them think what they want. You know me. Couldn't pay me to give a shit."

"It won't make you…dysphoric?" she asked meekly.

"Nah. Worst-case scenario, they'll think I'm just doing it for some viral internet challenge. Besides, if someone gives you a hard time, I'll deal with them." He took her hand and walked with her into the nearest makeup store, and Mia did not have it in her to protest. After all, she did really, really want to try out those lipsticks. In the store, River helped her find four shades that were exactly what she had been looking for, and they found a spot towards the back with a mirror. River held still, trying not to smile as Mia put the lipstick on him. She had to lean up on her toes to get the right angle. The aisle was narrow to the point that she had to press up against him. His eyes were locked on her the whole time she put on the lipstick. Her hand shook a little, from both general social anxiety and the fear of someone not liking that they were doing this, and she had to force herself to stay steady. This close to him, Mia could smell his cologne, the leather of his new jacket, his sweat, and she wondered if he could smell her lavender body spray. She bit the inside of her cheek and told herself not to return his gaze, looking only at his mouth. As she leaned in again, she felt her chest press up against his. It took her breath away for a moment, and she took a step back.

"Okay, and…done."

"What do you think?" he asked.

"It's a lot. Very bold. But I like the way it looks. I think I'll buy it." She handed him a cloth to wipe it off, then leaned in and whispered softly, "Thank you. You're the best."

They went their own ways after their trip to the mall, but the feelings stuck with River for a long time afterwards. He could not stop thinking about the look in Mia's eyes as she moved up that close to him and put the lipstick on him. His stomach had been fluttering the whole time, his head locked in a battle against itself, hotly debating if now was the time to tell her or not. Here she was, in a whole new light, and he didn't know what the hell to do with it.

But she looked nervous. Which she tended to be a lot in public places. Maybe he could wait until they were somewhere with fewer strangers around. After all, should the revelation of his crush be taken as bad news, she needed to be in a place where she could better handle it.

At work the next day, he kept thinking about Mia, wondering if she would even say yes if he asked her out. Would she even enjoy dating him? What if he wasn't her type?

Fuck, just shut up already, he tried telling himself. *Two weeks ago, she was just one of your best friends and that hasn't changed. She probably still sees you as just a friend, too.* It bothered him most of the morning on and off as he went about his shift, hardly aware of what he was doing and just going through the paces out of habit.

On top of that, he had a lot on his mind regarding the next steps for The History of the Disillusioned. Their biggest concert yet was coming up in a few weeks to promote their debut album's release. It would be taking place at a local venue, and tickets were being sold fast. After work, River crashed on his couch. It took him about ten minutes to get the energy to check his phone for any missed notifications. His heart skipped a beat when he saw he had gotten a text from Mia about half an hour ago.

Mia: Heya! Just thought you should know I got a couple of my friends to get tickets for the concert. I'm so excited!!

He could not help but smile as he began to text her back. He had made sure to help her and some mutual friends get tickets the minute they were on sale, and they had been spreading the word to help get The History of the Disillusioned more attention.

River: Thanks! I'm excited too!

Mia: Now I need to figure out what to wear. Last time I stood out like a sore thumb lol

River: Hey you can wear whatever you want. Don't worry about it!

There was several minutes' pause before he saw that she had started typing again.

Mia: I was actually thinking of wearing something real feminine, like a dress and even some makeup. Like…for the first time in public

River sat up straight as he texted back. Now his heart was pounding.

River: Oh my god, Mia, that's awesome!! Go you!

He sent it with a bunch of smiling and heart emojis. She replied with twice the amount of hearts.

River sank back into the couch. He felt like he was in high school again, collecting celebrity crushes like trading cards and raging puberty spinning his emotions in overdrive and in constant spirals. But this was a big deal. She was going to start showing the outside world who she really was, and that was not something to be taken lightly. And of course, in his own selfish way, he couldn't wait to see how beautiful she would look.

Chapter Twenty-Two

Tonight was a big night for both River and Mia, and for different reasons. The History of the Disillusioned's big concert was happening, followed by the album release party, which would be hosted at a nearby nightclub. A huge turnout was expected for both, and based on what Mia had seen on social media, the band had developed quite a large following in the city and surrounding area over the past few months, and it sounded like pre-order sales had been doing well too. In summary, a lot of expectations hinged on how tonight went down.

As for Mia, she must have spent two hours putting on makeup, then taking it off, then trying it on again, and on and on it went. The bedroom she shared with Grace had a large vanity table and mirror, and all sorts of makeup and hair products were scattered around it. At least one third of said products were Mia's, although the girls shared with each other as needed. Grace walked in just in time to see Mia grabbing the makeup wipes again.

"Woah, what's the matter?" Grace asked, frowning.

"I just want it to look perfect." She sulked. This was going to be her first time out in public with makeup and a dress on. Not just in front of friends and possibly friends of friends, but total strangers. Mia had chosen the night of the concert and release party for her, as it were, official 'debut' to the world as a woman. A great idea in theory. In reality, it left her scrambling with all the many styles and products and colors to choose from. It had to be perfect, and that's where the trouble started. Of course, it was a nightmare of her own making. She knew that. Still had to be perfect, though.

"Here, let me see…" She turned Mia to face her. "Oh, you look beautiful! Let's just add a little blush and smooth this out…and just a little more eyeshadow."

Mia relaxed and let her help, trusting her. She finished a few minutes later and let Mia look in the mirror. She had given herself heavy winged eyeliner and added a touch of pink eyeshadow to complete the look. Her cheeks had dewy highlights, and her lips looked plump and glossy.

It was a feeling she was still getting used to, seeing a face reflected back that finally looked like Mia. The real Mia. It still made her choke up sometimes.

"What do you think?"

"I think I'm terrified." She laughed.

"Hey, if you're not ready it's okay–"

"I'm ready! I'm more than ready. I just…it's a lot."

Grace smiled and gave her shoulders a gentle squeeze. With that, Mia got up and straightened her outfit. She had decided on a sleeveless pink plaid dress with a white top and black boots. It was the perfect mix of 'cute' and 'grunge', which is exactly what she was going for, a nice blend of two sides of her she wanted to combine into one.

"Okay, we'd better get going or we'll be late." Grace rushed her to the door. One of their friends from the support group,

Hailey, was waiting impatiently with their tickets and back-stage passes in hand.

They arrived at the venue about forty minutes before the concert. Once inside, the three of them were allowed backstage to the dressing room to say hello to River and the band. When Mia walked in, she saw River putting on his black eyeliner in front of one of the mirrors. He wore a black mesh tank top and black tactical pants with tears and chains all over, and his hair was slicked back. While Mia had been precise and careful with every stroke as she put on her makeup, he was quick and sloppy, and she realized that was very much on purpose. Messy eyeliner was the exact look he was going for.

Mia stared at him as Grace and Hailey went to go chat with the rest of the band, who were all also wrapped up in last-minute preparations. Her body began to tense up. She still liked him a lot; she knew that much. All summer she had waited eagerly to hear news from him whenever he could message her, but she had been so busy with work that it helped distract her racing mind. That, plus getting therapy and focusing on her own mental health and transition had been more than enough to keep thoughts of unrequited crushes at bay.

But all the old emotions rushed back in full force when she saw him again several weeks ago. Now, seeing him in his black leather garb, Mia realized the horrible truth: she couldn't kid around with herself anymore. Those feelings hadn't gone away at all, nor had they been watered down even the slightest. Nope. They had just been lying dormant, like a little old volcano in her weary heart.

Maybe part of her had hoped she would get over it. Be able to just see him as a friend and nothing more. But deep down, Mia knew better. She loved their friendship, but she craved more. She wanted to get to know him in other ways. She wanted to hold his hand and kiss him. She wanted *him*. Ugh.

When River saw her, he turned and smiled, and she immediately smiled back.

"You made it!"

"Of course we did! We wouldn't miss this for the world. We just wanted to say good luck. Also, what do you think?" She twirled her dress a bit for him, clutching her small shoulder bag, and when she did she realized just how much he was staring at her. His jaw was practically on the floor and he spoke in stammers.

"You look...holy *shit*. Sorry, just...you look amazing.". She had texted him many times about how today was her first day presenting as feminine in public, so there was no way this could have shocked him. But he still looked stunned by her appearance.

The last thing she should do, of course, was overthink his reaction. He just saw her as a friend. He didn't like her in that way. At least, as far as she knew. Had something changed? Or was she reading way too much into the way he was looking at her? Was it just wishful thinking?

Probably. She was nothing if not an expert on wishful thinking, on false hopes and dreams.

"I hope I don't stand out too much."

"You'll be fine, stranger. Hope you enjoy the concert."

"I'm so ready. Just don't forget to do my favorite song." She gave him a big wink.

"I wouldn't dare." Two of his bandmates walked up to him and muttered something about needing to do one last sound check. "Shoot, I have to go. I'll see you after, okay?"

"See you then!" Mia and her friends were ushered away from the dressing room and back to the main venue. Her excitement grew as more and more people filled the room. It was not large, and there was nowhere to sit down, but it was getting packed. Soon, they noticed other familiar faces in the crowd, including Hailey's little sister and her girlfriend, who hurried over to join them. As the girls began to chat and get to know each other, the venue filled up. People crowded around, many wearing shirts with the band logo on them. The more crowded it became, the more Mia began to feel shy, wondering if anyone would clock her. She knew better than to go down that train of thought since it didn't lead to anything good, but she couldn't help it. Hopefully, if anyone had a problem with how she looked, they weren't going to act on it.

Luckily, the concert soon started and any attention that may have gone to her was now just on the band. The room went dark, omitting a loud cheer from the crowd which Mia joined in on. Then the lead and bass began to start into one of their top songs, and the cheers grew even louder. When the lights came on they focused on River as he greeted the crowd.

Mia stared up at him. She had seen him and the band perform before at the craft festival, but this felt different. This was not just a small gig. This was their own concert, and tonight was the biggest night the band had ever had. Seeing him up there, bathed in the spotlight as he began singing the first verse to the song, Mia was mesmerized, finding it easy to forget that the lead singer on stage was her best friend and not some stranger.

It was almost jarring to see him take on his rockstar persona so well, getting the crowd excited and singing with him. Had this been Mia's first exposure to the band, it would have scared her. Seeing this huge guy in goth clothes all over the stage, screaming out dark, raunchy lyrics, watching him sweat so much she could see it drip from his hair onto the floor over and over. But instead, it gave her a huge thrill. She could see the appeal of going to concerts like this now, even without River on stage. All those girls in high school who never shut up about My Chemical Romance suddenly made a whole lot of sense.

The first song ended, and the band started up the next one, a sultry ballad about a family of cannibals. Supposedly it was a metaphor for late-stage capitalism, according to River, who explained it to her once and it went completely over her head. As the night went on Mia focused on enjoying herself, losing herself in the music and jumping up and down with her friends. She sang along to all the songs and cheered until her throat hurt. The concert ended with one of the band's most popular songs, one that was energetic and electric, and got the crowd roaring. When it was over, Mia and her friends started making their way to the album release party.

"Wow, you weren't kidding about them," Hailey said. "That was amazing! How have I never heard of them before?"

"Well, lucky for you, I have my sources and just happen to know the lead singer, and he'll be happy to sign your copy of the album," Grace said with an exaggerated wink.

"I just want to meet the bassist. She's my type." Hailey bit her lip as the others gave her a knowing look. "What? Can you blame me? I'm obsessed."

The conversation between the girls soon shifted to other bands, none of which Mia had heard of before, so she just listened. Her mind was already starting to slip into her previous thoughts which had started before the concert. Now that the distraction of good music was gone, self-consciousness trickled back in like an old wound. Not to mention thinking about how River had been looking at her earlier.

Fortunately, she knew exactly who she needed to talk to about this whole mess.

Soon they had arrived at the nightclub, along with the others who had been invited to the album release party. As soon as they found a table, Mia volunteered to go to the bar to get them some food and drinks.

"Grace, I need your help carrying everything," she said.

Grace gave her a look that meant she understood what Mia was really asking. Without a word she got up to walk with her. When the two were alone, Mia turned to her.

"So! Toootally random question," Mia began, knowing Grace would see right through that one, "but do you have any advice on asking a friend if they, I guess…if they like you?"

Grace raised her eyebrows and leaned against the counter.

"You're thinking of asking River out, aren't you?"

Mia blushed. *Dammit. She knows me so well. Too well.* She nodded a little. She should have figured Grace would get right to the point. After all, it had been Grace who called her out on her crush on him in the first place.

"Coming back after the summer has been…well. There's no other way to say it. I still like him. But I'm scared to tell him."

"Because you're afraid he's not ready to date yet and he'll say no and it'll make things really weird between you guys?"

Mia nodded again.

"I like being friends with him, and I don't want to ruin that," she said, tapping her nails on the counter. "But I don't know what I would do if he turned me down."

"Ever considered, and hear me out, that maybe he likes you too?"

She sputtered out a loud laugh.

"Come on."

"I'm serious. I think he does, and he hasn't been telling you for the same reason you're not telling him. But how do you know until you try?"

"Hang on. What makes you think *he* likes *me*?" Now Mia was really blushing.

Grace rolled her eyes. Their drinks arrived and she picked up two of them.

"So I had a hunch last spring, but it wasn't my place to say it, so I didn't. But since you're asking, I'm pretty convinced at this point. Especially since you're both back in town."

"Grace…don't do that to me. That's mean." Mia's body felt cold, not wanting to believe the conversation was headed in this direction.

"I'm not messing with you. I don't know how long it's been going on, but since you got back something's changed." Grace looked right at her. "All I'm saying is that I think if you ask him, you won't be turned down."

Mia really, really wanted to believe her. Because if Grace was right, that changed everything. Literally everything! It meant she could finally tell River how she felt about him. She could be more than a friend. She could get to know him in ways she had fantasized about for months.

But just the thought of pouring her heart out like that made her want to puke. There were too many ways it could go wrong. Her life was a long history of having aspirations dashed against the rocks, and people always say history repeats itself. Plus, she couldn't rule out the slight possibility that maybe Grace had read the signs wrong.

"I guess." Mia sighed. "But not tonight. Tonight is about the band."

"Oh, I agree. One thing at a time."

"I've never told someone I liked them before. Not like this," Mia confessed, thinking of the few dates with girls she had had in high school. Of course, those were all just to put on an act to prove to everyone she was just a regular straight guy and there was no reason to suspect otherwise. Needless to say, none of those had lasted long. This would be opening herself up for rejection on a whole other level.

"Maybe he will beat you to it." Grace shrugged, then offered her a small smile. "Come on. Let's go have some fun. We're celebrating!"

But Mia still felt dizzy, thinking of what her friend had told her and hoping, with all her heart, that Grace wasn't wrong.

Chapter Twenty-Three

Sometime later, the band arrived and were greeted with loud cheers. Mia looked up, watching as the band made their way to the large table that had been set up for them at the back, with CDs, shirts, pins, and posters for sale. They had barely sat down when people were getting in line to make their purchases. Hailey's girlfriend bolted up.

"I'm going to go buy one," she announced. "Anyone want to come with me?"

The others got up while Mia stayed where she was. She had too much on her mind right now to talk to River and ended up pulling out her phone to scroll through social media. Gradually, the noise volume in the nightclub increased as more people showed up at the party and, of course, people began drinking more. There was a constant buzz of activity around the table as fans bought merchandise and asked all the band members to sign them. Mia relaxed, sipping on a poor excuse for a chamoyada, too nervous to enjoy herself too much just yet and only confident enough to get up and order another beverage. Maybe the lemonade would be better here. As she hopped off her chair and turned around, her body collided with someone taller than her. She turned around to mumble an apology when she couldn't help but laugh at who it was.

"Hey, you!" She looked up at River. "Aren't you supposed to be signing some shirts?"

"I'm taking a short break." He smiled. His eyeliner was even messier than when she last saw him. Sweat had formed faint gray lines leading from his eyes down his cheeks. "Want to join me?"

"Of course!" Mia turned around and gave Grace a glance where she was dancing with Hailey. Grace just shot her a thumbs up and rushed back to her friends. Mia, happy to be in his company again, followed him back to their table and sat next to him. Tonight, River looked larger than life. Sitting there, radiant and glowing from the concert, shaking hands and accepting congrats from the fans who stopped by the table to say hello or hand him a marker to sign something.

A few minutes later, a group of three blonde girls with matching skirts and shoulder bags moved towards the table. They did not look or dress like typical fans of the band, but Mia supposed their music struck more than just the goth sub-cultures, which had to be a good thing. It meant they were growing and could hit a mainstream crowd. Two of the girls had bought band shirts and all three were holding a recently purchased CD.

"Hey, River. Could you sign our CDs and shirts, pretty please?" the girl in the middle asked in a strong West Holly-wood accent.

Mia watched the three of them, thinking to herself, *River actually has fangirls now. Okay, that makes sense. They're more into the band members than the actual music.* She imagined a bunch of girls who were more into basic pop, forcing themselves to endure The History of the Disillusioned's unique musical style for the sake of a crush, and found the idea amusing. She wasn't immune to it. Mia had long lost count of how much insufferable media she had consumed because of how smitten she was with one of the actors. The things people do for love and lust.

"Sure." He grabbed his black marker. "What are your names?"

One by one the girls introduced themselves. Three of the most suburban white girl names one could think of, Mia mused. Then they looked at her. River caught on and grabbed Mia's hand, interrupting his signing.

"This is my friend, Mia. She goes to the same school as me."

"Oh! Wow, you are so pretty!" one of the girls cooed.

Mia blushed, feeling light as a feather all over.

"Oh, well…thank you!" she said, forcing herself to elevate the pitch of her voice. She had fallen behind on vocal training, which she hated doing anyway, but tonight she had decided that anytime she talked to a stranger she would work on it. She also made an effort to dip her chin a little as, according to hours in front of the mirror proved, it helped her pass a little better. But what the girls said next made her freeze on the spot.

"When I tell you I'm obsessed with drag queens, I am…literally obsessed," one of the girls said. "I love going to the drag shows in the city."

"All you people are so fabulous. And so much prettier than me, too. It's so unfair," her friend chimed in. "I would love to see you perform sometime."

Mia felt her stomach ooze onto the floor.

Fuck. Oh fuck, no, not this. Keep it together, she told herself.

Suddenly, she wanted to die. She wished she had never done this. It was too soon to present in public. She should have waited longer. Mia began thinking of everyone who would have seen her tonight and wondered how many of them had thought the same thing these girls did, and the only difference was they were brave enough to say it out loud. Did everyone really just see her as a boy wearing makeup and girls' clothes? Is that all people could see when they looked at her?

Meanwhile, River's body stiffened and he sat up straighter.

"Well, she's not a drag queen, she's a woman. There's a big difference," he said in a tone that was quite blunt, even for him.

The first girl smiled and cocked her head at Mia.

"Well, you be whatever you want to be. Black, white, purple, green, gay, straight, it's all good!"

River started to scowl. He quickly finished signing the last CD and told them to enjoy the party. As they turned away, Mia heard them talking about River and the 'drag queen' with him. Like she was hardly a person, but just an act, a performer, someone to gawk at and take selfies with. Mia felt her throat throb. Her arms clasped over her chest, wanting to hide as much of her body as she could from the world.

That's what the world thinks of me. That's what they see. That's all they fucking see…

She felt River's hand on her shoulder.

"They're just idiots. You're way more of a woman than they'll ever be."

She nodded, but the tears were still coming. His compliment felt so empty and meaningless. Of course he was going to say a nice thing; he was her friend. He was just trying to cheer her up, not tell her the truth. She felt him lean in closer to her and, in spite of herself, a small shiver went up her back.

"Do you want Victoria or Emily to take you to the band's private room? You can take it easy there as long as you want."

Hiding somewhere safe sounded better than giving up the night altogether. Choking down more sobs, she forced herself to nod. River called over one of the band members from the other table. Then, to Mia's surprise, he stood up and approached the three girls who had just left.

"Wait. River…?" she croaked. But he was already there. His booming voice could be heard loud and clear over the music.

"Excuse me? Yeah, you were being really rude to my friend and you need to apologize."

The three girls blinked at him.

"Uh…I'm sorry?" the first one said, as if without the slightest idea of what he could be talking about. Either she was really good at acting or she truly didn't realize the hurt she had caused. Mia was unsure which was worse.

"I told you that my friend Mia is *not* a drag queen, that she is a *woman*, and yet you insist on calling her something she isn't. And you need to apologize to her for it."

"Okay, well, I'm sorry if I overstepped or said anything offensive. But I think you can understand the confusion. I mean, they're not really trying that hard." She held up her hands, waving them in front of her. "Besides, that's not me. I'm not that bigoted kind of person. My friends here will tell you the same. I'm just not that person! My cousin is gay! And I always tip the queens!"

"I don't see what's there to be fucking confused by. I told you who she is and I don't think you want to listen to me." River's voice was getting louder, but his hands stayed in his pockets. "And actually, you *are* being that bigoted kind of person. And I hope I'm not the first person to tell you that."

"Okay, wow, you know what? She is *not* a bigot, and you actually need as much money as you can get from allies if you're going to have any success. And just for that, I'm going to return this shirt. I don't want your merchandise if you're going to be a dick," one of her friends spat at him.

"We don't accept refunds, but I will accept an apology on Mia's behalf."

Mia huddled in her seat, hugging herself and wishing she could disappear.

"Why are you being such an asshole?!" the first girl yelled at him.

"Oh, my mistake. I think you can understand the confusion where I thought you were a nice person. But now I see that you're really a self-absorbed *cunt*." And as if that wasn't enough, River finished off his tirade with a loud, "So, where were *you* on January 6th?"

Another man's voice joined the conversation. Mia looked up. Two guys had walked over. She heard them asking the girls if this guy was bothering them and quickly put together that they must be the girls' boyfriends. In second, the heated conversation escalated into a shouting match as the boyfriends started accusing River of giving them a hard time, while he continued to insist that they needed to apologize.

Mia was about to get up to tell him to just forget the whole thing when *it* happened.

She saw a fist fly. Saw it meet the side of River's head. And just like that, two men were throwing hits at him. River barreled into them, like a bull charging at a red cape. Two chairs were knocked over. Almost instantly, the nearest partygoers saw what was going on and backed away, including the three girls. River was grabbed by the back of his shirt by one man while the other hit him hard in the ribs. Even with that, Mia saw him punch the guy right in the nose.

She bolted up. Her whole body hurt like it was being burned. She kept moving closer to where the three men were fighting, wanting to throw up and scream and burst into tears all at the same time.

River had already been hit a few times. His mouth was bleeding, but he was moving fast. One of the guys grabbed him by the shirt and slammed him against a table, while the other punched him hard in the ribcage a couple of times. Instead of backing down, River shoved the man back, hard, then hit him right in the left eye. The impact sent him stumbling backwards. River went for the other guy, punching him hard before receiving another hard blow to the face. That time he made a sound like that really hurt. Still, he kept going.

Mia watched, hands to her mouth, unable to breathe. She realized it was useless to beg them to stop, so she just looked away, the sight of blood making her nauseous. Luckily a few other guys who were bigger and stronger were moving in to break up the fight. As soon as they were separated, she ran to him. River was still standing, but bleeding from the face and breathing hoarsely. Mia didn't realize her hands and knees were shaking until River took her by the shoulder.

"Let's get the fuck out of here," he said.

Luckily they were able to get in the band's van and take off before any police showed up. Victoria got in with them and sat beside Mia while Oliver drove. One of them handed River a fistful of napkins so he wouldn't bleed all over the seats. Mia didn't know what to say or do so she just sat there, shaking all over. She had not seen that much blood or violence in many years, probably not since high school.

"I'm sorry…" River said quietly to her. His face was mostly hidden in the darkness, but she saw red blotches where he'd been hit, and blood around his nostrils and lips.

"River…" Without thinking, she grabbed his hand. "No, no, no. I should be thanking you for sticking up for me like that. You didn't have to."

"I couldn't help it."

"You were my knight in shining armor."

"Should we get him to the hospital?" Oliver asked. In response, Victoria moved to take a quick survey of his injuries, but River just shook his head.

"I'm good, I'm good. Just bumps and bruises."

"Are you *sure*?" Victoria made River look her in the eye.

"Yes. I. Am. Fine."

At his apartment, Oliver took River to the bathroom to help him clean up while Victoria and Mia stayed in the kitchen. There, now that the madness had ceased, Mia found herself bursting into sobs she had been holding in for the past thirty minutes or so. The girls' words from before came crashing down, mixed with the fear she felt watching River get into that fight.

Victoria grabbed her and pulled her into a tight hug. Mia just let herself cry and cry and cry.

"They said…I…"

"I know. I know. It's okay, Mia." Victoria stroked Mia's head. "Hey. You were very brave today, going out in public as your true self when people like that aren't going to understand. You are beautiful and radiant."

"Shut up. I'm not. I look like a…." Mia's chest heaved. The word she was thinking of hurt too much to say. It was the same word used against her as a teenager. A word she hoped she would be able to reclaim someday like some in the community could. And maybe someday it wouldn't hurt to hear it. But tonight, it still felt like a knife to the cut just at the mere mention.

"That's *not* true." Victoria was rubbing her upper back now. "I know a beautiful girl when I see one and that is you. You are kind and good and wonderful."

"You're a fucking liar." But Mia couldn't speak after that and just kept crying.

By the time Oliver and River were out of the bathroom, she finally got all her tears out and just curled up on River's couch, sipping from a glass of water Victoria fetched for her. River was shirtless, with some bandages and gauze on his sides as well as his face. Oliver, meanwhile, looked pissed off, his skinny arms flapping around as he went on his passionate tirade.

"A fight. On the night we drop our first album. Are you serious? I thought you were getting better about this, River. Why did you pick tonight of all nights to do that?"

River seemed to be coming off the adrenaline from the fight. He curled up on the other side of the sofa and kicked off his boots and socks. He stared down, looking as embarrassed as a puppy that had been caught chewing up the couch.

"You know what this is going to do to us, right? You know how your actions affect everyone in the band, *not* just you?!"

"Okay, that's enough!" Victoria cut in. "We can talk about this tomorrow. Let's just let everyone cool down for now."

"Yeah, you'd better sleep on it and think about what you've done." Oliver stormed out. "I'll be in the van."

Victoria watched him go with a sigh, then rubbed River's back for a moment and murmured something to him. Then she turned to Mia. Mia stared for a moment until she realized Victoria was waiting for her.

"Is it okay if I…"

"You can stay here for the night if you want," River finished for her.

"If that's okay?" she asked sheepishly. Tonight, River's apartment felt like the safest place in the world.

"Of course it's okay." He looked up at Victoria. "I'll call you in the morning."

Once she left, Mia felt the temptation to cry even more, if that was even physically possible. But this time, she was able to hold it down. She had cried so much her whole face hurt. These were not the sort of circumstances she expected a night alone with River to go. Her being all cried out and miserable, while he was beat up and the biggest night for his band all but ruined. Not exactly ideal.

They both sat there a while, just taking in the silence, both too drained from the night to say anything. After about ten minutes, River pulled out his cigarette pack and lighter and gestured to her. She nodded. They stepped out onto the small porch and smoked, just as they had done months ago at the party. Mia sat in the lawn chair, and River leaned on the railing.

That was another twelve minutes of silence as they each had two cigarettes, just easing their nerves and looking out at the city skyline. Finally, Mia felt she had collected her thoughts enough to speak.

"I shouldn't have picked tonight."

"What? Why do you say that?" River looked at her, the cigarette between his lips. The light flooding from inside made all his little freckles even more apparent. That, with the cigarette smoke and his messy hair, dried sweat, and yes, even his bruises…he looked gorgeous, and she was a mess.

Mia wanted him. She wanted him more than anything in the whole world. She wanted to kiss him good night and good morning and play with his hair and listen to him sleep beside her and be the reason he felt happy and alive in every sense of the words.

"It was your band's night. Not mine," she said quietly.

"That's bullshit. You picked a perfect night. I'm honored that you did."

"You are?" she asked, her hand shaking as she tapped her ashes into the empty flowerpot.

"Yeah. Coming out publicly is a big step in your journey. It's the Lollipop Woods."

"I'm sorry, the what now?"

"You know, Candyland? The board game?"

Mia grinned and began to laugh. It felt good. River began laughing with her. Seeing his big smile, in spite of his unkempt look, made Mia's heart melt.

Goddammit, River Solinski.

"And what is the…Molasses Swamp?" she giggled as she puffed on her cigarette.

"That's waiting to get on hormones. Cause those fucking doctors move as quickly as molasses to set up your prescriptions and insurance coverage." He laughed.

"That makes no sense!" Now she couldn't stop laughing.

"*You* make no sense."

Mia kicked his foot with hers and thought to herself, *If I had just an ounce less of self control, I'd tell you I love you right here, right now.*

When they both stopped laughing, River put out his cigarette and looked at her. She would have sold her soul to read his thoughts. To know if he saw her as more than a friend.

"We should really get some sleep," he said. "You want the bed or the couch?"

She hesitated, but she knew what the smart answer was.

"I can take the couch." She smiled weakly.

Chapter Twenty-Four

River did not fall asleep easily that night.

He wished the fight hadn't been broken up as quickly as it did. Just replaying their words in his mind brought back his rage and made him see red all over again. Oliver did have a point, though. He had been doing so well on his anger problems for the past few years, and that moment now felt like a relapse into an older version of himself he had tried to heal from. It felt like years of hard work had been erased in a split second.

But whenever he closed his eyes, all he could see was the look on Mia's face the moment she realized how empty and hurtful those girls' compliments really were. The way the sunshine in her eyes died out and her whole body looked like it had been grabbed by something vile. It had broken his heart.

And, of course, he understood it. He still had trouble believing he was handsome sometimes. At worst, being called handsome felt like fake praise. He knew that feeling. But at the same time, he wished Mia could see everything he saw in her. Her big heart that loved so deeply and so true. Her resilience to stay strong and help herself get better. Her compassion. How she listened to him when he had his breakdowns. How she didn't try to come up with a piece of advice and just held him until he came back. Her smile was so warm that it had to be partially to blame for climate change. Her laugh that she covered with her mouth because she got flustered and that made her even cuter. He understood why those things were hard for her to see, but at the same time, how could she not see how beautiful and perfect she was?

Around three in the morning, he got up and leaned out his bedroom window to have another cigarette, and he banged his forehead on the glass.

Fuck me.

The next morning, he woke up to a mountain of texts from the band. He sighed, groaning as he recollected what happened last night, as if the bruises weren't enough. As he got up, he found Mia still asleep on the couch. He didn't want to wake her, and she looked so adorable when she slept, anyway. So as a compromise, he found the nearest piece of scrap paper and wrote a note, telling her that he had to step out to go talk to the band but he would be back in a couple hours with coffee and breakfast sandwiches.

Less than fifteen minutes later, River dressed in a relatively clean pair of clothes he found on his bedroom floor and hurried to Emily's house, where the band typically met for meetings. He didn't bother to take a shower, so his hair was still a mess and he was still wearing a coat of dried sweat from last night. Once at the house, which was in a small neighborhood a short drive from his house, he found everyone standing on the porch, looking at him, and he had never felt so small. The cold, foggy atmosphere of the morning did not help, either.

"So," Emily began. "Last night. That was a fucking mess."

"It started when—" River began, but Victoria held up her hand, cutting him off.

"I saw it all, River. I told them the whole story already. And I get it. I really do. Those people were assholes. But you went too far."

"I know." River sighed, tousling his hair. He leaned against the porch railing, picking at a piece of chipped blue paint. "What kind of damage control are we looking at?"

Oliver held up his tablet and was scrolling through their social media feed.

"Well, the good news is there isn't any footage going around of the fight online. Bad news is some people who were there posted about it and there's been some discussion circulating. Fans are going to want answers. We're drafting up a response right now to clear up all the confusion. Because no one is officially sure of what actually happened."

"Just tell them the truth. I stood up for her and I got carried away. Fuck it, you can even throw in a line about how I've struggled with anger issues my whole life or something like that." River shrugged.

"I'll let everyone review it before I post anything," Oliver said curtly.

River began gnawing on his lip.

"Do you think…I blew it? Do you think I ruined every-thing?" he asked, hating how soft his voice sounded in that moment. He only sounded like that when he was around family.

Victoria shook her head.

"No. We just need to be transparent about what happened. Better to be honest upfront than do some bullshit cover-up and have someone else leak the truth. Some people are going to be pissed. We could lose a good number of the fanbase. But I think a good number of people are going to understand."

"We'll be okay," Cat added. "I did make some calls, by the way. No one is going to press charges, thank Satan, but the nightclub did make us pay a fee for the damages. And we can't perform there for a year."

"I'll pay for it," River said without hesitation. "It was all on me."

"It's over five hundred bucks. You broke a table and two chairs," said Emily.

"I'll...pay most of it."

Emily smiled a little and approached him, then pulled him into a hug. Suddenly, River began to cry.

"I'm sorry," he said, his voice muffled against her shoulder. "I don't want to be that person anymore. I want to be better. I just got so..."

"I know, bud." She rubbed his back to soothe him.

Mia was in one of her bad moods again thanks to the estrogen. It was the kind of day in which she had weird food cravings, everything made her upset, and she simultaneously wanted a bunch of hugs and to be left alone. Like a typical Mia Tuesday, times a hundred, but at least E had joined the main cast.

She had just finished her shift at her new job. Thanks to word of mouth, she had found a job at another car repair shop. One of the people in management at the shop was also trans, which made her feel much safer working here. So far, she hadn't officially come out to anyone except for said manager, and decided she would just answer the questions regarding her gender as they came.

After her shift, she was tempted to go home, curl up on the couch, and binge her latest rewatch until she fell asleep. But Mia felt too antsy today. Sitting around would drive her crazy.

She remembered River talked a lot about a lesser-known shore drive just a little ways out of the city. It was said to have some of the best scenic views of the coast and the lakeside cliffs overlooking the Pacific. She had told herself one of these days when she had a couple hours to burn she would drive there, get out of the metro and see some of the scenery around here.

Today was pretty much as good of an excuse as she was going to get.

Before she could change her mind, Mia filled up her car's tank and put in the directions on her phone. She drove out on the freeway for roughly forty minutes, taking her far away from downtown until slowly she became surrounded by beautiful forests. When her exit came up, she found herself on a little highway that made her really feel like she was in the middle of nowhere. She drove for some time, winding her way through the wilderness, until she turned the bend and suddenly the ocean was in view on her right, and a long shoreline with not a single person in sight.

As it turned out, River hadn't been wrong about the view. Mia rolled her window down to smell the salty sea and listen to the seagulls. It was a cloudy day, but she couldn't complain much. She just kept cruising down the road, enjoying the drive. So much so that she neglected to remember that she had not gotten around to buying a spare tire because other expenses came up.

Which meant that when she hit a bad pothole and her tire blew, she didn't freak out until she pulled over and looked in the trunk, only to find it was empty.

"Oh, for the love of…" she whispered under her breath. She had pulled over on one of the bends overlooking a large cliff side, so at least the view was nice. Before she realized it, she was on the brink of tears, feeling like the whole world was about to end over a silly mistake on her part. Of course, the one time she decided to treat herself by getting out of the city, this sort of thing would happen. Wasn't that just her luck? Served her right for 'having fun' and 'being adventurous.' Fuck it. Next time she got the urge to get out of the apartment, she was not getting off the damn couch.

She leaned against the fence along the edge of the cliff, looking out to the ocean and cursing under her breath. At first Mia wondered if she should call a tow truck to come get her, but that could be expensive, especially with how far out of the way she was, and she really couldn't afford that. Maybe one of her friends would be available to come help her out. The signal out here was a whopping single bar on her phone, so she was lucky her text even made it into the group chat.

Mia groaned with embarrassment at just sending her request for help. She had become the friend in her groups who you could come to with any car problems. She would swing by, make a quick diagnostic, and tell them exactly what part they needed so they didn't get ripped off at the shop. She accepted anything from an iced coffee to half a pizza as her payment. Which made it feel all the more embarrassing that she, of all people, did not have a spare tire on her. That was worse than the IT guy forgetting to plug in the monitor.

Several minutes later, River texted her, asking for her location. As soon as she sent it, he messaged back, saying he was on his way and would be there in just over an hour. Mia felt even more embarrassed but couldn't say no. What's more, just seeing his name appear on her new messages made her heart light up. She texted him back that she owed him big time.

By the time he arrived it was nearly sundown. Mia had begun taking paces back and forth along the dirt path beside the road. At this point, she was just forcing herself to enjoy the quiet and the stillness since she had nothing better to do. She also had to resist the urge to play music from her phone since she needed to save as much battery life as possible. Finally, River's motorcycle pulled up next to her car. When he took off his helmet his hair was messy and his cheeks flushed. Mia smiled.

"Love the jacket. You look nice in it," she said before she could stop herself.

"Thank you." He got off the bike. "I have to admit, you're the last person I expected to be asking for a ride."

She knew he was only saying it as a joke and meant no offense. But her day had already been so stressful on top of being stranded and having to wait in the middle of nowhere. Plus her anxiety as she imagined a stranger finding her and clocking her and doing something horrible to her. All things considered, his little remark, however sarcastic, was enough to push her over the edge. Mia covered her face as ugly sobs began coming out of her throat.

"Oh, no…I'm sorry! I didn't mean…shit." River ran up to her. "I didn't mean it like that."

"I'm okay!" She sniffled. "I've just had a long day and I'm tired and hungry and want a hot shower and I just wanted to go for a drive to feel better and now I feel worse!"

"Hey, it's okay." He rubbed her shoulder. "It happens to everybody. We'll get you home in no time."

Mia sniffled, ashamed at crying over such a silly thing in front of him. She tried to stop, but felt so weak. He moved his body closer to hers, and she breathed in his scent. He had officially upgraded from cheap body spray to something…a little nicer. Not triple digits in price nicer, but still. Character growth.

"Look, I'll give you a ride home on my bike. How about that?"

"But my car…"

"When you mentioned you can't afford a tow truck, I called one for you. They should be here any second."

"You didn't have to do that." She looked away. He was being too nice. Making her heart flutter too much. It wasn't fair.

"Well, too bad. I did anyway." Then, to Mia's surprise, he took her hand in his. "Come on, we can relax here and watch the sunset while we wait for them."

She nodded. They walked over to the fence bordering the cliff and found a large rock to sit on together. His timing could not have been more perfect. The sunset was starting and sinking into the west, casting rays of orange and yellow and pink across the skies. It was starting to get chilly out, but they still had time before it would become uncomfortably cold. River pulled out a cigarette and when he offered her one of his, she couldn't turn it down. Because of course, if her day wasn't bad enough, she had left her pack at home under the belief she wouldn't be gone this long. She shivered as she took a deep inhale.

"God, look at me being a...here." He took off his jacket and put it over her shoulders.

"Oh me, oh my, such a gentleman," she said, smiling. "Ugh, I really do need to quit smoking someday. But I feel like now that I'm a few months into hormones it's going to be even harder."

"There's never an easy time to quit. But you're right. I should quit too." He held up his pack with a small smirk. "As soon as I finish these, I will."

"Well, in that case, let me help you finish these off so you can quit sooner. It's only what a real friend would do." After they finished laughing, she stretched her legs down the slope of the rock, humming contentedly. His leather jacket sure was cozy. "I really can't thank you enough for saving my ass today. I thought going on this scenic drive would clear my head and all, but nope. That's what I get for getting out of the apartment and trying to have a dumb little adventure."

"The day isn't over yet. We can still save it."

Mia watched him hesitate. His hand was resting on the rock, just a few inches from hers. His fingers twitched like he wanted to move, but was stuck there. She balanced her cigarette in her left hand. Her right moved over slowly until she felt his fingers brush against hers.

River looked at her, his eyes large and earnest and wanting. Mia let her hand keep moving until it was folded over his completely and she could run her fingers on top of his. Her hand felt so small against his.

"You're my hero. I hope you know that," she said softly. Deep down she hoped she would never forget this moment.

Just the two of them in the wilderness, the woods behind them and the Pacific ahead of them. The sound of the ocean waves crashing against the cliffs and the distant cry of seagulls. The sun slowly sinking into the west against a gorgeous sunset, and his leather against her arms, and his soft breathing beside her, and the faint scent of his sweat and cologne. The way the fading sunlight made his eyes and skin and hair glow made her heart pound.

"Come on."

"I mean it. You saved me. In more than one way, too, you know."

It took her a second to comprehend what he said next.

"Well, it's because I love you."

She turned to him, the cigarette dangling from between her fingers. It fell to the ground, but she did not notice.

"You…I'm sorry, what?"

"I…I love you." It seemed that River finally understood what he said, too. He swallowed hard as he looked at her. Mia felt him lift his hand like he was about to pull away from her. Desperate to keep him close, she grabbed his hand and held it, lacing their fingers together. Even though they had hugged many times before, this felt like it was the closest she had ever been to him. It was making her head spin with exhilaration. This was really happening. She was holding his hand. Mia Reyes was holding River Solinski's hand.

"I love you too," she said without having to think about it. She meant it. She had meant to say it for so many months now.

"I mean, I love you as more than—"

"More than a friend?" Mia bit her lip and her vision suddenly blurred. *Goddammit.* Hadn't she cried enough today already?

"Yeah. More than a friend."

"Me too. I need to tell you something because I'm really on the edge right now, so I'm just going to." She let it out before she would have any second thoughts about it. If she didn't say it now, she never would. "I've been crazy about you for a while now. I really, really…*really* like you. If you don't want me that way, you can tell me, though, and it's okay. Or if you're not ready to date again because of your shitty ex, that's okay, too."

River put out his cigarette and moved closer to her. Mia reciprocated. And she closed her eyes as she felt his lips, soft and full and warm, press against hers.

Warmth rushed to the pit of her stomach, and it was as if the whole weight of the world had been lifted off her shoulders. He tightened his grip on her hand a bit before she felt his other hand move up her arm, gently caressing her skin.

But it didn't stop there. River parted his lips slightly and she felt him kiss just her bottom lip. She relaxed her jaw, letting her mouth respond to his movements. She was suddenly very aware of her body and how it was pulling itself towards him, wanting more. Mia reached up and cupped the side of his face to draw him in closer to her.

After a few moments River slowly pulled away, his eyes locked on her. His eyes looked a little cloudy, too. She had never seen him look this vulnerable before, this raw and open and wanting.

"I'm crazy about you, too. I love you, Mia…a lot."

Mia bit her lip, feeling the hot tears roll down her cheeks. Now that she had finally heard the words she had been wanting to hear for so long, she didn't know how to respond. Her whole body tingled with desire, like she had defied gravity and flown into the sun.

"You do?" she asked, her bottom lip trembling.

"I've been crazy about you for a long time too. Crazy about you since I met you. And I just didn't realize it until this summer when we were apart all those months."

"Are you…oh my god." She wanted to laugh and cry and dance and scream like a berserker all at the same time. "So let me get this straight. You're telling me that, all this time, we both liked each other, and we didn't do anything about it?!"

"I guess so." River swallowed hard and belted out a nervous laugh. "That's on me. I take full responsibility. I'm a real idiot."

But Mia wouldn't have it. No. No regretting the months their feelings for each other went unsaid, not even thinking it. She didn't care. She just wanted him. His best parts, his worst parts, his sleepless nights and lazy mornings, his favorite songs and least favorite foods…everything. No holding onto the months that could have been, only to the good times that were about to be.

"River, it's okay! We're saying it now. Just…just kiss me again," she whispered.

"I can kiss you again." River reached up and all at once both his hands were cupping her cheeks and he was pulling her in. Her shoulders relaxed, and she felt like she was about to melt into the ground. He tasted warm and sweet, and she loved how soft his lips felt. Without trying to think too much about it, Mia parted her lips and moved her tongue against the inside of his mouth. She tilted her head a bit to the side to make the angle easier and then he was probing her mouth hungrily, filling her with the taste of him, making her dizzy with exhilaration.

Which meant the tow truck could not have picked a better time to pull up around the bend and park loudly on the side of the road.

River pulled away and stared into her eyes for several seconds. Mia smiled softly.

"That was good. You're a real good kisser," she said, her voice shaking.

"You're good too." He took a deep breath, then got up. She watched him talk to the two drivers for a few minutes before they set to work hooking up her car. As River walked up to her he gestured to his motorcycle. "How badly do you need to stay at your apartment tonight?"

"I don't need to, actually. Are you offering?"

"I mean…yeah." He looked shy, his ears turning red as he shoved his hands in his jeans pockets.

She nodded. He tossed her his spare helmet before getting on his bike. The recent events had been so overwhelming that Mia did not even have time to get nervous about riding on a motorcycle for the first time.

"Hold onto me," he said. "It'll be okay as long as you don't let go."

"I won't let go. I promise. You'll have to pry me off with a crowbar." She wrapped her arms around his broad torso and snuggled her face against his back. As they took off, the roar of the engine sounded around her and the wind whipped at her hair. Even though she was scared, holding onto River made it exciting too. He could have taken her for a ride for hours and she would have been content.

Chapter
Twenty-Five

They got back to his place after dark. She didn't let go of him the whole ride there. When she finally got the spare and the tow company had left for the night, it was getting late. Once they got to his place, River parked his motorcycle around back and walked with her inside and upstairs to his apartment. Mia was tingling as she watched him, unsure of how long she could hold out.

Mia hadn't had much experience in sex. In high school there were a couple girls she went to second base with, but it had not been enough that she could constitute it as losing her virginity. But she felt ready now. There was no one else she'd rather have her first official time with.

As soon as he had shut the door behind him, she grabbed a fistful of his shirt and pulled him in for another kiss. She felt River wrap his arms tight around her, holding her close.

"River...I..." His hands were on her lower back. Mia reached up until her fingers were in his hair and she could grab fistfuls of it. Using her strength, she pushed him up against the door and kissed him more forcefully, wanting more.

"Mia..." he moaned. He moved his kisses down to her neck, making her gasp.

"Wait, wait…this is technically my first time," she said. "Doing the whole real thing, I mean."

"That's okay. I got my tubes tied, but I do have condoms I keep around, just in case."

"Good to know." She smiled as he took her hand and pulled her to his bedroom.

"Just let me know if you need to slow down or stop, okay?" He brushed her hair away from her face and kissed her on the lips again.

"I will."

River climbed onto the unmade bed. The only light was from the other room, but she didn't care. She knelt beside him, cupping his chin to kiss him again, still not over how amazing his kisses felt.

"I really love this…" she moaned.

"Yeah, me too." His hands moved to her shirt and began to pull it up.

Mia sucked in her breath as his fingers brushed her bare skin. She helped him pull her shirt off, exposing her small bra. It was a pastel floral pattern that had cost way more than Mia expected, but it made her feel cute. River took a moment to gaze at her body before he got up to undress. He was already breathing hard.

"Wait, let me help." Mia stood up and pulled his shirt over his head. "I love all your tattoos, you know…" She gazed at the ones on his chest and stomach. There was a raven encircled by a gothic font reading 'nevermore,' a heart pierced by a razor blade, a pair of dice, and a couple of small others. Her hands moved to his pants and worked on unbuckling him. As she stripped him down to his briefs, she felt his hands move to unsnap her bra. He was about to see her naked. No more hiding anything anymore.

"I'm glad you love them."

She pressed up against him, already turned on by the sight of him shirtless. She loved how strong he was and felt she could disappear completely if she was pinned underneath him.

He pulled her back onto the bed, making her squeal as her head hit the pillows. Mia shivered, feeling her bare skin against his, watching as he knelt over her. Their eyes met and they both smiled shyly. Her hair fell around her head like a halo, and the ends of his hair tickled her nose and cheeks with how close he was to her. Hands wandered along each other's torsos, to the sides of their stomachs and along their collarbones, exploring freckles and scars. Mia moaned with want, letting his hands wander all over her. In seconds she had kicked her pants to the floor, and she slipped her hand between his legs. She felt for him.

"Fuck!" he cried out and buried his face against the crook of her neck. He bit his lip, breathing in her scent.

"Real sensitive there?" She smirked and kept rubbing softly, loving how wet he was already. Every time he whimpered and moaned it vibrated against her neck. "You're dripping...are you wet for me?"

He just moaned in response, shuddering as her fingers explored him with almost a curiosity, wanting to find the places that would really send him over the edge with just the slightest touch. His chest heaved with deep breaths. She felt his wetness drip down her fingers.

"Start stroking me."

Without hesitating he reached down and slipped his hand under her panties. Her erection popped out and before she could move, he gripped her gently. Mia bit her lip and stared up at him, barely able to breathe. She felt goosebumps go up her arms. As he began stroking her, she curled her toes and kept her eyes locked on him, then resumed focusing on pleasuring him at the same time. Her body felt warm, and she saw beads of sweat run down his forehead and dampen his hair. It overwhelmed her. Her head swam with bliss, being touched so affectionately yet in a way that made her feel like she could drive the man insane with lust.

"River, please…please fuck me, I can't take it…" she whimpered.

"How badly do you want it?" He stroked her a little faster. "How badly do you want my cunt around your pretty little cock?"

Fuck, he's good at this dirty talk. She could have come right there if she had any less self-control.

"Please, River…*please.*" Mia bit her lip and lifted her legs, feeling so small and petite beneath him, and it felt so euphoric she didn't know if she could stand it. She watched him open the end table drawer and remove a condom. His eyes never left hers as he popped it open and gently slid the condom on, making her moan and whimper even more.

He folded his arms around her, and his body moved on top of hers. She cried out as she felt herself slowly move inside him. Wetness oozed down the sides of her shaft. River rested his head beside hers. Mia clung to his back. Once he had positioned himself in a way that felt the best, Mia felt him begin to thrust. It felt wild, having him ride her, like he was the one fucking her, the one who was really in control. Mia's eyes rolled back, and she reveled in feeling his body moving over hers, listening to his groans and labored breathing, listening to the obscene sounds his cunt made as he thrusted her cock inside him. He knew exactly how to move his hips so all she could do was lie there and take it.

"You feel so good. River…" She wasn't going to cry, but it felt so good, she wanted to.

He moved up and kissed her, muffling both of their moans. Mia grabbed fistfuls of his hair again. When his fingers moved to her hard nipples, she could not hold back the loud cry of pleasure.

"You really love to beg, huh?" River teased as he began kneading her breasts, his thumbs rubbing across her nipples over and over.

Mia couldn't even make the words come out. Her mouth hung open as she mewled and howled. She was seeing stars. She felt like she was floating. He thrust even faster and suddenly Mia was screaming out and her legs shook and she felt her orgasm hit her. Even as she came he didn't stop. With one hand he kept playing with her breasts and the other moved down to rub at himself. Mia noticed what he was doing and quickly took over. It only took a few strokes and he was soon crying out and grunting as he came hard all over her fingers.

"Shit, shit…!" He rested his head on her chest, panting like a wild animal.

"Oh, my god. I can't move…"

"Me neither." He rolled over to the side so he was lying next to her. "Fuck, that was really good."

"Good? It was amazing," she laughed. She inched closer to him and rested her head on his chest, soaking in his warmth. Mia felt him put his arm over her and she let out a soft moan of pure bliss.

"Hey. I love you," he said softly.

"I love you too." Mia closed her eyes. A few seconds later she felt him start to move, and she lifted her head.

"Sorry...I'm going to go clean up real quick before you fall asleep." River got up and slipped into the bathroom. Mia hugged the pillow as she waited for him, not wanting to move at all. When he came back out, Mia found herself admiring his naked body, all the perfections and imperfections. She realized he was staring at her, too. "You're staring..." he said with a shy smile.

"You're just so handsome."

"The magic of hormones." He climbed back into bed with her. Mia snuggled up to him, feeling drunk on the scent of him yet starving for it at the same time.

"Well, yeah, but it's more than that. I don't know how to use the right words, but...I just love you a lot."

"I love you too." He cupped her cheek and kissed her. "You're going to stay the night, right?"

"I mean, I do have a few other dates I planned to hook up with for the rest of the night, but...of course I'm staying, silly," she laughed.

"Good, cause you're a real good cuddler." He pressed up against her, pulling her body closer.

River woke up in Mia's arms after a long, interrupted night's sleep. It was the first time in a while he had been able to sleep without nightmares.

He stretched his legs, playing with his necklace, and was content to just lay there next to her, listening to her soft breathing as she slept. He looked at her, at the smudged eyeshadow from yesterday and the pink in her cheeks and her small, perky breasts. In his mind he knew, deep down, he had been feeling this way about her much longer than he thought. All those times during the summer he would log on to a wi-fi hotspot and start charging his phone, praying for a text from her. *I just think she's so pretty and funny and amazing, as a friend of course,* he would tell himself and his friends. And it took him that long to find out he was in love with her this whole time.

Mia woke up after a little while and blinked at him.

"How long have you been watching me?"

"Not that long."

"Creep." She smiled and kissed him on the cheek. "Hold me…"

He smiled and wrapped his arms around her.

"I love you." She meant it. She meant every word. As he held her close, she rested her eyes, a sense of protection and comfort all over her body. "You know, I slept real good last night. No nightmares."

"Yeah? Me neither," he said with a small smile.

"Maybe we helped protect each other from them. Or something corny like that, I don't know."

"No, that makes sense to me. I like it." He rolled over on his stomach and she flopped her arm over the middle of his back. "What would you say to some coffee and breakfast?"

"I'd love that. But not yet. I'm feeling lazy." She snuggled up next to him, lying on her side to get closer to him. "Stay here with me, just a little longer." Mia rested her eyes shut, relishing the bliss of a lazy, sleepy morning. She felt River do the same beside her, and she imagined she had a bunch of mornings just like this one to look forward to now. Mornings where they didn't have anywhere to go or anything to do and could just lie in bed like this all they wanted.

But she knew it wouldn't always be this good. Sooner or later, they were going to have bad nights again, with painful memories and long, sleepless hours. Some days would be the happiest moments of her life and some days, like the other night at the club, would have moments she would wish she could forget.

And that was okay. They were going to heal, and they were going to find the best part of themselves together, and that was what mattered. She could see her future brighter than ever now, and she would have him by her side. Not just River, but her friends too—Julian, Alan, Grace, all of them. She would never be alone again.

Chapter Twenty-Six

Within the week, River and Mia were officially out as a couple. As always, Alan, Julian, and Grace were the first to hear about it, followed by the rest of their mutual friends and the band.

For the first several days, their relationship was almost treated as a joke. The running gag was that they had finally both figured out what everyone else had known for months, and the joke was how long it took them to put two and two together. Fortunately, the joke got old quickly, and soon they were able to just be another couple in their friend circle.

In the next couple of months that followed, Mia had to come to terms with the fact that this was her first real relationship. A few dates in high school to try to prove she was a heterosexual man hardly counted. Now, she was in something for the long-term, with a person she already knew very well.

As it turned out, being in her first real relationship was a bit like learning a new language. She wasn't used to going on regular dates. Keeping things like a phone charger or a change of clothes at another apartment in the city. Having to have conversations about how they preferred to fold their towels, or why she needed him to text more than just 'we need to talk' or else it would make her have a panic attack. She wasn't used to suddenly having to consider another person's schedule, wants, needs, and preferences on top of her own, on a day-to-day basis. Before, Mia had imagined a relationship like this was just like friendship, with kisses and sex thrown in, but she quickly discovered it was so much more than that. That made the first few weeks a bit tumultuous for her, like riding out choppy waves. But it was River, who already understood a lot of her favorite things, her sense of humor, what excited her and what triggered her. And she had never felt more seen, more secure, or more at home than when she was with him.

Meanwhile, as she began to learn, River had had a long history of relationships going back to ninth grade. He used to have a habit of jumping from one to another, especially as he began dealing with his transition and his father's death, the latter of which only made it worse. By sophomore and junior year, he was solely engaging in hookups and one-night-stands, not necessarily with people he even liked. Just anyone who would give him that attention. By college, however, River began to change his ways and work on not using sexual relationships as a form of self-harm, and he started to get better. Until he met his ex before Mia, that is, the one who made him swear off dating for months by the time they broke up.

It wasn't always the perfect picture Mia had imagined it would be. Wasn't how it was depicted on the silver screen or in commercials. She and River had disagreements now and then, little things like when they preferred to go to bed or what television shows they would prefer watching on date night. They never fought or argued, but sometimes the little clashes would stress her out. Or worse, sometimes triggered one of River's anxiety attacks. But then, when things cooled down, River would take her into his arms and hug her and talk it out, and they would always circle back to being on the same side and working it out.

And through the messy days—days when she couldn't stand anyone touching her, or days when River's brain was going a million miles an hour, and no one could keep up with him—they learned more about each other. Quirks, qualities, and love languages. All the things they had been wanting to know all this time. And every day Mia woke up either to a good morning text or, better yet, to River making her coffee just the way she liked it, she found herself falling in love with him all over again.

But better yet, the more she fell in love with River, the more Mia realized, in a way, she was also falling in love with herself. Things that the rest of the world told her she needed to despise and try to change, whether due to her ethnicity or the gender she was assigned at birth. Things like her skin color, her jaw shape, her body hair, or even her laugh or her lips. Now those were the very things River told her time and time again that he adored about her, that drove him crazy, that made her perfect to him. And she learned to see herself in a new light when she looked in the mirror. To not only refuse to let the world's bigotry and hatred tell her they were flaws, but to celebrate them. Celebrate everything that made her 'Mia Reyes.' And little by little, the good days began to outnumber the bad.

Then the holiday season rolled around, and it all came to a head.

After clocking out at work one mid-November evening, Mia came over to River's apartment to find him staring at his laptop. She set the Chinese takeout she had ordered on the kitchen table and curled up next to him. By now, she had his three favorite orders memorized and also knew that he liked to circulate between the three. Today had been her turn to figure out dinner, and luckily for her (not so much for her paycheck), their favorite Chinese place was on the way.

"Hey, stranger. How was your day?" she asked him, planting a sloppy wet kiss on his temple.

But River didn't do his usual, typically something peculiar (but which Mia now found endearing) like licking her on the ear or biting her on the arm. Instead, he shut his laptop and ran his hands through his hair. She felt herself wince. Hands through the hair—not a good sign.

"My day was going okay until my mom messaged me."

"Uh-oh. About what?" Mia got up to dish up a plate for him.

"She wants to get the family all back together for the holidays at her home in New York. She's throwing a large party on December 23rd. And she's inviting everyone. She says you're invited too."

"Oh. Well, that's…good news, right? Good-ish?" she asked with a slight frown as she sat next to him. By now she had a general idea of his family, based on conversations he had had with her about them. She knew the names of his four brothers from oldest to youngest—Anthony, Nate, Brandon, and Dean. She knew his mom had two sisters, one of which was married with a daughter, and that his dad died in a car crash when he was a teenager. And finally, she knew that the Solinski's were a bit of a wild bunch, prone to reinventing the concept of 'family drama' tenfold. River had told his mom about his new girlfriend several weeks ago, but she had no idea how much the rest of the Solinskis knew, if anything.

"Yes and no. I mean…it's complicated. This is going to be a big deal to her. The whole family hasn't gotten together for the holidays since before I started college. But a lot of people are going to be there, including all my brothers."

"So it's not that great after all." She set down his plate of food and went to dish up her own. "If it's going to be too hard for you to go, I'm sure your mom would understand."

"I know, but it would let her down and she'll never stop giving me shit for it. Family means the world to her. If I don't go, everyone will know and I won't hear the end of it. I can't *not* go. But I don't want to. I haven't seen some of them in years and I don't know how I'm going to handle that. And the rest of my family, well, let's just say they can be all over the place."

"Then I'm definitely coming with you."

He looked up at her where she stood at the table, filling her plate with sweet and sour chicken and fried rice. The long pause in the air made Mia tense up.

"I mean, you wouldn't mind if I came with, right?"

"Yes! I mean, of course I'd love to have you come with. It's just…"

"What?" She sat next to him and began digging into her food. He hadn't even touched his plate yet. Another unusual thing for him. He sighed.

"Let's just say it's not exactly going to be something straight off the Hallmark Channel. Something always happens at a Solinski reunion. *Always.* And usually it's more than one thing. Dean and Nate are going to get into it about politics or Aunt Christie will scream at us because no one wants to eat her shitty potato salad or me and Brandon will fight about whatever new dumb hill he wants to die on. And that's not even, like, the top three things that are going to happen. And that's not even going into the in-laws like Anthony's wife Britney, who is a terrible person I wouldn't trust to babysit a fucking Furby. Britney's family is like all the worst parts about the West Coast thrown in a blender and topped off with all the worst things about New Jersey."

"Okay, maybe your family wouldn't cut it on Hallmark Channel, but the MTV reality show writes itself." Mia laughed at her own joke and was relieved when it got at least a small smile out of River. "Look…I don't care if there's drama. I want to meet your mom. I want to help you with dealing with seeing your family and everyone else." She stabbed a piece of broccoli from his plate. That seemed to finally get his attention, and he started digging in. "You don't want to hide me from your family, right?"

"No, Mia. Fuck, that's not what I mean at all! I just don't want any of them hurting you." He took a bite, forcing Mia to wait for him to explain. "My brothers didn't…take it well when I came out. Brandon and Nate are still dickwads who think binging conservative podcasts is a personality trait. My uncle Robin is the same way, just the same shit from a different generation. And even a lot of my family who are okay with it are still pretty careless and shitty with how they talk about it. I guess my point is…it'll be rough. If anyone said something real fucked up to you, I'd feel like it was my fault for bringing you along."

Mia grabbed his hand and squeezed it a bit.

"I get that. But I want to be there for you. And how about the food? Will it be good?"

"Oh, it'll be the best." He held up his index finger to make his point. "Now, that is *one* thing my family does right. We can have the screaming matches of the century and throw fights like no other, but dammit if we aren't great cooks!"

"And you don't want me missing out on good food, right?" she asked with a growing smirk. "Because that would just be wrong. I think it's actually one of the seven deadly sins."

"Good point." He shoved a forkful of food into his mouth. While he chewed, Mia rubbed at the back of his free hand.

"I'll come with you. And whatever happens, I'll be there with you." She stole another bit of broccoli off his plate. "Oh, and…one other thing. Does your family drink?"

"Oh, boy. Do they." He laughed, but it was not a happy laugh. A laugh that came from somewhere deep down. "My dad had me try my first beer when I was twelve."

"That's awful." Mia shuddered. She did not know what she would have done if her foster parents, who were neck-deep in that addiction, had tried to drag her down.

"It's not like that," River quickly said. "He was just having fun. The way he grew up, everyone around him drank hard and partied hard. It was normal to him. Most of my brothers ended up like that, too. They don't think it's a problem, and *that's* the problem."

"I understand that." She squeezed his hand. "We should make a pact, then. Neither of us will drink while we're there."

"I think that's a good idea. I'm okay with never drinking again, to be honest. Trouble always finds me when I do."

"Me too. Oh, and no fights, okay?"

"Fine, *Mom*." He shoved more food in his mouth, and she smiled at him. "I love you," he said with his mouth still half full, so it sounded more like "mm-luff-oo."

"I love you too."

They booked their plane tickets for the day after Mia's finals. As much as she was apprehensive about the family drama River warned her about, she was also excited. It would be her first time at a real family reunion and having a nice holiday dinner. Much like her first snowfall upon moving north, this was something she had only experienced by watching it on a TV screen. As in, not experienced at all.

It would also be her first time flying on a plane. That part scared the shit out of her. But River would be there the whole time, which helped shave off the worst of her fears. She would be caught dead flying alone.

Even so, she did take his warnings about his family to heart and began to mentally steel herself for what might happen at the Solinski reunion. She told herself she would do her best not to internalize whatever came her way, but her brain was nothing if not an expert on inventing worst-case scenarios, especially considering the description given of his uncle and two brothers. But whatever happened, she would be by River's side the whole time. Both to help remind her of her own strength and to comfort him.

Finals finally ended, much to Mia's relief, allowing her to relax her mind regarding school and just focus on the trip. The next morning, they were up early to head to the airport. Mia didn't feel too bad about it until they were boarding the plane and she could feel the hum of the engines rumbling through the floor. Suddenly every movie and news report she had seen about a plane crash flashed through her mind. She found herself leaning into River and grabbing his hand as they stepped inside, sweat making her grip slick.

"You okay?" he whispered.

"I'm going to die here, aren't I? This is it. This is the end."

"You're four hundred times less likely to die in a plane than in a car. And the odds of dying in a plane are one in over seven thousand. I'd say those are pretty good odds, wouldn't you?"

Mia blinked at him.

"You looked that up just to make me feel better, didn't you?"

"Is it helping?"

"I guess. Your motorcycle is logically way more dangerous than this." She glanced up at him as they waited their turn to keep walking down the narrow aisle. "Can I steal your hoodie?" she asked, as if she even needed to anymore. At this point Mia wore his hoodies and sweaters more than he did. It wasn't her fault how big and comfy they were.

Without a word, River pulled it off and let her take it. She squeezed his hand as they got in their seats. When the engines rumbled and they started to move, she began to whimper, her body paralyzed with terror. River smooched the back of her hand over and over and told her all his dumb jokes, whether it was a quote from their favorite show or his celebrity impressions that always put her in stitches. She was still scared, but it helped distract her. When they were finally in the air and the seat belt light was off, Mia leaned against him. River put his arm over her and held her close. Her body was still all tensed up, but having River close by was calming to her. She focused on listening to his breathing, to the way his fingers would idly rub her upper arm and shoulder or reach up and gently play with her hair. He felt so calm and steady, like nothing bad could happen to her as long as he was there.

As she began to drift off into a light doze, Mia began drifting to a sexual fantasy she had been thinking about ever since she found out they were going to be flying. It was far from realistic, but she liked to imagine them both sneaking off to the tiny bathroom on the plane and having sex. She imagined him dragging her in there and holding her tight, whispering in her ear that he was too horny to last even six hours without fucking her. She imagined him pinning her against the wall, his hand over her mouth so she wouldn't make any noise. It would feel so nasty and dirty but so much fun. Mia felt herself getting a little hard as she daydreamed about it.

Light sleep was mingled with her own dirty fantasies on and off during the flight. Mia only woke up to eat the meal provided and went right back to cuddling up next to River after that. He was content to let her rest the whole flight as he read the book he brought with him. In the last couple hours of the flight, he dozed off as well, resting his head on top of hers as her head was nestled on his shoulder.

Mia woke up feeling cranky and aching all over. River rubbed her shoulder as the cabin lights all flickered on.

"We're here. Did you sleep okay?"

"No. I'm hungry and I feel weird," she fussed, eager to be up and moving again. Once they were in the terminal, she stretched out her arms.

"My mom and aunt are picking us up at the baggage claim real soon."

"I finally get to meet your mom." She smiled and grabbed River's hand as they walked side by side. "Can you get me an iced coffee and a bagel? Pretty please?"

"Okay, but only because you're cute." He smiled and pulled her towards the nearest coffee place. Mia still felt gross all over and wanted to breathe cool, fresh air, but the food and drink helped her feel better. She slurped on her coffee as River grabbed their luggage, and they headed to where his mom was waiting for them.

Chapter Twenty-Seven

In a way, Liz Solinski was not who Mia had been expecting. For some reason she had pictured River's mom much taller and with softer features, whereas the woman standing outside barely reached River's shoulders. Beside her stood River's aunt, who had a long brown braid reaching to the small of her back and a gentle smile. Mia swallowed hard. But her anxiety began to dissipate as soon as she saw Ms. Solinski run up to her son and hug him tight. River was all smiles as he hugged his mom back. Hugs had to be a good sign, right?

"How was the flight?"

"Uneventful, so I can't complain." River pulled away after several seconds and put his arm around Mia's waist, leading her closer. "Mom, this is my girlfriend, Mia."

Mia smiled and waved her hand. Of course, River had told his mom that Mia was coming with him weeks in advance so everything could be ready, but it was still nerve-wracking. Mia had also given River permission to tell his mom she was transgender, as long as she didn't proactively mention it to the rest of the family.

"Uh, hi. Nice to meet you finally!" Mia said, using her best high-pitched voice, which was exhausting to do for long periods and she never felt the need to use it around River.

"Nice to meet you, too." His mom smiled, then pulled Mia into a hug. "Welcome to the family."

"I'm his aunt, Tami." She smiled warmly at them once they pulled away from the hug. "River, wow! The last time I saw you, you must have been about eighteen. You've grown!"

"Sounds about right," he said. Mia wasn't sure how River felt about this aunt in particular. From what she understood, Aunt Christie was married to the transphobic husband and had a daughter with him, while Tami had been divorced twice, never had kids, and now lived on her own in Colorado. She loved skiing and had a great job working for a media company located in downtown Denver.

"My goodness, your mom was right. You got so tall, and so handsome!" Tami pulled him in for a quick hug. That made Mia smile.

"Let's get going so we can beat traffic." Ms. Solinski opened the trunk of the car. "It'll be just the four of us today. Everybody else will show up tomorrow."

Once in the car, Mia realized it was probably the nicest and newest vehicle she had been in to date. She worried about spilling her iced coffee and gripped it a little tighter. And the ride was so quiet. Almost too quiet.

The drive to his mom's house took about an hour as they had to get out of downtown and head up into the north suburbs. During the drive, the conversation stayed casual for the most part. While Aunt Tami was enthusiastic about seeing River again, his mom was calm and collected. Tami had all sorts of questions, and it took them a long time to even begin to catch up. Eventually she was talking to just River's mom, and Mia took that opportunity to stare out the window at the beautiful city as they drove through, holding River's hand all the while.

His mom's house seemed like a mansion to Mia, even though she knew it technically wasn't. It was over eight thousand square feet and at the end of a cul-de-sac with other similar homes. There was a huge backyard with a small, wooded area out back and even an outdoor hot tub. Mia couldn't imagine how a family, even one of this size, could take up a house this big, but that was just her opinion she decided to keep to herself.

She got the full tour of the house first. Then they spent a quiet evening with a light dinner, followed by a card game. River and Tami got the most into it, making loud exclamations when certain cards were drawn, while Mia and his mom were more reserved, and found themselves enjoying the former two's outbursts and reactions more than the game itself. After the game, Mia was ready to turn in. She said goodnight to her hosts and rushed upstairs to the guest room to take a shower. Once alone for the first time all day, she took her time enjoying the hot water and cleaning up. All those dirty fantasies she semi-dreamed about on the flight had had her all pent up for hours, and now that she was by herself again, it didn't take long for her to start to harden. But before she could do anything to satisfy herself, there was a knock on the door. Mia yelped in surprise.

"It's the boogeyman," River called.

"Oh. Door's unlocked!" she hollered back. She resumed shampooing her hair as River stepped in.

"So, what do you think of them?" she heard him ask over the sound of running water.

"Your mom's so nice. Very smart too. And Tami is awesome. She's like the cool aunt I never had. She's such a sweetheart."

"She is pretty cool. Hey, I want to take a shower too."

"Come on in," Mia said, smiling. They had showered together many times already and had mostly figured out how to coordinate it so they weren't fumbling around each other.

River got in the shower and held his head under the running water until his hair was soaked. Mia grabbed his shampoo bottle and began washing his hair for him. It had become something she loved doing for him. He closed his eyes and moaned a little.

"What's it like being back in this house?"

"Brings back memories. Some good, some that could be better," he said quietly. "Honestly, it just makes me miss my dad more than anything."

Mia kissed him on the nose as she massaged his head.

"Are you okay?"

"I have you with me, so that's going to be a yes."

She smiled and had him lean his head up so she could rinse. They washed each other's backs, leaving small kisses on shoulders and fingertips and noses and chins. When they were both done, she grabbed a towel and began drying off. As soon as River finished drying himself she felt him grab her from behind and kiss the back of her neck.

"Oh, hello."

"You smell so good."

"I should hope so. I just showered." She giggled and turned around to face him. "So are you going to get on the bed so I can fuck you or what?"

"Make me." He smirked.

Mia bit her bottom lip and slapped him on the ass. He made a muffled cry. She grabbed him and began pulling out of the bathroom and towards the queen-sized bed.

"Lie face-down, baby," she whispered in his ear.

"Make me."

Again, Mia slapped his ass hard. Then she pushed him onto the bed. Even though he was much stronger than her, he willingly let her push him, submitting to her. Mia crawled on top of him and rolled him over so he was facing her.

"Fuck, I love you so much." She said it countless times a day every day, but never got tired of it. She meant it every time.

He stared up at her like he was in a daze, like he was a young boy love-struck for the first time. Mia's heart pounded as she leaned down and kissed him, caressing his chest and stomach. River reached up and cupped her sore breasts, making her moan out.

"They get a little bigger every day." He leaned up and began kissing one of her nipples.

Mia was about to moan when she remembered two other people were sleeping just down the hall.

"*Fuck*. River, we need to keep really quiet…"

"I know. I can do it. Can you?"

"I can try. And that isn't helping…" It was taking all her self-control not to cry out as he kept licking and twisting her nipples. Mia moved up on top of him, trying to rub her cock against his legs for a bit of relief. "I need to fuck you real hard."

"Bet you can't."

"Oh, you bet?" Mia smiled. She loved when he got feisty. She grabbed his legs and spread them, admiring him, before she began pleasuring him with two of her fingers. He bucked his hips and shut his eyes, chest heaving as he struggled to keep quiet. In seconds she started to feel his wetness pruning her fingers. "See, look how quickly you get wet for me, slut."

"Am I your little whore?" he moaned softly.

"Yes. All mine." She kissed him, muffling both their moans as she fingered him faster. He bit her lip, shuddering underneath her. Her hips began to rock against his and he wrapped his arms around her, pulling her close. It only took a few moments for Mia to position herself against him, put on a condom, and guide herself inside him. "Don't make a sound…"

"I won't." He was breathing hard. Mia nuzzled his neck, nibbling on his skin. Loving the little gasps and whimpers he made as he tried to be as quiet as possible. She grabbed his hips and began pounding into him.

But now it was starting to affect her, too. She bit her lip, struggling not to make a sound, her mind dizzy with pleasure. The way just a small move of her hips could make this man melt and unravel under her.

It didn't take either of them long to orgasm hard and she collapsed on top of him, breathing hard, shaking all over. Her head was spinning from how good it had been. She leaned up and planted lazy kisses up his neck. Something about having to not make a sound the whole time had made it almost better.

"That was…" Mia whispered breathlessly.

"Yeah. That was…"

"Really good," she laughed. "You have no idea how pent up I was all day. I thought I was going to go crazy."

"Me too." He rolled over on his side, pulling her with him so he could hold her from behind. She smiled and kissed the back of his hand and they laid there in silence for some time, just enjoying the moment for what it was, until they were fast asleep.

River knew today was going to suck. The only question was how much it would suck, and what level of sucking he would be able to put up with.

He got up early. As much as he tried to make himself sleep in as it was a holiday, his body decided that wasn't going to happen. Since Mia was still out, he tucked her under the comforter, put on a shirt and gym shorts, and headed downstairs. In the kitchen, River found that someone had already brewed a pot of coffee. Aunt Tami was at the counter sipping on some. When she saw him, she smiled.

"Good morning. Sleep okay?"

"I guess." He poured himself some coffee. He had always liked Aunt Tami. When he was young, she would babysit him while his parents were on a trip or a date, and she would visit the house often. Later on, after she moved to Colorado, his mom told Aunt Tami about his transition through their regular phone calls. But as soon as she got his email address, Tami reached out to tell him she supported him completely.

"I know, I never got to say this face to face, but...I'm proud of you, you know." She looked at him. "When you were little, I did have a feeling you were different in a way. That you were special. And when your mom told me you had started transitioning, a lot of pieces fell into place. It just made so much sense to me."

"Wait, really?" He blinked at her.

"It wasn't like I knew the whole time. But once I found out, a lot of the little signs that something was going on suddenly came together. And I just had to tell her, 'oh, of course. Of course he is a boy.'"

"Yeah, no kidding." River smiled and sipped his coffee. He thought back to those days. Tami and his mom's parents were the first people in his life to tell him that you could be whoever you wanted to be and love whoever you wanted to love. He owed them a lot for introducing him to that at a young age, paving the way for when he came out of the closet.

"How is she doing? Your girlfriend, I mean."

River wasn't sure how much he could speak for her, so decided to keep it simple. But last night over cards, Mia had already come out as trans to her, and she expressed nothing but love and support.

"She's doing a lot better. It was really hard for her at first. But she's come a long way." He thought about where Mia was about a year ago—unable to present her gender, depressed, suicidal, scars covering her arms and legs. And now she was dressing and wearing exactly what she wanted and glowing with new energy. The two were hardly comparable.

"That's really good. She's lucky to have you. You're a sweet boy with a big heart." She smiled.

"You're just saying that because I'm your favorite nephew."

Aunt Tami just laughed and helped herself to more cream in her coffee.

"By the way, how can you take your coffee black? It's disgusting. You're just like your mom."

"What can I say? Runs in the family."

Chapter Twenty-Eight

The morning was slow and lazy as they waited for the rest of the Solinskis to arrive. River took Mia for a walk around the woods out back, showing her what remained of the old forts and trenches he built with his brothers, and then they had a light breakfast. After that, they got to work with the first rounds of meal prep. River was more than happy to help in the kitchen, anything to keep his hands busy and his mind occupied. At first his mom told Mia she didn't have to help out and could go relax, as she was a guest and she was on vacation, but Mia was equally as stubborn. Eventually, in the most literal sense, she got her foot in the door and was soon helping too.

Then, in the early afternoon, the reunion officially began. Outside the large living room bay window, Mia saw a small caravan of cars pull up in the cul-de-sac. She swallowed and closed her eyes for a few moments.

You can't control what they'll say to you or your boyfriend, she reminded herself, just like how she had been taught to by her therapist. *All you can control is how you react to it. They don't know you. They're just idiots. You're going to be okay.* Then she left the kitchen, found River right outside, and squeezed his hand. She glanced up at him, noting the tension in his brow.

"Hey, you got this," she whispered.

He mumbled a 'mm–hm' under his breath as the front door opened. She saw Dean and Nate, who she recognized based on all the framed photos their mom showed her last night. Each of them was carrying a pie and roaring with laughter at a joke someone must have told on the way in. Anthony was close behind them. Wearing a nice coat, he quickly brushed the snow off, followed by his wife who had her hands full between helping her toddler inside and carrying a huge armload of food containers. Aunt Tami and his mom moved in first to help and exchange hugs and hellos, while River lingered in the back. But as it turned out, he didn't have to move a muscle. Anthony sauntered right up to him and smacked River on the back, hard.

"Hey, it's the starving artist! And wow, shocker, you got another shitty tattoo!" Anthony bellowed loud enough for the whole room to hear, and suddenly Mia knew way more than she needed to know about him.

"Hey, Ton'," River said, forcing a smile. "Long time, no see."

"No fucking kidding. Hey guys, look who finally decided to show up!" Anthony waved over the other two brothers, as River and Britney exchanged death glares from opposite ends of the room. Just at first glance, Mia already decided that Britney was exactly the type of person who hardly felt the need to shop anywhere else outside of Target, Hobby Lobby, and Nordstrom Rack. Meanwhile, Nate acknowledged River's presence with a slight nod then resumed chatting up with his mom, while Dean greeted his little brother with a big tackle that nearly knocked River to the floor. The two of them wrestled like teenage boys until their mother snapped at them to stop before they broke something.

The family had barely settled in when more filed in. Mia saw the last brother, Brandon, walk in right in front of Aunt Christie and her husband and adult daughter. Ironically, as they lived right down the street, River's grandparents were the last to arrive. All at once, a large house that had been dead quiet for the past several hours escalated into chaos, snow being stomped out and coats being thrown around and food hurried into the kitchen, hugs and laughter and jokes directed at long-seated insecurities piled on. The two little ones, Anthony's son and Aunt Christie's daughter, started chasing each other around, while the four brothers immediately opened the large packs of beer they brought with them. The two aunts, uncle, and River's mom and grandparents gathered in their own corner to chat before there was more work to do in the kitchen.

At the smell and sight of alcohol, Mia's body tensed a bit. It still triggered her sometimes, and as River had already warned her, it seemed 'Solinski reunion' and 'non-alcoholic setting' were contradictory terms. She had seen this coming, though, and went through her breathing exercises she learned in therapy to stay calm. As the family moved about the kitchen and living room, she never let go of River's hand. While she was watching the brothers crack open beers and insult each other's jobs or lack of girlfriends or whatever else, River gave Mia's hand a squeeze. As soon as he saw his mom and Aunt Tami return to the kitchen, he pulled Mia with him.

"Let's go finish helping them in there," he whispered. She barely heard him, over the sound of so many loud voices, but she nodded along. Mia was more than happy to help back in there. As they got to work, she saw River's grandmother walk in too, carrying a bottle of wine and a large pan of prime rib.

"River," she said, "you need to introduce me to this little angel from heaven you've got on your arm."

Mia flushed so hard she thought she would burst, as River hurried her over and introduced her as his girlfriend he met at college. River's grandmother was by far the most soft-spoken of the family. A gentle, but unyielding voice that commanded the entire room without having to escalate, which was a far cry from the four brothers and two aunts in the living room. His grandmother was barely over five feet tall, but when she reached out and touched Mia's arm, her grip felt firm. Mia couldn't look away from her.

"You have good hands. These are the hands of a woman who can change the world," said his grandmother. "Did you two meet at school?"

"Yes, about a year ago, and we've been dating for a few months," River answered. Meanwhile, Mia was swooning at the compliment, although she hardly understood it.

"Very good. Mia, baby, would you please put my coat in the closet? A lot of snow got tracked in out there and I don't want to slip."

"Of course, ma'am!" Mia nodded eagerly and made a mad dash for the closet, still trying to wrap her head around what she meant by 'good hands,' but supposed she'd ask River about it later. For the next half hour, they stayed in the kitchen to help until dinner was ready. With that, Aunt Tami rushed out and hollered out the big announcement that everyone, quote, had better get their asses to the table.

Now that she saw it all laid out at once, Mia understood what River meant about how well his family cooked. There were several kinds of meats laid out, including the huge turkey, the prime rib, brisket, and meatballs. To say nothing of all the vegetable side dishes, rolls, salads, and other appetizers. The dining table was huge, but they had managed to not leave a single square inch unused. In the ensuing several seconds of madness, everyone picked their spots. For a brief moment of panic, Mia rushed to River's side and grabbed the chair to his right before anyone else could. Plates and bowls were shuffled around as River's brothers, aunts, and uncles had to make room to set down the alcohol they had already started drinking.

Once they were all seated, River's grandfather sat at the head of the table, his wife on his left. Although the family was not religious (although Mia got the vibe that a few of them were Catholic), he said a few words, thanking everyone for taking the time to be here and get together as a family again. Much like his wife, he held the room's entire attention as he spoke, without having to raise his voice. The instant he was finished, the family resumed their previous speaking over each other and cracking jokes. Dishes were passed around in a rush. Mia kept her hands to herself so she didn't bump into anyone. River, noticing this, dished up her plate for her, and she mouthed a silent 'thank you' to him. For the first several minutes of dinner, they all indulged in the food, pausing only to drink or comment on how good it was. During the first pause of the meal, Aunt Christie piped up from where she was refilling her glass of white wine.

"So River. You haven't told us much about this new, ah…partner of yours!"

"Girlfriend. And you can call her Mia," he said, in typical loud-and-proud River fashion, which Mia now understood was typical Solinski fashion.

From the other end of the table, Mia caught Nate rolling his eyes before he glanced over at his uncle. She heard him mutter, "Here we go again," then something about how people these days are calling themselves whatever they like.

At first, that same cold feeling rushed over Mia's body. Much like when the guy in the elevator asked if she was the 'Carlos that wanted to turn into a girl.' Or when the girls at the nightclub called her a drag queen. The same helplessness, and horror, like the world had grown fangs and teeth and was closing in. Like it was all coming to an end, and she was being swallowed up into nothingness.

But before she could dip down back into that familiar, black pit, Mia looked around the table. Here was River, the love of her life, right next to her, holding her hand. There was his mom and Aunt Tami, both of whom had already expressed they accepted Mia for who she was and adored her. And there was his grandmother, the oldest one in the room, who had had no problem with seeing Mia as a woman. These assholes at the table weren't the only ones with a voice, and she had backup.

And more than anything, Mia knew who she was. No one could take that away from her.

So she lifted her chin, and when Brandon's eyes met hers, she gave him a small but sweet smile. He did not look pleased.

"Right, right, Mia. Sorry!" Aunt Christie looked over at her. "I heard you two have been dating for a couple months, but you said you knew each other for a long time before that. How did you two meet? How did the sparks start flying?" She folded her hands in front of her as she waited for one of them to answer.

River and Mia looked at each other and exchanged awkward smiles.

"I can tell it," said Mia. She laughed nervously and glanced around the table. "So I guess we first met when I first moved to the city and stopped in the coffee shop he worked at…"

And just like that, Mia was telling their whole story. A family-friendly version, of course, skipping the parts she did not feel comfortable bringing up to a certain number of people present. She told them about first meeting River at the coffee shop, and how they found out they attended the same college (and yes, how she had a crush on him from the time they first met). How their friendship blossomed over the next few months, including when they video chatted all the time during his trip to Italy. And how that culminated in them sitting on the side of the highway in the middle of nowhere and he somewhat accidentally dropped the l-word, and next thing you know, here she was meeting his whole family for the first time.

At the last minute, Mia decided to not just acknowledge that she was trans, but embrace it. Certainly enough at the table already knew, and she liked the idea of being honest about it. Of making certain folks have to endure listening to her celebrate her story. If nothing else, she had earned it.

And so, as her story of how she met and fell for River continued, she allowed her own coming out story to overlap with it. The way she had discovered her gender identity before coming to college, but was afraid to tell anyone or start transitioning. How she befriended Alan and Julian and they took her in like the two gay dads she had never had. And how, thanks to River, she began meeting others like her and making friends who were both accepting and part of the queer community. How she came out to River and their friend Grace, then their friend circle, and then how months later she finally got to start hormone therapy. And now, she had a good job, she was doing great in school, and had an entire network of support around her. She even found herself telling them that she was already looking at gender affirming surgeries in the upcoming future.

When Mia finished her story, she glanced around the table. She suddenly worried she had said too much, or got way too personal for a holiday dinner. But Aunt Christie just smiled warmly at her. She also saw River's mom and grandparents nodding politely in sympathy and understanding. Even two of the brothers, Anthony and Dean, seemed to like hearing her story. As for the rest at the table, they were not making a sound.

"That is a beautiful story. Sounds like you two were meant for each other," said Aunt Christie.

"Yeah, something like that, I think." Mia beamed.

"Wait a hard-boiled minute here," Dean interjected, who sat directly across from River. "So you mean to tell me that it took him over a *year* to realize he liked you back?" He pointed an accusatory butter knife at him, but he had a teasing smile. "What the hell, dude? I thought we raised you better than that."

"To be fair, it took your dad just as long to ask me out," River's mom said with a small smile.

"So it runs in the family. Like father, like son," Aunt Tami teased. To that, Mia saw more eyerolls from a couple of the brothers and the uncle, the disgust that she had called River that out loud. But it didn't scare her. And it made Aunt Tami's affirmation of them all the more meaningful to her, knowing it would not be met with complete approval of the others present.

"Exactly! Besides, he may be an idiot, but he's *my* idiot." Mia proudly grabbed River's hand where they all could see.

After that, Anthony changed the subject to start talking about his company. His uncle had his own opinions on how to run a business, and shortly after, the two had taken up the table in their own heated debate, complete with everyone else's snide comments and jokes.

River glanced at Mia and smiled before shoving an entire roll into his mouth.

Chapter Twenty-Nine

A while later into the dinner, Dean snatched his third helping of brisket, which Mia passed to him. Down at the other end of the table, Brandon was arguing with Britney about something, but Dean paid them no mind.

"So, Mia, question," he said. "Where did you come from? And how about your family?"

She had been preparing for this question, as it was bound to come up at some point. She took a large bite of turkey drenched in gravy before answering him.

"Well, I grew up in a small town, nothing real special. But I worked hard in school and that's how I ended up getting into college, thank goodness. It was one of those kinds of towns where there was nothing really there for me, you know? I knew I needed a change, and this was my dream school."

"That's cool. I never got into my dream school, but that's because I was a lazy ass in high school." Dean laughed. "And you did it all by yourself, huh?"

"Well, yes and no?" Mia shrugged, then grabbed another dinner roll. "I didn't have any real support in middle school or high school, so that was pretty much all me. When I got here, I was broke, scared, and all by myself. But I started making other friends, and I got the support I needed. I don't know how I would have gotten this far if I had to do it all alone, honestly. I mean, you can only work so hard before you need someone to help you up, you know?"

Dean had been nodding and saying 'uh-huh' so much while she talked, it irked her. But it pleased her to see him agreeing with her, at least. Unlike the other three brothers, who dressed in cardigans and dress shirts that looked rather pricey, Dean had on an old music festival shirt under a trucker jacket, grime under his nails, and a small partially faded tattoo near the base of his neck, and he smelled of gasoline and strong tobacco. Mia decided that, until further notice, he was her favorite of River's brothers.

"Totally. I get that. Having friends who are there for you can make all the difference. None of us were born to be islands," Dean said. "And what's your major?" By then, their little conversation had gotten the attention of Anthony and River's uncle, who listened in when she answered.

"Mechanical Engineering," Mia said rather proudly. "I'm looking into a career in aerospace engineering or automotives. I keep changing my mind on that one, though, so who knows. There's so much I'd love to do." She shoved the dinner roll in her mouth, practically swallowing it whole.

"Damn, engineering? That's fucking awesome." Dean looked at River. "You found a smart one for a change, thank god. Helps balance it out with your, uh, lack thereof."

"Oh, fuck you. You didn't even go to college!" River threw a piece of broccoli at him, but Mia saw the playful delight in each of their eyes. Dean threw a meatball at him, and River was about to retaliate when their mother scolded them, with an offhand reference that she would not have another food fight at her table. Before Mia could ask what she meant by 'another,' River rubbed her shoulder a little. "She's great with cars too, by the way. She can literally fix anything. I've seen it."

"Maybe you can help me with my car. It's been making a funny noise." Dean gulped down the last of his beer. "I'm joking. Probably."

"I accept payment in coffee and free pizza," Mia teased right back.

As the evening went on, she paid close attention to the folks around her, weaving in and out of either joining in the chat or just sitting back to listen. Eventually the conversation morphed into the rest of them catching up on what they had been up to since the last family reunion. The more she learned about this family, the more she became fascinated by their rich histories and adventures, even the ones she didn't particularly like. Mia began to realize that they could sit here for literally days and would probably come nowhere close to sharing all of their stories.

Slowly, their stories painted a vivid picture of the family. Anthony was the oldest, the most successful, the first one to give their mom a grandchild. He was the one with the pretty wife and the adorable kid who, at least on the surface, had everything going for him. Nate, the second oldest, worked for their uncle and seemed to know exactly how to make as much money as he could while doing the smallest amount of work, while Brandon hopped from the next big brilliant idea to another off the backs of family loans and offers. Dean, the fourth in line, was the most blue-collar second only to River, working as a truck driver and sharing an apartment with a couple of friends in a small town a few hours away. Mia also got the impression that Anthony was the hard-headed one who decided to take on the role of father figure after their dad died. If Nate and Brandon suffered from middle child syndrome, they were certainly making up for it by bragging about their money, girlfriends (who were noticeably absent from the reunion, of course), and how good they had it, happy to befriend whoever they had to in order to get to the top. Then there were the two littlest brothers, Dean and River. The troublemakers, the partners in crime, the rowdiest and messiest and least financially successful of the family. Coupled with that were the three sisters—Liz, Tami, and Christie—who could not be more different. Liz was level-headed, sturdy, calm. Tami was all over the place, but enjoyed every moment of it. Christie was somewhere between, bridled only by the domineering presence of her husband, Robin. River's cousin, named Summer, was about the same age as Brandon and didn't seem to get along with anyone save for Anthony's wife.

Hours felt like minutes as the evening went on. When he got the chance, River caught them up on how his band had been doing. Their fan following grew a little more all the time, and they were up to thousands of subscribers on their social media platforms. Soon, they hoped to tour the West Coast with some other bands. Maybe they could make it really big in the near future, but it was too early to tell. Either way, though, Mia was always going to be the band's number one fan and show up to every single concert.

His news about the band had mixed results. His brothers all made more 'starving artists' jokes, but Mia detected varying levels of how much was in jest and how much they really meant it. It felt the most in good humor out of Dean, and partially

Anthony, but the other two had that hint of venom in their tone. The implication was they not only didn't want River to do well, but they would enjoy watching him fail. As for Nate, he leaned back in his chair, cutting River off when he tried to tell them that the album was selling well.

"I'm just saying, there are thousands of bands that never make it. Just don't take it too hard. Besides, it's not like your brand is popular. That one punk band lost its edge when the lead singer said he was a—"

"The only music you ever listen to is dubstep and post 9/11 country, so you're not exactly the expert in the room," River cut him off.

Dean burst out laughing at his comeback. River and Brandon looked ready to fight right then and there when Aunt Tami interrupted them, saying that dessert was ready. But even as the aunts rushed to grab the pies, the brothers kept giving each other dirty looks. Quickly, Mia grabbed River's hand under the table, running her thumb over his knuckles just the way he liked.

Luckily, there was nothing like several pies and cakes to distract the family from their disagreements and dig in. Mia had thought she couldn't eat anymore until she smelled the apple, caramel, and eggnog, and suddenly she decided she had room for just a bit more. Soon the conversation shifted into which desserts were the best and who needed whipped cream or ice cream with theirs, and save for Aunt Christie's small meltdown because her pie was the last one anyone helped themselves to, the dinner finished out rather smoothly, all things considered.

After dessert, the family moved to the living room. River and Mia filed in behind everyone else. When she got her chance, she grabbed his hand and gave it a gentle squeeze.

"Hey," she whispered, "you doing okay? Your one brother was…"

"Yeah. This is normal for him." He stopped walking so they could have a moment of privacy, standing in the space between the dining room and kitchen. "But…I'm actually doing okay, I think. A drink sounds really, really good right now, though."

"It does. But we have our pact." He sulked, and she rubbed his biceps. "Try not to start a fight, okay? You've been doing so much better about that. You haven't had one since the release party."

"Yeah…you're right." He took a deep breath. "Wish me luck." In the other room, they could hear everyone else laugh at yet another funny story someone was telling before they refilled their glasses of wine. Mia just got the tail-end of it, and it involved something having to do with Nate's stash of weed and nearly setting fire to an old shed near the edge of the woods.

"Ready?"

He nodded again and laced their fingers together as they walked in, taking a vacant spot on the edge of the couch. Mia thought she would be nodding off by now with how late it was and how much she had eaten, but the dinner party had only just started. A few of them—notably Aunt Christie, Dean, Anthony, and Britney—had already had a lot to drink and were growing louder and sillier. Someone decided to bring out the karaoke machine, at which point Mia had been having such a good time that she grabbed the mic without thinking twice about it. She felt like she did a pretty good performance of some early 2000s pop songs. Then River pulled her into doing a duet for an old love song which, she had to admit, did make her teary-eyed to sing with him. During their performance, she had her eyes only on him and ignored the sour looks she knew certain family members were giving them. After that, the song choices progressed into more and more energetic, fun tunes, in-between tall tales and reminiscing about the past.

About an hour in, Mia wondered if they were really in the clear. If the family drama River had gotten so worked up about was just paranoia. Then she saw the uncle, Robin, start telling a story from years ago, and instantly, the atmosphere took a dark turn.

The story started simple enough. It was about the four brothers playing in the woods out back. Both River and Summer, who was visiting the family with her father, were invited to play with them, only to realize their involvement in the game was being 'hunted down' by the brothers.

River remembered it very well. It was just one example of the many times his brothers teamed up against him. There was a period of a few years where they would push and push until he broke down crying, then laugh and tell him it was just a joke and to stop being a baby. When River got a little older, he would start to fight back before the tears came, throwing swings and tackling them to the ground instead of letting them see him cry. Right around that same time he came out, and it all took on a new dimension of harassment and abuse.

He felt Mia keep looking at him, as Uncle Robin recounted the two of them being chased through the woods, being shot at with the boys' airsoft guns and rocks and pinecones thrown at them. River clenched his jaw, hands balled into fists. Summer, too, was leaning against the wall and glared at her dad as he described seeing the four boys surround them and shoot at their feet to scare them, then pretend to 'execute' them as prisoners of war. As if all of that was bad enough, Uncle Robin was using his former government name over and over. When he did correct himself, he made a big show of it, as if he found it amusing.

About halfway through the story, River finally couldn't take it anymore. The second Uncle Robin paused to chug back some more beer, River cut in by saying loudly,

"Yeah, I don't think me or Summer found it very funny."

"Oh, come on. We didn't actually hurt you," Nate said. "It was just a game."

"Easy to say when you're the one carrying the airsoft gun," Summer muttered before grabbing another beer. "Remember when we played 'Battle Royale' and we ganged up on you and Tony? You were pissed off the rest of the week."

Nate bristled at that, squeezing his beer bottle.

"You know what the problem with your generation is?" Uncle Robin said. "You don't know how to take a joke. You act like using the wrong name or whatever is a hate crime and that you deserve a Purple Heart just for being gay."

The words had not changed. They were all the same people River had grown up with. The same people who compared him to the scum of the earth. He remembered the way Uncle Robin had screamed at his parents about how they were making a big mistake by letting River start hormones, and the way his brothers watched the kids at school call him horrible names and not only did nothing to stop it but joined in on the laughter. He remembered the last family reunion and the way Brandon had blown up in his face the moment he dared mention his transition, saying it made him sick to his stomach, and they had started attacking each other before Anthony and Dean were able to pry them apart. Everything was happening exactly as he feared it would happen.

Did his uncle deserve a punch in the jaw for this? Maybe. Probably. But River had made a promise to Mia, and he did not want to be someone who went back on his word. Besides, his uncle wasn't the only one here. He had people in his family who loved him and saw him for who he was. And they were the ones worth spending time with.

So River smiled at him and walked over to the closet just outside the entry door. Sure enough, one of the old footballs was still in there. He had long lost count of how many times this had hit him in the face, on the back of the head, or in the solar plexus.

"Okay, Uncle Robin, I'm not going to have this conversation with you. I'm going to take the football outside. Anyone want to join me?" He glanced around the room.

"Me! I call team captain!" Dean leaped over the couch, already grabbing his coat.

Summer smiled at her cousin and set down her drink.

"I'm in," she said, pulling her hair back in a ponytail.

"Why the hell not?" Anthony gulped down the rest of his beer. As he got up, he glanced at the other two brothers. "Come on, you losers. Let's go play!"

"Well, while you're all having fun, I'll go start cleaning up in the kitchen," their mom said. Aunt Tami, who was still sober enough to get up and walk, joined her, and Mia took her chance to slip away with the two women. River stole a passing glance at his uncle, who silently fumed that he had not been granted the dignity of a comeback, before they rushed aside.

Outside, in the backyard, the six of them played a classic game of football. Just like they used to as kids, only now both River and Summer could play with them. It only took minutes for all of them to get soaking wet from the snow. None of River's brothers held back on how hard they tackled, so River didn't either. He kept up with his teammates, Dean and Anthony, and although he loved the competition, he also didn't care if he won or not.

Because in the back of his mind, River imagined his dad watching from the porch, smoking his cigarettes like he used to, a smile on his face as he watched his five boys play together.

Chapter Thirty

They rushed back inside when the game was over. Soaked hair, beet-red faces, and all but River and Summer bursting with drunken laughter, stumbling over each other. After they dried off, those who had already been drinking had a couple more as the evening winded down. As for River, he collapsed on the sofa with a can of soda and put his arm over Mia. He kept a close eye on his uncle, who had moved to the back to chat with Anthony and Britney. Let them. River didn't even care what they were talking about.

It was long past midnight when the family finally started heading out, too exhausted to go any further with the party. On Ms. Solinski's insistence, most of the leftovers went home with the family instead of staying behind. All she wanted was some pie and enough for River, Mia, and Aunt Tami to eat until they went home in two days. Of course, this was partially because she had no room in her fridge to keep all of it. Even sending home huge containers with all of them, they still had more than enough leftovers.

River's grandparents were the last to leave. Aside from a single glass of wine each, neither of them had had anything to drink. Meanwhile, empty beer bottles and cans piled high against the trash bin, remnants of a long history of living hard and not seeing another way of living. Even with how drunk many of the brothers were, succumbing to the cheapest and most immature jokes, they all still quieted down and exchanged hugs to say goodnight.

As they headed out, Mia was even surprised to get goodbye hugs from both his grandfather and grandmother. Each of them pulled her in, holding onto her gently but firmly.

"Welcome to the family, Mia," River's grandfather said in a soft voice.

"Wait…really?" She blinked at him.

"Of course." He pulled away and smiled at her, his hands on her shoulders. "You're one of us now. If you or River need anything, we're only one phone call away. You call me anytime, any day. Got it?"

"Uh…sure. Got it." She smiled meekly. She walked with them out to the car, carrying their leftovers for them, and behind her, she heard Dean telling River a joke about something that happened during their football game. With a glance over her shoulder, she saw the two brothers standing side by side, smiling, like it had always been this way.

The house was quiet again, and River could not sleep.

He headed back down to the kitchen around one in the morning to have another slice of pie, and found his mom was still up, too. One of the lights in the dining room was on, and she was looking through an old photo album as she sipped from a glass of wine. He put his pie on a plate, grabbed another can of soda, and pulled up a chair beside her.

"Hey…" She looked at him, rubbing her eyes. "You okay? I'm sorry about your uncle. You know how he gets."

"I know. I'm just glad he didn't come for Mia. But next time we see him, he probably will." He sighed. "Can't force them to change, but some days I really wish we could."

"I know. Me too." She reached over and squeezed his hand.

"What are you looking at?" he asked, then started working on his piece of pie.

"Oh, you know. Just...old photos. Seeing all of my kids back together just...brings back the old memories. Your dad would have loved to be here tonight." She flipped the book over to the most recent photos. Here, River saw one of the few photos taken of him with his dad when he had been living as a boy and already started transitioning. His hair was short, and he wore a Chicago Bulls basketball jersey and huge Tripp pants. They were standing together at one of the many car shows his dad loved to attend, and his dad's arm was over his shoulders. The exact same way he would pose with his other boys.

"This is a good one. Even though my clothes look god-awful. Jesus." He laughed.

"Tomorrow, we can go through his things together. Take home whatever you can fit in your luggage."

"I will. Thanks. And hey...just for the record, I didn't pick a fight with Uncle Robin tonight because I'm really trying to be better at that and I promised Mia I wouldn't. But I can't say I'll do that for next time."

"Well, maybe next time I just won't invite him." She shrugged and sipped at her wine.

When River returned to the bedroom, Mia looked fast asleep. She was lying on her side, her back turned to him. Careful not to disturb her, he slipped into his old shirt he used for pajamas, kicked off his pants, and climbed into bed, pulling the covers over himself. She still didn't move, and just when he thought he wouldn't have to wake her up, he heard a high-pitched squeal.

"What? What's wrong?!" He jolted back.

"Your feet are freezing," Mia said, just before letting out a laugh. She rolled over to face him and gazed up at him. Her eyelids were droopy, and her hair was messy. "That was…a lot."

"Honestly, it wasn't quite as bad as I thought it would be. Maybe they were just saving it for next time."

"Maybe. But I'm proud of you. You did really good." She gave him a kiss on the nose.

"Good enough that you'll let me warm my feet on your back?"

"Don't push it," she laughed, biting her bottom lip.

He wrapped his arm over her, pulling her close, and wouldn't let go, not even after both of them had fallen asleep.

Several days later, back home in Oregon, the year was in its final hours.

They had spent two more days at his mom's home before their flight home and were still burnt out from the trip. As a result, Mia and River decided to spend this New Years' alone. Just the two of them. No relatives, no crass jokes, no alcohol, and no long-winded conversations about music or money or the past. Not even Alan and Julian's promise of a lot of good food at their New Year's Eve party could convince them this time, although Mia did plan to visit them real soon and bring a nice gift.

They found the perfect spot. The resort lodge was a little way out of the city, where, according to the reviews online, one could get a perfect view of the firework show not far away. They found a place near one of the lodge's huge floor-to-ceiling windows and waited for the show to start. There were plenty of others who had had the same idea tonight, but luckily it wasn't too crowded, and they had some space to themselves. Mia was wearing her new favorite outfit for the winter: a cream-colored thick sweater with a few small heart outlines on the front, large enough she could hide her hands under the sleeves easily. She also had her black leggings that kept her surprisingly warm and finally, and her prized knee-high dark brown boots. Beside her, River wore the evergreen knitted sweater Mia gave him for Christmas, and his favorite black pants and boots. He brought her some apple cider in a mug and stood beside her in front of the window.

"Hey, so good news," Mia said in the last handful of minutes to midnight, to help pass the time. "I got the lab results back from my blood test this afternoon. They said the levels look good, so they're upping my estrogen a little. And then just a few more months and it'll be a year since I started."

"A year already? Wow." River smiled. "That went by fast."

"I know! It's crazy." She grinned. "But it feels good. Really, really good. I never thought I would make it this far. It felt like it took forever to get here, and now it's happening so fast."

He stared at her. The way she glowed. It seemed that with every day Mia found a little more of that happiness she had been looking for her whole life. More of that sense that she finally felt at home in her own body for the first time, more comfortable with how she presented herself to the world and how people saw her. All the things he had experienced years ago, now he got to see happen for her in real-time.

And in truth, it made him fall in love with her over and over again.

"I bet it does," he agreed.

"And then there's the legal name change, and the surgeries I might want to get...ugh. I get a headache just thinking about all the paperwork and the costs. But I know it'll be worth it."

"And there's Cat and Emily. Both of them can really help you with finding a surgeon, working things out with insurance, aftercare and recovery...you know what I mean."

"I know. I can't wait." She grabbed his hand, holding it tight, when something came to mind he had been wanting to bring up for a while.

"Should we go on another trip for spring break?" River asked.

"Oh, I haven't thought that far ahead. But yes, we should. Where should we go?" She set her apple cider down and smiled. "We could go anywhere. Not super far away since I don't have a ton of money to spare, but something small. I don't need a huge trip."

"Me neither. Since I took you to meet my family last week, it's only fair you get to pick where we go next."

"Ooh, that's a lot of pressure to put on one girl. Hmm...maybe San Francisco? I've always wanted to see it, hit up all the gay bars that Julian has told me about. Or maybe Disneyland."

"Tomorrow we can start coming up with a list of ideas. How does that sound?"

"Sounds good to me." She looked up, then quickly pulled him with her to the window. "Oh, hurry! It's almost midnight!"

The final countdown started. Everyone inside the lodge moved closer to watch the start of the fireworks show. With just a few seconds left of the old year, River turned to her and cupped her face in his hands. His thumbs traced her freckles, her dimples, as she smiled up at him. And he dreamed that this time next year, they would be doing this all over again. And that they would be a little happier, a little kinder, a little brighter, a little more healed, and a little more at peace with themselves. A little less chained down to bad habits and old ways of living, in favor of a new chapter they had both been trying so hard to ascend to. That they would continue to renew the best parts of each other until the past were but scars they could kiss away every night.

"Our first New Years' kiss," Mia said. "My first, well…ever, actually. I've never gotten to do this before." She reached up until her hands were over his, tracing his fingertips.

He smiled, suddenly overcome with shyness. This was his first New Years kiss he wanted to happen, and he wanted to make it perfect. Especially since it was her first at all.

"Ready to start the new year off right?" he asked.

She nodded. A second later, cheers erupted as the clock struck midnight. He pressed his lips against hers and she melted into the kiss, pressing her body against his. Both the group chats on their phones exploded. Alan, Julian, Grace, Victoria, Oliver, and everyone said goodbye to the old year and welcomed in the new.

As she slowly pulled away from the kiss, they looked into each other's eyes. River felt his heart skip a beat just from the way she looked at him. It wasn't going to be an easy year; he knew that. The road would twist and turn as she progressed further into both her physical and social transition. New challenges would come up, especially when the possibility of the surgeries and name change grew closer. She had the rest of college, and they each had their own careers to worry about, too. They had his family to worry about. All their friends and their mutual friends, too.

But they were in this together. And they would never be alone again.

"Happy New Year," Mia beamed up at him. She gave him another kiss, grabbing onto him. Then they turned to watch the fireworks display, arms wrapped around each other, as they both reflected on the uncertain but hopeful future that lay ahead.

Acknowledgements

Many thanks to family and friends who sat down to read my creative writing over the years. The time you dedicated to letting me share my work with you gave me the courage I needed to pursue my writing as a career. Whether you were there to let me overexplain the latest make-believe world I had invented overnight, or took the time to offer me constructive criticism and notes on my writing, it all helped me get to where I am today.

Thank you to my friends in the LGBT+ community, who supported me when I first came out and began transitioning. This book is a love letter to the community and the people in it, and is an unapologetic celebration of all of our identities.

I also want to thank all the folks who left heartfelt comments and kudos on all my fan fiction over the years. I have been active in online fandom spaces for over a decade, and I have crossed paths with so many kind, wonderful, creative people. Seeing your reactions to the stories I wrote about our favorite characters (whether they were space wizards, scoundrels, or fandom crossover fusions) inspired me to one day share my own original stories with the world. Seeing the way these stories resonated with you, comforted you, and helped you feel less alone, made me realize I wanted to bring that experience to a wider audience. Thank you for sharing your love of fandom with me.

I want to extend an extra special thank you to my mom, who homeschooled me all the way from Pre-K to high school graduation. Mom, thank you for seeing the storyteller in me from the beginning. For not only letting that fire keep burning, but giving it the strength it needed throughout my education. For every writing course you enrolled me in. And for letting me write all those short stories for extra credit, especially when I did it at the expense of my Algebra homework.

Lastly, thank you to my partner and the love of my life, who inspired me to write this story many years ago. How much has changed since those days, and yet how much has stayed the same! What started as a fun little idea on a shared Google doc blossomed into this, and I couldn't have done it without your support or your companionship.

About The Author

Tatum Schroeder was born and raised in the upper midwestern United States, and currently resides in the Atlanta metro area with his partner and two cats. From the age of four, he knew he wanted to be a storyteller, and began by drawing short fiction on blank print paper. By age seven, he won second place in a national writing contest. He completed a Bachelors in English at age 18 from Thomas Edison State University.

Until You Say My Name is his debut novel. In addition to prose-length novels, he also enjoys writing short fiction and poetry. He previously had a short story, "The Long Way North," published with Scarlet Leaf Review in 2021. As a gay trans man, Tatum enjoys exploring queer themes and stories in his work, as well as tapping into themes such as existential horror, subverting societal expectations and values, and the tenacity of the human spirit.

Outside of writing, he enjoys playing video games, traveling, curating Spotify playlists for his original characters, and deep diving into the lore and minutiae of fictional worlds.

Excellent LGBTQ+ fiction by unique, wonderful authors.
Thrillers
Mystery
Romance
Young Adult
& More

Join our mailing list here for news, offers and free books!

Visit our website for more Spectrum Books
www.spectrum-books.com

Or find us on Instagram
@spectrumbookpublisher